Amid the brooding mountains of Glen Coe and the bleak windswept Rannoch Moor, the bitter enmity between the families of the Campbells and the Mac-Donalds blazes ever fiercer. Though it is fifty years since that first terrible massacre, Catriona Campbell, daughter of the Laird of Darna, has been taught to fear and hate the 'black-hearted' MacDonalds. So when she meets Rorie the 'Red' MacDonald, she is amazed to find that he is not the monster she had always supposed him to be. But how, in the face of her family's implacable opposition, can she ever have the courage to live with the man she loves in that hate-ridden atmosphere?

Wild Wind in the Heather

Valentina Luellen

MILLS & BOON LIMITED
London · Sydney · Toronto

First published in Great Britain 1983
by Mills & Boon London Limited, 15–16 Brook's Mews,
London W1A 1DR

ISBN 0 263 74303 9

Set in 10 on 10½ pt Times Roman
04/0683

Photoset by Rowland Phototypesetting Ltd
Bury St Edmunds, Suffolk
Made and printed in Great Britain by
Cox and Wyman Ltd, Reading

For James,
with love

CHAPTER
ONE

THE weather changed suddenly, from a bright sunny day which Catriona had intended to use to the very last hour of daylight, to one of overcast skies and dark grey clouds which heralded the approach of rain. She would have to abandon her visit to her brother Murdoch and the Stewarts, she thought regretfully, looking down at the lightweight riding habit she wore. From where she was now, only a short ride from Rannoch Moor, the house was another hour away. She suspected she would not reach it, or her own home, before the rains came. Thank goodness she had been sensible enough to bring a cloak. Some protection at least, should those menacing clouds open up.

Always here, she mused as she reined in her horse and stared at the desolate countryside about her. The sun never shone for long over the brooding mountains of Glen Coe. Already she could see the mists sweeping down from the hills, rolling along the valley floor like a silent beastie from a childhood nightmare—intent on driving her from its domain.

Her old nanny had always insisted that the silent, creeping blanket of mist contained the spirits of all those poor souls massacred by some of her kinsmen over fifty years before. They were searching for anyone rash enough to venture close to the place where, on that infamous night, written in blood in the memories of the people of the glens for miles around, innocent men, women and children had been cruelly put to the sword.

Those fortunate enough to escape suffered cold and privations in the blizzard which raged through the unfriendly, snow-clad mountains as they struggled to safety.

Catriona did not believe in ghosts or beasties, but even she shivered as her gaze wandered over the approaching mists, now totally obscuring the pass and the mountains beyond as far as the sparse, desolate land she had just ridden over. She loved to ride hereabouts, but only to the edge of Loch Ba, for in the other direction, beyond Glen Coe, lay the lands of the hereditary enemies of the Campbells—the MacDonalds.

For as long as Catriona could remember, there had always been hatred existing between her family and a certain family of MacDonalds that lived the other side of the valley. The bloody death feud between the two families spared no one. Many a night she had seen the sky alight with the flames of burning crofts as MacDonald raiders laid waste to Campbell lands. She closed her ears to the grisly tales which ran rampant through the house after such attacks, shut her eyes to the sight of her brother and father leading their clansmen out on an equally devastating raid.

The origin of the bad feeling had been lost in time. Some said it came about when a smooth-tongued Campbell stole the wife of a MacDonald chief and then left her to die in the attic of his house after he had spent all her dowry and grown tired of her.

Other sources claimed old, dormant prejudices flared to life with the ill-fated uprising in 1715, in support of James Stuart, when defeat to loyal Highlanders brought about near ruin for many clans, but for the canny Campbells came land and wealth in abundance for services rendered. Thirteen years after the infamous massacre of the MacIan MacDonalds, it fed the already raging fire with more fuel.

In sunlight Rannoch Moor was a pleasant place where

she could forget her troubles, sit aimlessly by a burn listening to the music of the water or ride across the wind-swept moor, but once the mists began to roll across the peat-bogs, obscuring vision in all directions, they brought with them an eerie silence which she found unnerving. A spot of rain fell upon her hand. She wheeled her horse about, but had scarcely covered a mile before the heavens opened and she was soaked to the skin and forced to take shelter from the blinding rain beneath some trees.

Wherever she went, since early childhood, Catriona had always been accompanied by armed clansmen, dedicated to the protection from harm of the daughter of the Laird of Darna. Not on the orders of her father, who had sired a daughter he did not want, but on those of James Campbell, the eldest son, who idolised his baby sister and protected her from the outside world at any cost.

As she grew older however and her spirit developed, Catriona had refused an escort, deliberately ridden far from the house without men to guard her, much to the chagrin of her brother. For her seventeenth birthday he had given her a chestnut mare which was her pride and joy. Within a year she could outride both her brothers and almost anyone else who dared to challenge her. Such unladylike antics brought instant condemnation from her father's lips. By the time she had reached the age of ten Catriona had acknowledged the fact that he would never love her. Nothing she could ever do, no matter how hard she tried to accomplish the most difficult task in order to please him as a son would have done, he would never accept her. There were times when she saw him watching her and knew he was wishing she had died in the place of the beautiful, fragile creature who had given her life. And so she developed her own little world which lay outside Darna. Hers and hers alone, despite the dangers.

Today, disturbed in her mind, she had left the house early, even before the servants were awake. She had roused a stable lad to saddle her horse and ridden away hoping to find peace. Beyond the house, out of sight of her father's reproachful gaze and scornful words, it was easy to find herself as one with the world which surrounded her. To enjoy that first moment of freedom experienced when she gave her horse free rein, was her sole claim to happiness these days.

She brushed the wet hair from her face. Darna was still at least ten miles away. She knew every back track, every rocky crevice and marshy patch of ground which led into the glen, so she was not afraid to continue, but the deluge of rain had soaked her and she began to shiver, wishing Murdoch and the Stewarts had been closer. She would have given anything at that moment for the warmth of a fire and some dry clothes.

It was still quite early in the afternoon, but the sky was so dark it could have been night. Soon the rain would abate, she suspected, and then the cold, clinging mists would descend, slowly, silently—treacherously, for those who did not know the right paths. Strangers could be led into bogs or marshy ground to lose their mounts or even their lives, or to wander aimlessly until the white blanket disappeared as quickly as it had come.

Whenever she went missing from the house without a word, James would know something was troubling her. He would wait by the bridge which forded the stream just below Darna and they would talk before returning to the house together. She prayed he was there now. She needed to unburden herself after the unpleasantness of the previous evening.

The rain seemed ceaseless. She stared at the grey sky in despair. Then, without warning, as was so typical in this part of the Highlands, it stopped. The mists closed around her instantly. There was no sound. It was as if she had suddenly been transported to another world.

Her horse was well trained; it would make its own way back to Darna without faltering. Her saturated clothes clung to her, chilling her to the bone, but she shut her mind against the cold. She had been out in such weather before and knew from past experience that the sun could break through at any moment. A challenge from the beasties of Glen Coe, she thought as she urged her horse homewards. If they were to lay claim to anyone this day, it would not be her.

'Stand fast and identify yourself.' The voice came off to her left. She reined in instinctively and then found herself wondering why. A strange voice under such circumstances should have sent her racing down the glen. 'Stand fast, I say. Who are you? Kirsty, is that you?'

A shape materialised at her side as dripping wet as she was. A hand grabbed her bridle and she caught her breath at the sight of a drawn sword. Close at hand, even through the swirling mists, the red and blue plaid, interlaced with green, was unmistakable. A Mac-Donald! A thousand thoughts raced through her brain. What was he doing this side of the valley? Were there more? She could hear no other sound, but that did not mean there were not others lying in wait out of sight. Who was he? Would he recognise her? Could she spur her horse away and break his hold? As if he read her thoughts, the man raised the blade of the claymore upwards to menace her.

'Climb down!'

Catriona had no intention of doing so. Bluff was her only chance of escape. For this man, whoever he was, to discover her identity meant . . . She was not sure. She could only go by what she had been told would happen to her if she was ever captured by the MacDonalds. Ransom, if she was fortunate. If not, captivity among men who would use her for their own pleasures, taking revenge for all their old grievances, and then cut her throat. Not that her father would care!

Instead of obeying the command, she raised a hand and swept back her hood. Long, blonde hair, free from confinement, tumbled about her wet cheeks and shoulders. She heard a startled oath as the man stepped back.

'Who are you, sir, to detain me thus?' she demanded in a frosty tone. 'Is it no longer safe to ride in the lands of the Stewarts and MacDonalds without being accosted?'

'Hold your tongue, girl, I mean you no harm. You are not the one I am seeking,' came the harsh reply.

'Really? Then allow me to pass. I am wet through and wishing I was at home this very minute.' Catriona's audacity amazed her. Inwardly she could feel herself shaking as she gazed at that naked blade and then watched it slowly returned to its scabbard.

The man was tall. Taller, she estimated than her brother James who was himself six feet. And well built. Apart from that she could see little else of him. His bonnet was drawn well down over his face, totally obscuring his features, apart from his mouth which she saw was closed in a tight, suspicious line.

'You—are detaining me, sir. Pray, for what reason? Please allow me to go on my way.' She was shaking, yet her voice still remained steady. MacDonalds so near Darna! Was there to be another raid? She had to warn James!

'You have no reason to be feart of me so long as you answer my questions truthfully. Where have you come from?'

She hesitated. The weapon was sheathed, but the tone of the man told her he was past patience.

'From friends . . . Tamsie Stewart . . .'

'You are heading towards Glen Creran, bonny lass. Since when were the Stewarts of Appin any more akin to the Campbells than us MacDonalds?' came the slow, insolent answer.'

'Creran!' The tremor in Catriona's voice gave credibility to the fear she felt. He had taken her words to indicate she was some relation of the Stewarts in the next glen. It saved her further explanations. 'I am lost! The mists came down so quickly . . .'

'Aye and they may have trapped more than you,' came the grave retort. 'I hope my men have better luck than me in their searching. Turn your horse about, I will take you back to the right path.'

'You—you are looking for someone?' Catriona faltered. So it was not an attack, as she feared.

'Aye. A young girl about your own age, also taken to riding in these parts in unpredictable weather. Have you seen another rider? Anyone at all this past hour?'

How Catriona wished she could distinguish the dark features before her, but it was impossible. He sounded so concerned, as James would have done had she been lost on the moors. A human being capable of emotion like anyone else—so different from the MacDonalds she had been taught to fear and hate.

'No one. But would she have strayed this far?'

'Ordinarily? No, but she was distraught. Faith, when I lay my hands on her she will not be able to ride for a week.'

'You sound like my brother,' Catriona ejaculated, momentarily forgetting her fears. 'He always sounds like a bear when he is angry, but it doesn't last. He is really a very gentle man.'

'Well, if he doesn't take you to task over today, then I will,' came the dry retort. 'Stay here while I fetch my horse and then we will ride back together. I want to meet this soft bear.'

He turned away and Catriona watched him clambering over the rocks at the side of the road until he disappeared from sight. She waited no longer. Digging her heels into her horse's flanks, she galloped on as if D'hommil Dhu himself was after her.

James Campbell was waiting for his sister at the bridge

in Glen Creran. Not alone, but with a dozen or more
armed clansmen about him. Catriona flung herself from
her horse and into his arms, breathless, sobbing with
relief. Her clothes clung to her, yet her skin beneath his
touch was hot and his grip tightened in sudden anxiety.

'James—oh, James. I wasn't sure you would be here.'

'Another few minutes and we would have come looking for you again. Where the devil have you been?'

'Again?' She echoed, raising her head from his
shoulder.

The soft bear, the MacDonald had called him. There
was nothing soft about the tense, pale man facing her in
the half-light. It was well known in the surrounding glens
that James Campbell was not a patient man, except
where his sister was concerned. She could do no wrong
in his eyes and had never aroused in him the temper
which made him widely feared. But at this moment she
wondered if she was not about to feel the full force of it.
She was six years his junior, yet they could have been
twins. Both had inherited the blonde hair and fair
colouring of their beautiful mother.

'Yes, again, dammit! And why did you come riding
down this road like a fool? In this weather your horse
could have put its foot into a hole and thrown you, and
then God knows how long it would have taken to find
you. I thought you had gone to see Murdoch. You left no
word. I rode over there as soon as the weather turned,
only to find you had not been there. I suppose you were
on Rannoch Moor again. I've told you time and time
again about riding so far from the house without an
escort.'

Catriona said nothing in justification of her thoughtless actions. He had every right to take her to task. He
never fully understood the intensity with which she
loved the wild, desolate countryside about her, nor the
necessity to experience that feeling of freedom that she
could only feel astride a horse.

'There are MacDonalds not a mile from old Andrew's croft. One stopped me. He was looking for a girl about my age who is lost,' she interrupted, and brushed damp hair from her eyes.

As she did so, her self-control began to return after the hectic ride which followed her narrow escape. She noticed what she had been too distracted to see before. Four silent clansmen stood grouped beneath the trees to her left and lying at their feet, wrapped in someone's plaid, was the unconscious form of a young girl.

'You have found her! She must be the one he seeks!'

'If I'd known she was a MacDonald I would have left her where she was. I'll have her taken back to the high road. She'll be found before morning,' James said tersely, turning on his heel.

'You will do no such thing,' Catriona protested, hurrying after him. Instant pity filled her as she knelt beside the girl. It could have been herself had she not been so familiar with the countryside.

'Leave her,' James ordered as she bent to brush away the long dark curls shadowing a face bereft of all colour.

'James! She could be badly hurt, besides you have brought her this far.'

The audacious insinuation that the girl should be conveyed to Darna made her brother's eyes widen with incredulity. Catriona pointed to the trickle of blood welling from beneath the girl's hairline. She had never felt so helpless in all her twenty years. Her lips compressed determinedly as she looked up into his face. The stubborn trait in her was something else she had inherited from their mother.

'Damn your soft heart, you'll have all our throats cut for such stupidity—if we survive Father's anger, that is. If the MacDonalds stopped you at the head of the glen, then the fact they are searching this far afield means she is important to them. Important enough to ride up to the walls of Darna itself perhaps.' He swore beneath his breath and the nearest clansman looked uncomfortable and moved several paces backwards. 'You wouldn't like us to deliver her to them in person, would you, then you could introduce yourself to them properly.' Kneeling beside the girl, he laid a hand over her heart. He was frowning heavily and more ill at ease than Catriona had seen him in many months. He cared, but it was more than his life was worth to show it in front of the men watching him.

'She can ride in front of you,' she replied, ignoring his sarcasm.

She wheeled about, calling for their horses to be brought, afraid he might overrule her and send the unfortunate girl back to where she had been found. She would die of exposure, if she was not already dead by the time the Campbell men had finished with her. Catriona saw by their expressions that they thought she had lost her senses.

James mounted, his features impassive. He said nothing and she held her breath.

'Give her to me,' he ordered and no one dared question it. He did not speak to his sister on the journey home and she did not bother him with talk, only too aware of how his gaze continually swept the surrounding countryside as if suspecting they might at any moment be set upon by the enemy.

Not until they came in sight of the impressive house, built on the softly rolling slopes of the glen, did she sense he had relaxed again. Not so the men riding with him. The fires would burn well into the night as they discussed her folly and James's apparent show of weakness. She could see it, gazing into their closed faces. They would never forgive her for offering sanctuary to a Mac-Donald!

It could have been her, Catriona reminded herself again. She was right!

'James, for the love of heaven, show her a little

gentleness,' Catriona protested as he dismounted and strode towards the house. The girl in his arms moaned in his tight hold.

'She's a MacDonald. Would you have me treat her as kin?' he demanded ungraciously.

'The MacDonalds may act as animals with our womenfolk, but is that any reason for us to do the same?' she flung back angrily, running to keep pace with him.

'I wonder if you would feel like that after an hour with one of them?' James retorted.

Their arrival with their semi-conscious burden aroused great curiosity among the servants and there was so much noise as Catriona sent them scurrying to carry out preparations of a room for their injured guest, that Fergus Campbell came out of his study, demanding to know the reason for the uproar.

James paused at the bottom of the staircase and looked at his father, his lips twisted into a wry smile.

'My sister has a soft heart, even for our enemies. We found this girl on the moors—a MacDonald by all accounts—and she's hurt. She needs a doctor.'

'Are you out of your mind to bring her beneath my roof?' Fergus thundered, his eyes almost starting out of his head. He rounded on the listening servants, sending them in all directions with his threats. At times like these, Catriona realised from where James had inherited his temper.

'It's too late to worry about that now. She's here and she needs help. If the worst happens, she will make a fine hostage when the MacDonalds come looking for her.'

'Father—no!' Catriona protested. She was shocked at James's attitude over a defenceless girl no older than she was herself.

'Go with your brother. Tend the girl if you must,' Fergus said coldly, 'but if we are to be held to account for this ministering, she will find no mercy at my hands. You will not interfere with your brother. He and I are in complete agreement.'

Catriona went upstairs, acutely conscious she had disgraced herself before family and household. No one gave aid to the murderous MacDonalds!

James had taken the girl to a room which adjoined her own suite and laid her on the bed.

'Remember,' he warned as she tried to make her charge more comfortable. 'I give way this far and no further. She shall have a doctor and all the attention she needs to get well, then she will be given a horse and sent on her way. Pray the MacDonalds do not discover her whereabouts before then, little sister.'

'Thank you, James.'

'You will not thank me if this house is raided. You will wonder whatever possessed you to be so stupid.'

'She is not our enemy, James,' Catriona said softly. 'Look at her! She is no older than I am.'

'Doubtless she has a family who hate us and would destroy us without a twinge of conscience,' her brother returned, tight-lipped. 'Are you being deliberately awkward?'

'As you would, without a second's thought, destroy them, my brother. Are we so different?'

James stared into her pale, set features. He had seen these stubborn moods before. He shut his mind against the infuriated man waiting for him below and his gaze wandered across to the unconscious MacDonald girl. Catriona did not like the look which crept into his eyes, but she wisely held her tongue.

She had gone against father and brother to bring the injured girl to safety. To offend either of them was foolishness. James would protect her against her father's wrath. James would ensure a doctor came to attend the injured girl. James would be her ally until she pushed him too far. She embraced him silently and ushered him out. If only he had not stared at the girl so boldly. She was beginning to fear she had made a bad mistake!

'Your patient is doing well, I hope?'

Fergus Campbell looked down the length of the dining table at his silent daughter, inwardly cursing her for her audacity. Then, as his eyes studied the carefully arranged hair, the jewels glittering at her throat, ears and wrists, his mouth tightened into a bleak line. Memories, painful memories flooded back to him, of a wilful, golden-haired girl who had gone against her own family to wed him. She had given him two fine stalwart sons and then life had departed from her frail body, bequeathing it instead to this firebrand with eyes which shone like sapphires in the candlelight as she turned to answer his question. She was beautiful, like her mother. More so? No! No one could have been more lovely. He hated this apparition which haunted his dreams, this daughter who for so long had begged for his love, for one little sign of affection and, when she had been denied it, had withdrawn into herself and now haunted him every moment of the day with her presence. The very sight of her was distasteful. She was nothing to him, would never rouse one iota of feeling in him.

Her life had meant death for the only woman he had ever loved. He thought of the marriage he had arranged. A good marriage, with many advantages for him. She would go to Andrew Fraser with a generous dowry. He would have spent anything to be rid of her. The man was infatuated with her. Heaven only knew why, when he was reputed to be a notorious womaniser and had his choice of females throughout the Highlands. In return the Fraser had given a promise of arms and men. Fergus Campbell in his wildest dreams, still imagined a triumphant victory over his MacDonald enemies. With the Fraser's help and James at his side, how could he lose?

Catriona felt James's eyes on her as she stared at her

father. Tolerance, they pleaded. He has been patient this far.

'Very well, Father,' she answered. 'Her injuries were not serious. A gashed leg and small graze to her head, but the doctor thinks she is not a strong girl.'

'What else did he say? When can she leave?'

'He thinks it unwise to move her just yet. For at least a week. He fears she may catch a chill and I agree with him.'

'You will do well to remember she is here on sufferance, my girl. She goes as soon as she can walk. Do you hear?'

'Father is right, Catriona, we cannot keep her here for long. She has been missed already and by now the MacDonalds are putting two and two together,' James interposed. 'However, I urge restraint, Father. Would it not be better to return her to them alive and well, singing our praises, or at least those of my soft-hearted sister, than for them to receive her half dead? We would surely be blamed for that as if we had left her out in the heather to die.'

'By God, do you think I care what the MacDonalds think?' Fergus thundered, staring at him incredulously.

James stared back without flinching.

'I do. If you are not concerned with the welfare of this household, I am! The MacDonalds would be upon us like a pack of wolves the moment they suspected ill treatment to one of their own. For once we have turned the other cheek. Let us see what happens, shall we?'

Oh, dearest brother, Catriona thought gratefully. Again you come to my rescue.

'No, by God! No! She leaves by the end of the week. I care not if she falls from her horse and breaks her neck. You have a short memory of late, James. Have you forgotten not two weeks ago the crofts of our closest tenants were fired, their livestock stolen and their women abused or abducted? Among the attackers were many like her upstairs. What has made you suddenly so noble?'

'Perhaps a growing distaste for this wanton destruction and bloodlust that is going on around us almost every day.' Catriona was surprised to see a slow flush stealing beneath her brother's cheeks. As yet her suspicions that he might be harbouring some grudge towards the injured MacDonald girl had proved unfounded, although twice she had found him in the girl's room and had sent him storming from her presence with her angry accusations ringing in his ears. 'You have a taste for it, Father, and you raised me in your image. It is expected of me, but you overlooked one thing. I will stand by your side, I will avenge our people when they are attacked and killed. I will take up a sword and fight, but none of that will change what is in my heart. I know there must be another way and I would like to find it. If this girl is treated with respect and kindness, it might be the turning point in our relationship with the Mac-Donalds.'

'This is your doing!' Fergus glared down the table at his daughter. She looked back at him without a trace of fear. 'You've wrought mischief in this house since the day you were born. I shall be well rid of you.'

'If I thought that was the only reason you had agreed to the Fraser's marriage offer, I would oppose you, even at this late stage,' James said, his eyes narrowing sharply. 'It is true I have always listened to Catriona's point of view. It differs so greatly from your own which I am always hearing—and my own in the beginning. There is no hatred in her, no malice, no desire for revenge . . .'

'As yet she has not experienced MacDonald hospitality.'

Catriona laid a hand over James's. He was tense and ready to fly at his father. She had unwittingly begun a chain of events that threatened to arouse in him something which had deeper roots than just his disgust for the retaliatory raids against their enemies. He was deeply troubled and it was her fault.

'No more, please,' she whispered. 'I will go upstairs. Stay and drink with him. You know how he enjoys your company.'

'And try to pretend we are from the same mould?'

'No. You are father and son. He loves you.'

'And treats you like a stranger. How can I?'

'Soon I will be gone from Darna, James. You must think of yourself now. In four days it is my betrothal ball. In three months I shall be a wife.'

'Chained to a man you do not love, who is marrying you for the fine dowry you bring with you and, I suspect, the fact that he knows he cannot get his hands on you any other way. If I was wrong to agree to this match, tell me now and I will stop it.'

How easy to do just that, Catriona thought, staring into his face. She had been appalled when her father had told her she was to marry Andrew Fraser, a Captain with an Argyll regiment billeted in Inverness. Twelve years her senior, Catriona had met him several times, but knew him better from the reputation which had preceded him. A gambler, always in debt. A ladies' man, faithful to none. He drank too much and was coarse in his language when he did so; at other times he was an overdressed philanderer. Her father spared no details and she had shrunk from the smile on his face as he recounted them. Tearing her away from Darna and the brother she loved, from the countryside which gave her so much pleasure, to isolate her in some town house for the sole amusement of one man who gained nothing from the liaison but money, and perhaps power, was revenge enough for being born a girl, instead of the third son he desired.

'Do not antagonise him further on my behalf,' she said to James and rose to her feet. 'It is too late to change the way things must be.'

After three days, Catriona still knew as little about her patient as when she had been brought unconscious to the house. When the girl recovered her senses, she stared sullenly at the wall, refusing to look at anyone or answer a single question about herself. No amount of cajoling from Catriona or threats from Nan, who grew quite indignant at such an attitude after all her mistress' kind ministering, brought forth a reply. James, Catriona noticed, stayed in the background. Always there, yet never offering advice. That was unusual!

Catriona knew, although she hid it well, that the girl was terribly afraid. Constantly the dark brown eyes watched the door or windows as if she was forever weighing the chances of escape, and on one occasion she had caught her silently weeping into the pillows.

As she entered the sick-room an idea was forming in her mind, so wild and audacious it could possibly work. It was not fair to expect James to continually side with her against their father in this case, and so she intended to say nothing of her scheme—if it was put into action —until it was all over. Whether the poor girl was well enough or not, Catriona suspected her father intended to turn her out of the house by the end of the week.

'How is she, Nan?' She looked into the pale face of the girl sitting still and quiet in the huge canopied bed, her hands clasped tightly together in front of her. The middle-aged woman who rose from a chair, gathering up her sewing, pulled a wry face.

'Silent as usual. I gave her a wee drop of warm milk not long ago to help her to sleep.'

'That was good of you, considering you, too, I know, disapprove of what I have done.'

'It's not my place to say aye or nay, mistress, but there's talk below stairs that you have brought bad luck upon the house by bringing her here. They care little the lass was hurt, only that she's a MacDonald. Like the old

Laird, some of them have long memories and old scores to settle.'

'Which will not be settled now. Go to bed, I will see to her myself.'

As the door closed behind the woman, Catriona advanced to the bed and said in a firm tone:

'My father is of a mind to turn you out of the house within a few days. That is not my intention, nor my brother's. Trust me! Be honest with me and tell me who you are. You will be returned to your family unharmed, I promise.'

'I heard you—you and your father quarrelling over me. The woman was asleep and I crept out to the stairs. Why?' The voice was almost lost amid the huddle of blankets the girl pulled around her shoulders and once again Catriona was swept with an immense feeling of shame. Such fear! The same fear she would have felt had she found herself a guest of the MacDonalds! Yet when she had found herself alone on the moors with a man who bore that infamous name, she had experienced more compassion than fear. Her father would never understand how she felt or why. And James had burdened himself enough with her troubles.

'I was on my way home when I was stopped by one of your clansmen, looking for you. He could have been my own brother searching for me because I had ridden too far, as I often do, and became lost in the mist. Don't you understand what I am trying to say? I don't know what you are to him, but I know he cared about you. I could tell by his voice; perhaps as much as James cares for me. He worries if I am out of his sight for even a few hours. By whatever name we are called, that makes us little different from each other. We are human beings with emotions too, emotions that sometimes prove over-whelming.'

A faint smile touched the lips of the other girl.

'My brother would die laughing to think a Campbell

capable of decent feelings. Until now you were only a name to me, to be feared, despised—and avoided.'

'And I was reared on grisly tales of MacDonald raids and abductions, of needless slaughter that made me think the whole world had gone mad. Out on the moor, I encountered a man whose face I could not see, but who bore a name I was taught to hate. I saw him only as a very wet, tired, concerned man looking for a young lost girl. Yet because of what I had been told, I pretended I had come from Appin. Had I not ridden off he would have escorted me back there. He wanted to take my brother to task for allowing me out in such weather.'

'That sounds like my brother. He is very strict about where I should ride, but we had quarrelled and I wasn't thinking, or caring where I went. He wants to send me back to my aunt in Paris to become a lady and I refused. It's horrible with her. She keeps taking me to parties and balls in the hope I may catch the eye of some rich French aristocrat and make a good marriage. I am not going back.'

'Your brother?' Catriona echoed softly. The girl was coming out of her shell. The barrier between them had been broken by the honesty of her words.

'My name is Kirsty MacDonald. I am sure the man you met was Rorie. My other brother Donald would not have been so polite. I believe you call Rorie "MacDonald Ruadh"—the "Red" MacDonald, do you not?'

Catriona felt as if a chasm had suddenly opened up beneath her feet. She had brought into her father's house the sister of his worst enemies, the MacDonalds who lived on the edge of the wild, sweeping Forest of Mamore.

'I have shocked you.' Kirsty's voice was now tinged with mockery. 'Did you expect me to have horns—or fangs? Like you I am perfectly normal, with brothers who love and protect me too. Are we still alike, Catriona Campbell?'

'If I was to send word to your brothers that you are alive and well, would they believe me?' Catriona asked, spurred on by a strange impulse she did not fully understand, but was unable to ignore. 'Or would they raid the crofts of our people and kill and plunder until you were returned to them?'

'Believe you? No, that is too much to ask, surely you realise that.' Kirsty sat bolt upright in bed, her eyes brightening. 'But they would believe a letter written in my hand. Can it be done? What is it, you look so pale?'

Catriona passed a hand across her eyes, aware of the enormity of what she was about to attempt. Failure could not be contemplated.

'Nan has a son who is a groom here. His cousin is married to a MacIan girl in Glen Coe. If we can only reach them, I'm sure a message could be delivered to your brother. I shall need Nan's help to get it out of the house, but I know she will arrange it. She has raised me from birth and we have no secrets. The timing is perfect.'

'Why?' Kirsty leaned forward growing more intent.

At first she had been sceptical at this offered hand of friendship, but now she realised the risks Catriona would have to take in order to help her and knew it was a genuine offer. An offer she grasped at eagerly in the hope of being returned quickly to safety.

'In a few days my betrothal ball is to be held here. The house will be full of people. If your brothers come for you that night, you will be able to slip away without being seen . . .'

'And avoid the bloodbath we both fear could take place,' Kirsty interposed quietly and Catriona nodded. 'Bring me pen and paper. I will write whatever you want.'

'No. Put down your own words otherwise he will know.'

'How long did you say you had spent in my brother's company?' the girl asked, her eyebrows arching.

'A few minutes—why?'

'Rorie is a canny man. He has an instinct for people, yet few have ever been able to assess his character so well as you have after such a brief meeting. You have succeeded where others have failed and I find that—interesting.'

Catriona rose to her feet, shutting her mind against the consequences of failure as she gathered up writing materials. Not only had she brought an enemy into the house, albeit a helpless girl, but she was about to compound the felonious crime by allowing her to communicate with the one man her father hated above all others. The 'Red' MacDonald! Oh, God, am I doing right, she thought fearfully? Then, as her mother's stubbornness won through, she turned back to the bed and handed them to Kirsty.

CHAPTER
TWO

FERGUS CAMPBELL had spared no expense for the betrothal ball of his daughter to Andrew Fraser. He invited
everyone who had once enjoyed the hospitality of Darna
and with whom he had all but lost touch since the last
troubled times. There was the clan piper and musicians
from Inverness to provide a variety of music. The sump-
tuous array of food for the guests had come from half a
dozen places and from as far afield as France. Catriona's
dressmaker had been ordered to make her a gown fit for
a queen and women from the village had been working
on it for a whole month.

She looked elegant enough to be royalty, Catriona
thought as she stared at her reflection, yet she still felt
like a piece of unwanted merchandise being bartered for
sale. Her father's generosity was a farce and she hated
him for that. She knew he wanted to hear her beg for the
wedding to be cancelled, but it would not happen. Pride
forbade her to grovel before him and she suspected
he would only have laughed in her face had she done
so.

She would voice no argument against the marriage.
She had to accept it for James's sake at least. He should
be thinking of taking a wife for himself, but being always
at loggerheads with their father over her gave him little
time to think of himself and his own needs.

She knew so little of the world which lay outside
Darna, she was more than a trifle afraid of what lay
ahead for her. Apart from a few visits to Inverness and

Edinburgh over the past few years, always suitably chaperoned by Nan or her brother, she had lived all her life within the sanctuary of Darna's walls. Her lack of worldliness made her feel awkward and incompetent in Andrew's company, forcing her to resort to a sharpness of tongue that was totally against her nature.

Sometimes, when he was sober and too arrogant to care what she thought of him, he did not retaliate, but when he had been drinking, he would turn on her and on more than one occasion had reduced her to tears with his crude comments on how life with him would be once she was his wife.

The last time, the evening before she had set out to see Murdoch and instead met Rorie MacDonald, James had come upon them in the garden, seen Andrew holding so tightly to her shoulders—she was biting her lips in pain—heard the slurred oaths and threats which fell from his lips. He had hit him hard, just once, and left him lying amid the rose bushes. Catriona saw the look in his eyes and realised in that moment James would have killed for her had she asked it. That frightened her more than anything that had ever happened before. One wrong word—a look—and she could have turned her brother into a murderer! No, she would not oppose the marriage any longer. She would do nothing, say nothing to antagonise her brother into going against their father's wishes. He was too precious to her.

For a second time a servant came to the door and Catriona was aware of Nan sending him quietly, but firmly away.

'Your father is asking again that you present yourself. My lady, you must go down. The next time the Laird might come himself.'

'I doubt that, but you are right. I must show myself. How do I look?'

Catriona turned slowly before her, knowing she would receive a truthful answer. Her gown was of pale yellow satin, a shower of lace dyed exactly to match gracing the wide neckline and bordering the sleeves. She wore pearls around her neck and in her ears and several more adorned the combs which secured her hair in a gleaming cascade of long curls over one shoulder.

'Lovely, as always. You'll make the Fraser a bonny wife. Far better than he deserves, if you ask me. The village women are wondering why you have no' chosen the material for your wedding gown yet.' Nan made a final adjustment to Catriona's hair, her expression thoughtful. 'It's not to your liking is it—this match? Tell me to mind my own business if you like, but these past weeks I've watched you growing more miserable, and tonight, when you should be radiant with happiness, you linger here, neglecting not only your guests, but the very man you are to wed.'

'No, the marriage is not what I want,' Catriona returned, gathering up her fan. 'But I must obey the wishes of my father. Don't worry, I won't leave you behind when I go. I want you to come to Perth with me . . . But I am not lingering here because of that. Oh, Nan—why have they not answered our letter? Do they care so little for their own flesh and blood?'

'They?' The woman's nose wrinkled in disgust. 'Oh, you mean the MacDonalds. What did you expect? Did I not tell you it was madness to communicate with them? Likely they will wait until the poor lass is dead before they rouse themselves. Perhaps with their evil minds that is their very intention. It will give them the excuse they need to rouse their kin the MacIans and descend on Darna in full force.' Nan crossed herself fervently.

'James tells me it is Father's intention to send Kirsty home tomorrow with an escort of four armed clansmen,' Catriona replied. 'You share my fears that she will never return to her brothers alive. Four men to escort her . . . Nan, we both know what will happen—we must not allow it!'

'How can you prevent it, child? Haven't you done enough?'

'Perhaps James was right and we should have left her out on the moor—she might have been found. Perhaps I am not a true Campbell, Nan, because I like her and I want her returned home safely. Dear Nan, you have helped me so much already, I hesitate to ask more from you . . . but if Kirsty is to live, she has to leave here tonight.'

'Then tell me what I must do and go downstairs. I'd not put it above the Laird to drag you down himself if you do not. You are spoiling his evening,' Nan returned dryly.

'Bless you. Thank God, there is someone in this house I can trust.'

Catriona thought of James as she spoke, but she assured herself she was in no way being disloyal to the close bonds which linked them together. He must know nothing of what she intended to do. Her father's wrath would escape him this time and she had nothing to lose, for she would soon be leaving Darna anyway.

'Tell Alistair to have a horse saddled and waiting in the stables at eleven o'clock. By then everyone should be enjoying themselves too much to notice if I am missing for a few minutes. I'll tell Kirsty now. You will bring her down by the back stairs. I will be waiting. Is that clear?'

'Aye. Away with you now and don't linger too long with the lass,' Nan warned.

The last person Catriona expected to see as she entered Kirsty's room was James. She had thought him to be downstairs with everyone else. He sprang from the couch beside Kirsty, his cheeks reddening beneath his sister's penetrating gaze. He had been holding her hand—and looked for all the world as if he had been about to kiss her! And she had trusted him!

'Devil take you, Catriona, do you have to steal about

the place like a shadow,' he reproved sharply. 'And don't look at me like that. There is no cause.'

'Don't be alarmed.' Kirsty rose quickly to her feet in defence of the man at her side. 'James came only to pay his respects. I was glad. I—I wanted to thank him for his help. I have not forgotten it was he who found me in that awful weather. I owe you both a debt I can never repay.'

'Between friends there is no talk of debts,' Catriona answered, forcing a smile to her stiff lips. Kirsty and James—surely not! 'I would like to speak to Kirsty alone. Will you wait outside for me, James, and escort me downstairs?'

'As you wish.' As he passed her, James halted and stared full into his sister's face. 'I haven't touched her,' he said quietly. 'Ask her yourself if you don't believe me.' His features darkening he wheeled towards the door, then with an oath that made Catriona inwardly wince—for he rarely swore in her company—he turned back. 'No, dammit! Why should I pretend to you of all people,' he declared in a fierce tone. 'Kirsty and I plan to continue seeing each other after she has returned home.'

'No,' the girl cried, her expression growing distraught. 'You said that. I did not agree to it. I have already told you it is impossible.'

'Anything is possible,' James said, frowning. 'You want to see me again. You said so not a few minutes ago when I held you in my arms.'

'James,' Catriona whispered, 'you do not realise what you ask of her. The risks, to you both.'

'Risks I am willing to take. I seem to remember not long ago you risked our father's anger when you had me bring her here. I think Kirsty has your kind of courage too.'

She had never seen her brother this way before. In growing amazement she looked from one to the other. Was it possible in such a short time that love had blossomed between them?

'Before you say anything else, there is something you must know,' Kirsty said, paling considerably as she spoke. Catriona's heart went out to her. 'I have two brothers, James—Rorie and Donald. If I am not mistaken, you know them both well.'

Her young face took on a defiant expression as she gazed at him yet the brown eyes begged, Catriona thought, for gentleness and understanding.

She saw her brother stiffen, slowly absorb the shock of her words in silence and then, to her amazement, he smiled.

'And what is in a name, Kirsty MacDonald? Are you so feart to be seen in the company of a Campbell? If so, be honest now and let this go no further.'

'I will be honoured to see you again, James. If you will risk your father's anger, then I will risk that of my brothers.'

Catriona burst into a peal of laughter and flung her arms around her brother's neck.

'Bless you for making this evening something to remember. And you, Kirsty.' She hugged her friend warmly, blinking back bright tears. This was her night, yet she was finding more pleasure in the future happiness of these two people than her own. Suddenly the smile vanished. She had no choice now, but to tell James of her plans. 'Tomorrow, as you know, it is Father's intention to send Kirsty from here with an escort of four men. I trust neither his word that she will arrive home safely, nor the men who are to go with her. I have arranged for her to leave tonight.' The words tumbled out in a rush.

'There was no need,' her brother said, with a tight smile. 'It was my intention to ride with them. Unlike you, I trust Father's word, but the interpretation of it by the escort could leave a way open to something violent and unpleasant. What other plans have you made? I swear, Catriona, you grow more secretive every day. How have you arranged everything, tonight of all nights? Yet . . .' He nodded slowly, understanding. 'With so many people in the house, yes, it would be a good time. Who rides with her?'

Kirsty sent a despairing look towards Catriona. Should their secret be revealed, even to the man she had grown to like and trust?

'Word was sent to the MacDonalds that Kirsty is safe and well.' Catriona swallowed hard before answering. James's favourite she might be, but she had placed Darna and all its occupants in danger. Her father would have killed her for such a confession.

'I did it. The note was in my hand,' Kirsty interrupted as James's face darkened with disbelief. Already he was envisaging the consequences of such an act of folly. 'Rorie would not come otherwise.'

'You had the stupidity to ask the MacDonalds to come here?' James snapped. 'You will see a bloodbath that will either exterminate Darna or Kirsty's brothers and their kin. Little fools! Do you think they will come alone? Are you that naïve? I cannot believe my sister could be so irresponsible—so thoughtless for the lives of others . . .'

'A few minutes ago in this very room you asked me to trust you. Where is that trust now?' Kirsty demanded, her hands clenching into tight fists at her sides. 'Is your sister the only one who wants peace between us?'

'You are both children,' James retorted angrily. He had made his own plans, now ruined by Catriona's schemes. 'Catriona is right to suspect you would not return home alive, which is why I intended to ride with you. Neither will your brothers believe the note, even written in your hand, was done of your own free will. They will think we forced you. Did neither of you consider that? If they come, it will be expecting to find you dead. They will come with murder in their hearts, seeking revenge.'

Both girls exchanged dismayed glances. So eager to

achieve their aims, neither of them had given considera-
tion to that fact.

'What have you arranged, Catriona? Don't fence with
me, it is too late for that. If bloodshed is to be avoided, I
must act fast.'

'James, no!' Kirsty cried. 'You do not know Rorie. I
asked him to come alone and he will.'

'You have two brothers,' came the grim reply. 'Both I
and my brother Murdoch have reason to know them
well. I am waiting, Catriona.'

Already James's mind was racing ahead to discover a
way out of the dilemna which faced him. He had men in
the house who were loyal to him alone and would obey
his orders without question. He would place several on
the walls and at all the gates leading into the inner
courtyard. If the MacDonalds came in force he would be
ready. And if they came alone, two worried men seeking
their sister? No, the idea was too preposterous even to
consider.

He had killed many MacDonalds on the raids he and
his father led into their lands and could never deny they
fought well. Many had died cursing him with his last
breath. But they were a different breed of men.

He remembered one particularly bloody and savage
night after two families had been massacred by the
MacDonalds. The fury inside him could not be satiated
and he rode out with his father, his senses immune to the
brutality and death he was about to witness—and to take
part in. That night he inadvertently cut down a young
girl who came screaming at him out of the darkness,
brandishing a claymore. Saw too late the girlish features
twisted with hate as his own weapon slashed downwards.
Heard the cry of pain and saw what he had done. He
would never forget that moment or forgive the father
who had congratulated him on a good night's work
without realising the anguish and disgust which was
tearing his son's heart in two.

He had never confided in Catriona. Now he wished he had done so. As yet she had not experienced violent emotions capable of turning a normal human being into a mindless animal, devoid of any feeling. He had tried once to broach the subject, but the overwhelming nausea which overcame him at the mere recollection of that night, the fear that she might turn from him in revulsion, magnified his sense of guilt and he shied away from unburdening his soul. He did not want her to look at him as that girl had looked at him as she fell beneath his horse's hoofs.

'I thought that by eleven o'clock it would be safe for me to slip away. Nan is to take Kirsty down the back stairs to the stables where a horse will be waiting for her. I am going to have Alistair ride with her as far as the Stewarts, as no one else has appeared. She knows Tamsie and once there she will be safe.'

'The more you meddle the less you realise what harm you are doing,' James retorted, and the hazel eyes glinted with anger. Catriona dared not ask why, although she sensed another, deeper reason for his agitation, as she had done once before. 'I will escort Kirsty myself, as far as possible. My men will be on the gate to ensure no questions are asked. If we are seen by another of Father's servants, I am merely escorting a guest home. You will remain in your room, Kirsty, until Nan comes for you. And you, my sister, will now accompany me downstairs and be nice to your guests and in particular to your betrothed. Do I make myself quite clear? One thing more,' he added. 'If this goes wrong, or Father realises what we are about, he will ensure Kirsty does not leave Darna alive. Are you both willing to take that chance?'

'I am, if it means being united with my family again,' Kirsty declared. 'Give me a horse and let me go alone and I will take my chances. I cannot ask you, Catriona, to risk anything further, or you, James, to face your father's anger and the contempt of your kinsmen by protecting me tonight—or as you so gallantly intended, tomorrow. If you lived, you would be disowned, an outsider, and I cannot even offer you the thanks of my brothers. They are inclined to think as your father does.' Her lips quivering, Kirsty laid a hand on James's arm. 'Just let me go.'

If her brother was enamoured of this MacDonald girl, then she was doubly so with him, Catriona thought, and knew a moment of envy as she watched them. Her own presence was totally forgotten as James covered the slim fingers pressing tightly against his sleeve with his own. Such tenderness in his eyes. Tenderness as she had once dreamed of seeing in the eyes of the man she loved. But she had never known love—and never would now! She would tolerate, but never love the man she was to marry. Endure his mastery of her body and bear his children, but never give herself in total surrender. He would take her and it would satisfy him, leaving her unsatisfied, disappointed, disillusioned.

'The soft bear,' she murmured, tears filling her eyes.

James looked across at her, only half aware she had spoken.

'Did you say something?' He released Kirsty with some reluctance and stepped to her side.

'I was just remembering something someone once said to me. It is nothing important,' she said quickly. Would the memory of that encounter forever haunt her? 'Please take me down now, James.'

At the head of the wide marble staircase which led down to the Great Hall, James felt his sister grow tense and saw she was exceedingly pale. He tucked her arm beneath his with a reassuring smile.

'Don't worry. You have done all you can. Now it is up to me. I promise my men will be in all the important places when we leave. I am fond of the girl, Catriona, though how it came about I fail to comprehend.'

'She is everything I could ever wish for you,' Catriona whispered sincerely. Dear James, he thought her still to be thinking of Kirsty, not realising her attention was centred on the man standing beside her father at the bottom of the stairs.

Andrew Fraser, although in his mid-thirties, boasted he could outrun and outfight any man ten years his junior. His coat and trews were hand-made to make light of the growing paunch. The powdered wig and queue hid, she knew, receding lank hair. Narrowed eyes scrutinised the slender figure who halted before him, and Catriona forced down her anger as he declared in a loud voice:

'At last you daughter presents herself, Fergus. If she is this late on our wedding day she will not find me waiting for her at the altar. I shall find something better to do.'

'Does my appearance not meet with your approval, sir?' Catriona inclined her head slightly to one side, inspecting him with the same frankness as he was her. He always aroused this deep rebellion in her. She could not avert the marriage, but by heaven she would not bow to his arrogance and rudeness. Immediately she felt James's fingers curl warningly over hers. Their father's expression was like a gathering storm. 'Tonight and my wedding day are great occasions for me. Surely I may be allowed your indulgence in order to please both you and my father who has done so much to make our marriage possible,' she continued in a meeker tone. Was he the only one to notice the sadness in her eyes, James wondered?

Here he was revelling in the most wonderful thing that had ever happened to him, while Catriona was sick at heart. She could not go through with it. He would not allow it! She had been so adamant that she was not averse to the match when it had been first proposed. She had concealed her true feelings from him completely. Only as the fateful day grew closer and the fears inside her multiplied, could she no longer hide her distaste.

'Father, I must speak to you urgently,' he began, but Fergus shook his head.

'No, James. I have been neglecting our guests waiting here for your sister. We will speak later if it is important. Go with Andrew, girl, and be sociable. Many of these people have come a long way to be with us tonight.

'Yes, Father.'

Disengaging herself from James's protective grasp with a brave smile, she gave her hand to Andrew Fraser, steeling herself not to flinch as his fingers closed over hers. She always felt he wanted to assert his authority over her whenever they were together and was only protected from it by the fact she was not yet his property. Would her strong will survive his domination? Oh God, she thought, if it does not I shall die!

He was in his element, she realised as they moved among the assembled throng. Marriage to the daughter of the Laird of Darna, not to mention the dowry which accompanied her, had given the son of a dressmaker new status. He strutted and boasted about the room like a peacock, expecting congratulations to fall naturally from the lips of everyone he spoke to.

It was a full hour before Catriona was able to leave his presence. She retired to the table where punch was being served and partook of two glasses, one after the other. Only when the strong mixture of heavy-bodied wine laced, she suspected, with ancient, traditionally home-brewed whisky, intended to enliven the gathering, burned her throat and stomach, did she begin to recover her composure.

Andrew had been doubly difficult, refusing to allow her to leave his side for a moment. She had been forced to made idle conversation which held no interest for her whatsoever, to discuss her forthcoming marriage with a show of enthusiasm no one ever guessed was totally false.

All evening she remembered the look on her brother's face when she surprised him with Kirsty—the tenderness and affection in his eyes and in those of the girl she had befriended as she stared at the man Catriona cared for most in the whole world. They had found something to be cherished and protected from unfeeling men like her father and the Fraser. Oh, Kirsty, how I envy you the love you have found, she thought.

'Young ladies of good breeding should know it is not considered seemly to partake of strong spirits, especially in front of the Misses Buchanan, who are the worst gossip-mongers this side of Inverness,' a voice declared in her ear. 'However, having tasted the punch myself, I should say it is treated with some of Aunt Agatha's fire-water and well deserving of another sample. Have another glass yourself and then you might begin to enjoy yourself.'

'Murdoch!' Catriona flung herself unashamedly into the arms of the brother who had left Darna three years before. 'I didn't know you would be here. Thank you for coming. Are you staying? Have you made peace with Father after all this time? Is that why you are here?'

Murdoch Campbell was twenty-four years old. He was more slightly built than Catriona or James and he possessed none of Fergus' characteristics—except perhaps for the shrewd brown eyes which surveyed and absorbed every detail about him. He was an outcast from Darna of his own free will, and nothing Catriona had ever said to him had brought him back to the fold. Once he had shared the same love and affection as James in their father's eyes, something she had always been denied, but that had ended a short time after he returned home from university, with a crippled, useless hand. Her father tolerated no weakness of any kind! The son for whom he had once made so many plans was no longer of value to him. Now, only James remained. When their father learned of his attraction to one of the enemy, what then? Would he be disinherited too? If so, Darna would know no heir! The line would be ended.

Murdoch's arm tightened around her shoulders as he kissed her on both cheeks. The fingers resting on her bare skin, she knew had no feeling in them—the result of a sword fight during his student days. She wanted to reach up and cover them with her own, but dared not, knowing how sensitive he was about his disability.

'How could I stay away, tonight of all nights? Say hello to Tamsie and then let's have some more punch. Father's friends are as dull as the music. Is this supposed to be a gay occasion or a wake?'

'Murdoch, you promised,' the girl at his side chided gently and he turned in her direction, a disarming smile on his young face.

'Tamsie, my sweet, I swore I would be the soul of discretion and I will, provided I am not provoked.'

'Which I will ensure you are not. We have not seen each other in over a week and I intend we should get very drunk together—if the ladies will permit,' James declared appearing at Catriona's elbow. He leaned forward to brush her cheek with his, whispering in a voice too low for the others to hear. 'It is all arranged. We leave at eleven as planned.'

'Secrets?' their brother murmured amusedly.

'Everyone has them,' James returned and Catriona saw Murdoch's eyes darken with shadows. There were times when she thought she did not really know either of her brothers. They spoke quite openly in front of her whenever they were all together, yet she often sensed secondary implications to their words as if they shared something of which she was ignorant. 'Well, are we going to stand here all evening? Let's get to the serious matter of drinking now before it is all gone,' James insisted.

'Tamsie, my love, you must excuse me,' Murdoch laughed softly, and Catriona was relieved to see him relax. She embraced him again and he looked at her with a crooked smile. 'Enough, you will make my true love jealous. When I fall flat on my face, little sister, have a servant throw me over my horse and point it in the direction of home,' he called back over his shoulder as he moved away.

'Don't heed him,' Tamsie Stewart said quietly as Catriona's lips tightened. 'It is only his way, you should know that by now.'

'He has no right to bring you here and then desert you,' Catriona declared. 'He can be an unfeeling brute at times. You, of all people, who cared for him when he was sick, stayed faithful when he deserted you for over two years, and then welcomed him when he walked back into you life as if he had never been away. Tamsie, what is it about me? I have never known such—such devotion—such love. You and Murdoch share something very special and I know he loves you, although he would cut out his tongue before admitting it—and now . . .' She broke off. She would not reveal James's secret even to her closest friend. 'Oh, Tamsie, I am desolate! I am soon to be married, yet I feel nothing! If life holds nothing for me, then it cannot be worth living.'

'Dear Catriona, I know how miserable you have been from the very day your betrothal was announced, but I cannot offer you comfort and you would not heed my advice. If I thought you would, I'd tell you to go where your heart dictates, whatever the consequences. Don't look at me like that. I have loved Murdoch from the age of twelve when we all used to play together. When he came to my father's house, broken in spirit, a crippled hand tearing his heart apart, I nursed him. He cursed me and when he was well, he left. A year ago he returned. Not the Murdoch I had known, but a self-assured, confident man who took me to his bed the first night he was back. I am still not sure, as you are, that he loves me, we never discuss it, but I love him. I am his mistress and will remain so until he discards or weds me, and your badgering will not make either day come closer. Crippled hand or not, I shall never know another man like him. I never want to.'

'Are you—suggesting I have an affair outside my marriage?' Catriona gasped, appalled.

'Before, if it pleases you. If the man pleases you. If he is what you want, then take what is offered while you can and enjoy it. Life is short, Catriona, and happiness sometimes very difficult to find. If it comes your way, reach out and grasp it with both hands, unafraid.'

Catriona was silent. Tamsie, she now realised, was not only older in years, but also in the ways of the world. Perhaps she spoke foolishness, perhaps wisdom. She might never know, for she suspected she would never have the courage to act in such a fashion as her friend had done. Tamsie was tall and rather plump, with dark hair drawn back from a surprisingly thin, pointed face. Plain, yes, but the inner warmth radiating from her had reached Murdoch's heart all those years ago, remained with him during his absence and brought him back to her side. Not to Darna, his home, to the sister and brother who sorely missed him and had prayed for his return— but to Tamsie Stewart.

'I was not aware you had been invited.'

Catriona wheeled about apprehensively as she heard her father's cold tones behind her. He had come face to face with his youngest son at the punch table and the encounter did not please him. She should have known. James, not her father, had invited him, bringing all three of them together beneath Darna's roof once again as she had always wanted.

'I was not—not by you at least. Someone else remembered my existence, thank God! I hope I have spoiled your evening,' Murdoch returned slowly, smiling, but not amused. Father and son hated each other and no longer bothered to hide the fact.

Fergus glanced around at Catriona's anxious face, at James whose expression, dark with his own thoughts, told him nothing, and back to the sardonic smile of the son he had disowned. He wanted to hit him for daring to appear, for flaunting that useless sword-arm before his gaze and that of his guests.

'You are not man enough even for that,' he snapped and was pleased at the anger which sprang to Murdoch's eyes. Before the evening was out he would teach the young pup a lesson and ensure he never set foot in Darna again.

'Getting rid of little Catriona is giving you so much pleasure nothing else can spoil it, eh? A pity, I would gladly have given my other hand to have ruined to-night for you. Be careful, Father, Darna is becoming a house fit only for ghosts. But then you live in the past, don't you? The present and all those dwelling in it, including your own children, are unimportant to you.'

'Get out,' Fergus thundered and curious onlookers drifted away, not wanting to be drawn into a family argument. 'If you are not gone from this house within the hour, I shall have you, and your fancy woman, thrown out.'

'No, Murdoch!' James's fingers fastened over the hand which reached for a dirk. 'You promised Tamsie. Besides this night belongs to our sister and I will not allow anyone—anyone at all, to spoil it for her. That includes you, Father. Murdoch is here by my request and he will stay. The room is big enough for you to avoid each other, is it not?'

For a long moment Fergus considered his eldest son. He was all that was left to make his dreams come true. He needed him, needed his support in the years ahead, needed the wife he would bring to Darna, the grand-children they would raise. Heirs for Darna! Without him there was nothing left. He would do anything to keep

James at his side. Without a word he turned on his heel and walked away.

Catriona watched her brothers refill their glasses and move across to the far side of the room. She turned to her companion.

'Tamsie, I must apologise for my father.'

'Why, my dear? I am Murdoch's woman without a ring and open to whatever insults men and women choose to fling at me. I will not deny it stings, but I no longer cry as I once did. I knew what I was doing when I stayed with Murdoch a second time. He gave me that choice. I have never regretted it.'

'You are wonderfully, foolishly brave,' Catriona whispered in admiration.

'I am a woman in love. I have chosen my man and I will be true to him. Please excuse me, Catriona, I am going to retire to the gardens for a while, out of sight of all these gawking wives before I am accused of trying to steal their husbands.'

Catriona wished she, too, could slip away for a little peace and quiet, but it was not yet ten o'clock and she suspected she would be missed at once. She forced herself to dance with the bevy of young men who sought her out. It was one way of avoiding Andrew, who she saw was growing more and more unsteady with the steady consumption of punch. Hopefully when the evening was over he would collapse into a chair somewhere as he had done several times before after a hectic evening and be put to bed by his servants.

When people began to make their way into the dining room to partake of the delicious refreshments provided, she found herself able to slip outside into the cool night air. The sky was clear and a full moon bathed the gardens in a silver cloak. There was no sign of the heavy mists which often descended over the glens on these early summer's evenings.

When she was married she would live with Andrew

mostly in Inverness where his regiment was billeted, also in Perth. She had only seen the house there once. The visit had been on a rainy, dull day which did nothing to endear the gloomy, grey-stoned building to her. It was set in the middle of the main street, indistinguishable from the next in line. The interior was cold and un-friendly. Not even the warmth of her reception by the servants, who at least smiled and seemed pleased she was to be the new mistress, brought her comfort. She was being dragged away from Darna and all she loved. There was nothing to compensate for the great loss she must endure.

'My lady.' Someone touched her arm and she turned reluctantly, her peaceful moment shattered. Had she been missed so soon?

'Yes, Calum, what is it?'

'I must speak with the Laird, but he's closeted with the Fraser and I was sent away—twice. I dare not disturb him, my lady, but I must—it is of the greatest import-ance.' The man's face looked grey with fear in the bright moonlight—or was her imagination playing tricks? What was there for him to fear? 'There—there are MacDonalds at the gate!'

They had come after all in response to Kirsty's letter! Catriona's heart somersaulted unsteadily.

'How—how many are there?'

'Two, but there are more skulking in the trees. I heard the sound of many horses. They demand to see the master and were not too polite in their manner of asking. They say they have come for the girl we have here. They mean trouble.'

'Follow me,' Catriona demanded and strode off be-fore the bewildered man could argue. Taking a side path which led her around the house, she entered the main courtyard through a small wooden door, shutting her mind to the terrible risk she was about to undertake and the inevitable consequences for everyone in the house if she was wrong. 'Bring the two MacDonalds to me and be quick about it before anyone else realises they are here and then return to your quarters. If anyone asks what is wrong, you are ill and I have told you to go to bed. Speak of this to no one. You have seen no one, heard nothing. Do you understand?'

'No. I mean, yes, my lady.'

The man hurried across the cobblestones, too amazed to think clearly. MacDonalds in Darna, and being received by a slip of a girl who had never before asserted such authority. Like her mother used to be, the old retainer thought proudly. Quiet, but strong—and totally unpredictable.

CHAPTER
THREE

As SHE waited, Catriona carefully smoothed down the skirts of her gown and pushed a strand of loose hair, tugged free by a strong breeze, back behind the jewelled combs. She must appear calm and confident, yet at the sound of a foot-step behind her, she caught her breath.

'James.' She was overcome with relief as her brother appeared, his expression full of curiosity.

'What are you doing out here? Have young Michael's attentions driven you away or did I interrupt something?' His eyes swept the darkened alcoves and door-ways about them. 'He's a persistent lad, isn't he? Three dances in a row. I thought Andrew would call him out when he refused to relinquish his hold on you the last time.'

'The MacDonalds have come for Kirsty,' Catriona interrupted his light-hearted banter. Her cousin Michael had monopolised her, but she forgave him because she liked him and knew, whatever anyone else might think, that he had no interest in her at all, being already pledged to an Admiral's daughter from Edinburgh. 'They are at the gate now.'

'And you intended to meet them alone,' James ejaculated in a low, fierce tone. 'When will you take heed of what I tell you about them. Go back into the house and leave this to me. Fools! Why did they have to come? I should have had her safely home by morning.'

'Or perhaps you would have met them half-way and

never returned,' Catriona answered. She saw his fingers steal beneath the lace ruffles of his sleeve. Concealed there was a slender-bladed knife, as deadly as his ability to use it. 'That is not the way, James. They are here now and we must get Kirsty away with them before they are seen. They must be reasonable men or they would not be here. They risk their lives in doing so.'

'If you believe that then you are a fool. They will have men waiting nearby to attack once they have her safely away. Damn them! They have put all our lives at risk.'

'Calum did say he heard the sound of other horses hidden in the trees beyond the walls,' she hastened to say, wishing he did not sound so confident in his assessment of the situation, and James swore under his breath.

'You might find your betrothal ball turned into a funeral,' he muttered as two horsemen came out of the shadows in front of them. He drew a deep breath as their features became distinguishable. 'By heaven, it's the devil's twins themselves. The "Red" MacDonald and his brother Donald, no less.'

Catriona was aware of ten, perhaps more, figures moving behind the arrivals in a half-circle, blocking their retreat as they dismounted. She felt dwarfed by the two tall frames which confronted them.

'Do you come in peace, MacDonald? If you have death in your heart you will not leave here alive,' James said in a cold tone. 'There are men all about you.'

Catriona noticed he addressed himself to the man who stood perhaps a foot closer to him than his companion. One to guard the front, the other the rear, she thought, and was momentarily taken aback. Years of being taught to believe this particular family were worthless scoundrels, cattle thieves, and perpetrators of destruction and murder were making her think like everyone else.

From Nan's wild tales, often exaggerated, she thought she had half expected some wild beasts, seven feet high, belching fire and smoke. She remembered how, several times, she had been whisked off a street in Inverness and into the protection of a shop, so that she could not gaze on those MacDonald monsters, who roamed the streets in search of liquor and women, and appreciated neither.

They lived on the edge of the sweeping Mamore Forest in a house the 'Red' MacDonald had built for his mother, now dead. As a baby, she had been one of the few survivors from the massacre in Glen Coe. Taken to the safety of the Isle of Rhum, she had lived there most of her life, married and had a family, which she promptly returned to the mainland along with herself and the considerable fortune left to her on the death of her husband.

Never, until that day in the mist, had Catriona been close enough to one of them to be able to touch an arm, a hand, a cheek. Now she was given the opportunity to see for herself the evil they were said to represent.

'By God, brother, did I not tell you this was a trap,' the furthest MacDonald snapped.'

'The Campbell is no fool, Donald, he knows by now we did not come alone and what will happen if we do not leave with our sister—unharmed. Where is she?'

The quiet, hard voice which answered James made Catriona stiffen with shock. The moon was behind him, making it difficult for her to see his features any more clearly than she had that last time, but she would never forget the voice. Had it not haunted her sleep for many nights since?

'So she did not lie, she is your sister,' James breathed. There was a tenseness about him Catriona did not like. These men were old enemies. 'She is upstairs.'

'And well, I hope, for your sake. That sounds a bonny gathering inside. It would be a pity to interrupt it.'

She could just make out a hand tightly clutching the hilt of a claymore. James was right, they had come expecting to walk into a trap—prepared to fight their way out, killing as many Campbells as was possible on the way. But they had still come!

'You and your brother are welcome here, Rorie Mac-Donald. We gave you our word you would be received hospitably and allowed to leave unmolested with your sister,' Catriona said, moving slightly to one side of her brother. The mocking undertone in her voice which in no way betrayed the unsteady pounding of her heart, made the man give her his attention for the first time.

'You have a habit of straying a long way from Appin,' he answered, gazing at her steadily. He had recognised her too! She dared not look at James, although she knew he was staring at her intently. 'I should have realised when you lied so adroitly that you were akin to the Campbells. They are all accomplished liars.' The scathing comment far outweighed Catriona's attempt at sarcasm and she felt a rush of fierce colour to her cheeks, which grew more acute as he added, 'Are the men hereabouts all cowards that they send a child to speak for them?'

'Child?' Donald MacDonald murmured with a deep-throated chuckle. 'Rorie, this light deceives you.'

'I am no child. Address yourself to me,' James snapped.

'James, be calm.' Catriona's hand rested on the fingers groping for the dirk, stilling their progress. 'They would like this to be a trap. It would satisfy the bloodlust they feel towards us. No doubt their men are only waiting for some prearranged signal, to fall upon the house and kill us all.' Anger overcame the embarrassment these men made her feel. Carefully picking up the skirts of her beautiful gown, she tossed back her head, stared directly up at Rorie MacDonald and said in the frostiest tone she could muster. 'Come, I will take you to Kirsty. If you are not afraid to follow this child, Rorie MacDonald.'

She heard James's bitten-off expletive at her impudence, but she moved away from him quickly, heading towards a side door which would lead them upstairs without being seen by any of the assembled guests. She had to get them out of the courtyard!

Her fingers were reaching for the catch when they were roughly coupled in a grip which made her wince and she was brought abruptly to a halt.

'We are not fools to follow blindly, even after such an innocent face,' Rorie MacDonald hissed in her ear. 'You lied to me once before. Why should I trust you now?'

Catriona fought down the impulse to resist him. She had no reason. Soon he would see how wrong his suspicions were and then she would demand an apology for his ill-mannered behaviour.

She cried out as there came the sound of steel striking steel and James's dirk clattered to the floor at her feet. Wide-eyed she saw the claymore of the second Mac-Donald at his throat.

'Treachery, brother. This one tried to dirk me in the dark.'

'He is afraid for me—as you are for your sister,' she flung back. 'What kind of men are you? We find Kirsty and bring her here. The doctor comes from Dalness to attend her and I go against my father's wishes to send you word she is safe. For what? Instead of thanks there are threats. You come with murder in your hearts instead of gratitude.'

'We have tasted Campbell hospitality before,' the man holding her replied humourlessly. 'My mother's family, men, women and tiny babes were murdered by one of your kin, if you remember. If you speak the truth and Kirsty is unharmed, we will leave in peace. If she has been hurt—or disposed of . . .' He significantly left the sentence unfinished. 'Take me to her. Your friend here . . .'

'My brother,' Catriona interrupted.

'So this is the Laird's precious little daughter, the one

he is giving into the safe keeping of that old lecher, Andrew Fraser. Now I can see why he is so anxious for the wedding,' Donald laughed softly and James swore at his helplessness.

'Don't,' Catriona pleaded, recognising his frustration. 'We will do what they want. We have nothing to fear.'

'Upstairs.' She was pushed roughly through the open door towards the staircase. 'One sound and you both die and we'll take our chances where we stand.'

'Brave words, MacDonald and what of your sister when the four of us are dead?' Catriona flung back. 'I am beginning to understand why our families have been feuding for so long. You and my father are much alike. When you have satisfied yourself Kirsty is alive and well, perhaps you would like me to introduce you to him, as you have so much in common.'

'Be quiet. What part of the house are we in?'

'This staircase will take us directly to the landing where your sister has a room. Do you see how easily I give away our secrets, MacDonald.' Catriona was becoming amazed at her own audacity. She failed to comprehend how two men could be so blind and distrustful and yet so brave as to walk into the house of their enemy fully expecting to be cut down without quarter given at any moment. How they must love their sister. Yes—as she and James loved each other. Understanding this she momentarily forgave them their numerous other failings.

She was aware of James watching her in disbelief. He had never seen her this way before. Rebellion before their father was understandable and he had grown accustomed to it over the years, but to deliberately antagonise two armed and dangerous MacDonalds was madness.

'Walk ahead of me slowly.' Catriona felt the touch of a knife blade against her skin. 'A mere precaution,' Rorie muttered, the shadowed features creasing into a smile. 'You are too bold, mistress. Remember, you will die quickly and silently if this is a trap, and your brother will follow you.'

Acutely conscious of him behind her every step of the way, Catriona slowly mounted the stairs. More than once she stumbled in the darkness of the twisting stair-case used mostly by the servants, her mind dwelling on the terrible predicament in which she had placed her brother. If only he would contain his temper, stay calm and make no foolish moves until they were safely in Kirsty's room.

To her horror as they reached the passageway, one of the kitchen maids appeared from the room, a supper tray in her hands, and moved in their direction.

A strong arm encircled Catriona's waist, drawing her backwards into a recess where the light from the flicker-ing wall torches a few yards away did not reach. The sharp point of his dirk touched her breast just below the neckline of her gown.

'If she suspects a thing I'll kill her,' came the threat in her ear as her mind fought for some way out of this unexpected crises. 'Donald—hide, man.'

Before her mind had begun to function again, she was pressed back against the wall and held helpless by the weight of his body. Her hands thrust upwards against his chest in silent horror, but they were imprisoned to her sides as his mouth fastened over hers, effectively silen-cing the cry which rose to her lips.

Catriona had not been kissed many times before. James always kissed her tenderly, lovingly. The man she was to marry usually gave her the feeling he cared little or nothing that he bruised her soft lips so long as it was enjoyable to him. Andrew was a soldier, used to having women where and when it suited him. Had it not been for her father's name and influence, she had often thought she would have been considered in the same light.

No one had ever kissed her like this! She wanted to

fight this man who dared to lay hands on her, but she was held immobile. She wanted to cry out, but his lips remained on hers without mercy until they parted and came alive beneath his and, for the first time in all her twenty years, she experienced a deep fire within her, urging her to surrender to the moment, enjoy it, return his kisses! Who would know?

She could not move—think! She was in the power of a totally unknown force! It was frightening and yet enjoyable. Shameful, yet more wonderful than anything she had ever experienced before.

The maid came upon two figures, locked in what appeared to be a passionate embrace. She could not see either of their faces, but the material of the woman's exquisite gown was unmistakable. She had risked boxed ears to sneak up from the kitchens to peek at the guests and had returned, declaring Catriona to be the most beautifully-dressed woman there.

'My lady—I'm—I'm sorry,' she stammered. 'I thought—I mean . . .'

Catriona was so breathless she could scarcely speak. As she raised her head, the pressure of the dirk increased.

'Go about your duties, girl. You have not seen me. I shall know who to blame if word of this reaches my father's ears.'

'Oh, no. Not me . . . I wouldn't . . .'

She was gone in a flurry of white petticoats, a hand against her mouth, and Catriona, as she was released, fell back against the wall, sick with apprehension.

'She will never keep silent. She is the worst chatterbox in the house. Within the hour everyone will know I was up here with—with another man on the very night of my betrothal ball.' Sanity came flooding back and with it the reality of the train of events this man had unwittingly set in motion. What she had felt in that mad moment was forgotten, extinguished like a candle-flame as she thought of her father's reaction to this tit-bit of gossip—and Andrew!

'That is your problem,' her companion returned callously. 'With your ability to lie you should have no trouble getting out of an awkward situation. Where is my sister's room?'

'At the end of the passage.'

'Show me—or are you afraid of what I shall find?' came the contemptuous taunt.

With a muffled sob, Catriona fled along the carpeted passageway. Without pausing in flight, she flung open the door and ran into Kirsty's room, fighting back a flood of tears. So many emotions were raging through her, she did not know whether to cry or resort to temper.

Kirsty leapt up from a chair drawn close to the fire with a cry.

'Catriona, what is it? What's wrong? You are early.' And then her voice trailed off at the sight of the tall man whose frame blocked the doorway. 'Rorie! Oh, Rorie, you came after all.'

Regardless of the open door behind him, forgetful of the daughter of his enemy, the 'Red' MacDonald crossed the room in three long strides and gathered his sister in his arms.

'My God, you are safe!' He buried his face in her loose hair. 'You can't imagine what I have been thinking.'

Catriona was moved. This was the kind of relationship she shared with James. There were tears in both their eyes. MacDonald men capable of emotion like normal human beings. It was unheard of!

In the fully lighted room Catriona was able to study Rorie MacDonald clearly for the first time. Her assessment of his stature had not been exaggerated by the shadowy courtyard. He was perhaps a little over six feet. His thick hair was as red as the flames dancing in the hearth, yet as he moved his head the candlelight caught strands of burnished gold. His features were darker than

Kirsty's, the bone structure more prominent. The mouth was lean, the firmness of the jawline indicating more than a hint of ruthlessness. As she had already discovered, a man not to be disobeyed. Giving orders, but not taking them. The kind of man others looked to in times of need—or trouble.

As he became aware of his surroundings again, Rorie eased himself away from his sister. Tawny eyes, flecked with green, fastened on the silent figure in yellow satin, and swept her from head to toe with an intent stare that made her blush to the very roots of her hair.

He had heard the Laird of Darna's daughter was headstrong and wilful, spoilt utterly by the father and brother who adored her. The colour staining her cheeks surprised him. After her sarcasm and bold front he had expected to be confronted by a brazen-faced woman of the world, not a child, embarrassed by the frankness of a man's eyes.

A child? No, Donald was right there. Young in years perhaps, but already a desirable woman. In the mists he had met a dishevelled, soaking wet creature. Now he was looking at an elegant vision of loveliness he knew he would not forget overnight. Was he mad to allow such thoughts to enter his mind, clouding his judgment? She was a Campbell. The pretty face no doubt hid the mind of another scheming woman, although she carried the pose of innocence well. He reminded himself she was to marry Andrew Fraser. No woman who had ever come into contact with that man remained virtuous for long. His brother's description of 'old lecher' was how he was known behind his back in Inverness and across the glens as far as Mamore. The men under his command were equally as rapacious, given free rein by a man who had no respect for womanhood. Age was immaterial to the Fraser.

'It would appear I made a hasty judgment.' The words fell hesitantly from his lips—begrudgingly. But she had helped Kirsty. 'If so, I offer my apologies for my rough manner.'

'If so,' Catriona echoed in a contemptuous tone. Dear heaven, these MacDonalds were proud. They could not bend one iota. 'Your sister stands beside you alive and well. Is that not proof of our good faith?'

Rorie's eyes gleamed mockingly in the candlelight.

'Downstairs there were at least a dozen armed men ready to strike at us from behind. Where will they be when we reappear? Waiting in the shadows to finish what they intended then? That's the only Campbell hospitality I have ever known. You little fool, did you think we would believe Kirsty's letter? We came prepared, so if you or your brother have any devious plans for us, I suggest you think again. You will both die long before we do.'

'With two such important hostages leading the way to freedom, we have nothing to worry about—we can kill them later at our pleasure,' Donald MacDonald drawled from the doorway behind them.

Catriona spun about apprehensively, but at the sight of James with him, she slowly relaxed again. He was pale, she saw, but thankfully in control of himself. She had to match his calmness and keep her wits about her. 'We hid in a closet until that fool girl had gone.'

'Put up your sword, Kirsty is safe,' his elder brother said.

'So I see. The moment I get home, young woman, I intend to put you over my knee and if Rorie has any sense he'll ship you to France immediately. Have they touched you—this one in particular?' He indicated James, his lip curling. 'Don't be afraid to speak, I'll slit his throat if he denies it.'

'I have not been harmed,' Kirsty insisted. 'Why will neither of you believe them capable of kindness? Catriona has been an angel. She has faced her father's anger and the animosity of almost everyone in this house to care for me. At no time have I been molested, or even threatened.'

Catriona noticed she did not look at James, almost as if she dared not for fear of giving herself away and she was aware of the 'Red' MacDonald staring intently into his sister's face. He was no fool! He knew the Laird's daughter did not carry sufficient weight to prevent her being killed. He raised his head and looked directly at Catriona, his eyes shadowed with suspicion, but before he could put voice to his thoughts, Donald chuckled.

'We must think of a way to repay her, must we not, brother.' He looked at her and Catriona shivered inexplicably. Of the two men she found she feared him most, although from the tales Nan had told her, the reverse should have applied.

'We have what we came for,' Rorie said tersely. 'Lay a hand on the girl and we will have to fight our way out.'

'Touch my sister and I will see you both roasted in the fires of hell,' James threatened.

Rorie looked at him sharply. So James Campbell had an Achilles heel after all. He had always thought him too selfish to care for anyone but himself. That could prove useful.

'Stop this! I am ashamed of you both,' Kirsty interrupted, her features pale and distraught. 'Can't you see Donald is spoiling for a fight, Rorie. Please take me home before you are discovered.'

'We have already been seen,' Catriona said, thinking of Morag, the servant girl, as she spoke. 'I suspect by now most of the servants are enjoying a juicy piece of gossip.' They had to leave now. If they were seen and the alarm raised, there would be no time for explanations. Her blood and that of her brother would mingle with the MacDonalds' before sanity prevailed again.

James too, was only too aware of the predicament they all faced. Had he ridden through the gate with a hooded woman at his side, no one would have thought twice about it, but his men had seen the MacDonalds, knew they were now inside the house. For all he knew one of them had lost courage at the last moment as he waited in the darkness and slipped inside to warn his father. There could be armed men on the staircase and in the corridor outside, waiting to cut them down. His mouth grew dry at the thought of Catriona beneath the sword of Rorie MacDonald.

'There is a way out of this still,' he said, addressing himself to the man at Kirsty's side. 'I never expected you to come, but now you are here . . .'

'You had men waiting for us . . .' Donald growled, but he was waved to silence.

'As you brought men with you, not believing your sister had written to you willingly. Why should you trust us, we do not trust you?'

'James,' Catriona protested.

'At least let us be honest with each other for a few minutes—it may be all we have unless we are sensible,' James continued, ignoring her interruption. 'I do not agree with everything my sister has done and well she knows it, but nor do I agree with what my father had in mind.'

'And what was that?' Rorie asked in a low tone.

'To send your sister from here with an escort of our men. We are not fools, MacDonald, I can only guess how you would have received her and it was not to my liking. I intended to secrete her out of the house tonight while everyone was occupied and get her safely to the Stewarts' house in Appin where my brother lives. From there her journey would have been a short one. At the time I did not know of my sister's wild schemes.'

'Had you met us on the road you would be dead now.' Rorie weighed the words carefully. They had a ring of truth to them. Kirsty was nodding her head vehemently, her eyes pleading with James to believe them.

'As you will be if you are seen. Allow Catriona to go downstairs and tell father you are here and wish to express your gratitude before leaving. He cannot refuse to receive you. Our laws of hospitality forbid it. I give you my word, I will allow no man to draw a sword against you while you are beneath this roof.'

Donald MacDonald swore violently. Even Catriona could not suppress an incredulous gasp. Have the Mac-Donalds present themselves in the Great Hall? It was madness.

'The alternative,' James continued as a heavy silence prevailed, 'is to go back the way we came and take our chances.'

There was a knock on the door which transfixed them all rigid. Even as Rorie's dirk appeared to menace Catriona, Nan exploded into the room, her face red from the exertion of rushing upstairs.

'Here you are! I've been looking everywhere for you, my lady. The Laird is nigh tearing out his hair at your absence and the Fraser is so drunk he can scarcely stand. What are you doing up here with these . . .' Incredulity, amazement and then fear registered on her features as she paused for breath and for the first time recognised the tartan of the two strangers—saw the wicked-looking blade held not two inches from her young mistress' throat.

'In with you, woman, before you rouse the whole house with your blathering.' James snapped. He grabbed her by the arm and pulled her into the room so violently she lost her balance and toppled sideways into a chair.

Donald ducked his head outside, then closed and locked the door.

'It's too late for that now,' Rorie said grimly.

'Man, what are you worried about, there's no one in sight. We can be away in ten minutes. If there's trouble, we have the girl and her brother and the fat old biddy will make extra cannon fodder if necessary,' his brother chuckled.

'Dear heaven, we are all going to be murdered,' Nan wailed, crossing herself.

'You—Campbell,' Rorie turned on James, his face an expressionless mask. 'Away downstairs and tell the Laird of Darna The 'Red' MacDonald wishes to pay his respects. Return alone with his answer.'

'Let my sister go!'

'No! I have no fear you will betray us while she is with me.' A smile touched his lips. It was not a pleasant smile and too late James realised his vulnerability had been detected.

'Go, James. I am not afraid to remain,' Catriona said bravely.

'Then you are a fool,' Rorie answered, pushing her towards a settee. 'Sit down and keep quiet. That goes for you too,' he added as Kirsty opened her mouth to protest at his rough treatment of the girl she had come to regard as a friend. 'If it was not for your foolishness we would not be here now, risking our necks.'

He glowered at her as she sat down and slipped an arm reassuringly around Catriona's shoulders, but he said nothing more.

Donald took up a position by the door as James left, sword drawn. His head was tilted back against the wooden panels, his eyes fastened on Catriona. She hated him for the animal thoughts she knew were in his mind.

His elder brother also saw that scrutinising stare and began to grow uneasy as the minutes ticked past with interminable slowness. He knew if his brother made a move towards her he would be forced to intervene, even though he cared nothing for the girl, but there was more at stake than just the satisfying of Donald's appetite. Oh, God, he thought, laying his sword within fingertip reach, let there be one honest Campbell. Hurry. For God's sake hurry, James Campbell.

*　　*　　*

'James, where the devil have you been and where is your sister? I sent that maid of hers to find her a full fifteen minutes ago and she hasn't returned yet,' Fergus said irritably, when James sought him out and drew him into a quiet corner. 'Andrew is drinking too much again, damn the man. Find Catriona and have her stay with him. I won't have my friends upset by his coarseness.' He was tired and in no mood for conversation. James frowned as his hand was shrugged off. 'Well, don't just stand there, do as I say.'

As a son-in-law Andrew Fraser would take an un-wanted daughter off his hands, but there was no love lost between them. Each knew he was using—and being used by—the other. Fergus silently detested his future son-in-law more each day they met. His manners were becoming too crude, and his conversation tonight was often illuminated with the coarseness brought about by years of soldiering.

'Listen to me, Father, and listen carefully. Say nothing until I have finished. We have two MacDonalds in the house. They have come for their sister. Now, either we let them take her, or we spill the innocent blood of others here tonight by involving them in our quarrels.'

'MacDonalds in Darna!' Fergus gaped at him disbelievingly. 'My God, this is treachery. Who has betrayed us?'

'Keep your voice down,' James insisted as curious looks were directed at them. His fingers closed like a vice over Fergus's wrist, holding him fast. 'There are only two in the house, but more wait outside our walls. They came in peace, Father. They wish to thank you for caring for their sister. Receive them.' His grip tightened and Fergus winced in pain. He had almost forgotten this forceful side of his son's character, it so rarely showed itself these days.

Despite his anger, his disbelief at what he had been told, he felt a fierce twinge of pride. He had been like this once, strong, fearless, dominant. Yes, James was his son, his heir. He would remind him of it soon. With Catriona gone, he should take a wife, have children.

'I will not receive them,' he said stiffly, but already in his mind he had accepted that he must, or risk a massacre of friends and relatives, the like of which Darna had never seen. 'Who do they think they are to demand an audience with me?'

'Tis the "Red", MacDonald himself, Father, that's who. Kirsty is his sister. He is a powerful man, with much influence in the glens. There will be many here tonight who will think you wise to declare a truce. Do I fetch them, or are you prepared to spill blood—and mine will be the first—by refusing? They hold Catriona hostage upstairs. You know they will not hesitate to kill her if we send men against them—and I will surely die avenging her.'

Fergus swore blindly. When he spoke his voice was hoarse with frustration. As much as he wanted to wheel about and call his clansmen to storm upstairs and cut down the enemy, he knew he could not for fear his son's life would be ended in its prime. Not for one moment did he consider the plight of his daughter.

'Damn you, James. When this night is over you will answer to me. You and your sister. Don't attempt to protect her. This is somehow her doing, I know it—her and that MacDonald bitch! Bring them to me, but I warn you. One false move from any of them and I will have them slain at my feet and risk the consequences.'

Catriona raised her head and looked at the two silent men opposite. Donald seemed half-asleep, but she knew he was still watching her and avoided his narrowed gaze. Rorie MacDonald stood by the curtained window. Unlike his brother, his expression betrayed none of his thoughts.

Kirsty's fingers squeezed hers, but she found no comfort in the gesture. James had been gone too long. Surely he would not have betrayed them? Death—she had never considered it before. Now she was realising she was closer to it than at any other time in her life. It was a terrifying thought.

As if of a similar mind, Rorie turned and looked at her, the green-flecked eyes thoughtful. He was prepared to fight—and die—she realised. He had been brought up that way. Part of her abhorred his courage, part of her envied it. His resemblance to James had stunned her at first. Both he and James had sisters they adored and would go to any lengths to protect. The bonds between them went deeper than any blood-ties. Only a name separated them.

Donald straightened suddenly, raised his claymore and swung wide the door. Catriona took one look at her brother's face and knew he had been expecting to find the worst upon his return.

'He's alone.'

Rorie's hand relaxed about the hilt of his sword. He was puzzled by the attitude of the girl he had watched during the prolonged absence of her brother. Despite his insistence she remain silent, Kirsty had filled his ears with praise of her. He found such an angel of virtue too good to be true! He owed her a great deal, but he was not as trusting as his sister. Beneath the innocent pose, behind those blue eyes that stared at him with such disdain, she was still a Campbell—treacherous!

'My father is willing to receive you,' James declared and Catriona's eyes widened in disbelief.

'With a hundred men ready to rush at us the moment we show our faces. Rorie, for the love of God, don't listen to him. It has to be a trap,' Donald cried hoarsely. 'Is he willing to go first with my dirk at his back?'

'I am.' Catriona stood up. Her legs felt like water, but she forced them to hold her upright. 'If you believe it to be a trap then you are not only fools, but blind fools!'

'You and I will test your father's word,' Rorie snapped. Sheathing his weapon he crossed to her side and tucked her arm beneath his. 'Follow us with my sister, Campbell. You bring up the rear, Donald. If he so much as blinks in the wrong direction, kill him!'

Catriona froze as they reached the head of the staircase. The pressure on the arm Rorie held in a vice-like grip grew exceedingly more painful.

'Afraid? Do you not trust your own father?' he drawled in her ear.

'You are everything I have ever been told you were— cold, callous, immune to the decent feelings of others,' she spat the words at him, roused to rebellion once more by his taunts. 'Like your brother, you would like treachery, would you not? The pair of you would die in a blaze of glory, the minstrels would sing of your courage as you cut down helpless men and women and at some future time, your kinsmen would descend on this house and annihilate what was left of us. No, MacDonald Ruadh, we will not satisfy your lust for destruction. As distasteful as it is to him, my father will receive you and my friends here tonight will not raise a finger against you. It will give me great pleasure to watch you humble your MacDonald pride and accept Campbell hospitality. The memory of it will stick in your throat forever.'

'And one day you will pay for those words, you bitch!' Rorie replied tight-lipped.

He stepped forward, pulling her so close to him it would appear to everyone below they were descending arm in arm. Ruthlessly he forced her down the first stairs. She fought to free herself in silence, failed, and as startled eyes swept upwards, submitted to this final act of humiliation.

CHAPTER
FOUR

THE tartan being worn by the man at Catriona's side was too obvious to go unnoticed for long. Conversation lulled—mouths gaped, expressions were incredulous and finally the minstrels in the long gallery ceased their playing. The Great Hall waited. Disbelieving eyes watched Catriona and her companion cross the floor to where Fergus stood in front of the enormous fireplace, his features as granite as the stone behind him. Hands reached instinctively for weapons, but none were drawn as James declared in a loud voice,

'Peace, my friends. These men are our guests tonight.'

He had given his father no choice but to step forward and acknowledge the MacDonalds. It angered him beyond all reason, his son saw that, but it had to be done.

'Father, I think you already know Rorie MacDonald and his brother Donald.' Catriona's voice shook as she followed James's lead, conscious of Andrew shouldering his way from the back of the room, only to have his way barred by Murdoch and two of her brother's closest friends.

Rorie felt the relief which surged through her, the relaxing of her hand in his, and his gaze swept the sea of hostile faces, ignoring the hatred in the eyes fastened on him, until he found the face he sought.

Andrew Fraser was being persuaded to step into a side-chamber by four men who surrounded him. Forcibly persuaded, Rorie saw with a moment's amusement as the man was unceremoniously propelled backwards through the half-open door, which was immediately closed after him. His eyes narrowed as he considered the man who stood guard before it. The youngest son, Murdoch! Was he to be for ever haunted by men whose sole purpose in life was to see him dead?

'We are already well acquainted.' An uneasy murmur ran through the onlookers as Fergus refused to offer his hand. 'My son tells me you have come for your sister. You are satisfied she has been well cared for, I hope?'

One day, Fergus thought, staring into the berry-brown features before him, I will have my blade in you for this night. And you, my daughter will rue the day you were born. I will deal with you first and then Andrew can have you with my blessing.

'Satisfied and grateful,' Rorie returned politely. He knew well what was in the old man's mind, for every threat was mirrored in his eyes for all about him to see. He would have given anything to see him dead at his feet, to toss his remains over the walls for his men to find, but he dared not. 'I admit such concern was unexpected. Once again, my thanks.'

'It is my daughter who should receive your thanks, sir, although she'll get none from me,' Fergus declared, making it plain to everyone he was no party to this farce. 'I am of no mind to shelter anyone bearing your accursed name.'

James squeezed Kirsty's hand as she darted an anxious glance his way. Damn his father, could he not bend? Thank heavens he had had the foresight to tell Murdoch what he was about and warn him to get Andrew out of the way. That drunken loud-mouth could have incited a massacre within the space of minutes.

'So you will not accept my thanks and take a dram with me,' Rorie asked and his voice grew very quiet. When he received no answer, he deliberately motioned forward a servant, took a glass of whisky from the tray he held and waited for Fergus to do the same. Quickly Catriona took a small glass of wine. Forcing a painful smile to his lips, Fergus picked up a glass. He cared not what it contained, wishing it would fall to the ground and shatter before it touched his lips.

'May you rot in hell,' he said between clenched teeth and swallowed the whisky.

Turning on his heel he waved to the minstrels, indicating they should continue with the music and sought solace with his closest friends, his back towards them.

Rorie stood unmoving as did Catriona, and James behind her. For a few minutes none of them could believe they were still alive. Behind them all, Donald let loose a string of obscenities about the rudeness of their host.

With Kirsty on his arm, James stepped past them, turned and looked back at the tall man holding fast to his sister's arm.

'You wanted him to refuse your toast, that I understand, but he did not. You have drunk together. You have accepted his hospitality, for what it is worth, and must continue to do so or every hand will be raised against you when you leave this room. Remain for a while longer—as my guests, if not my father's. My promise still stands.'

'Please, James, you ask too much,' Kirsty broke in. The look Rorie directed at her for such familiarity made her quickly look away, her cheeks bright with embarrassment. James's touch gave her renewed courage. She said, not looking at her brother, 'Dance with me. Just once before I go.'

'We are leaving,' Rorie snapped, scarcely able to believe his ears. 'Now.'

'So soon, when the evening has just become interesting,' Donald murmured, his eyes intent on a pretty girl across the room. 'I suggest you take the advice of the Campbell and enjoy the Laird's hospitality a little longer. They dare not harm us.'

He moved away in the direction of the girl and a moment later she was in his arms in the midst of the dancers. Many withdrew, leaving them almost alone on the floor.

'The fool,' Rorie said bleakly, despairing at his brother's weakness—not the worst one he could name, but sufficiently provocative to give the watching men a reason to turn against them.

'My brother has given you his word there will be no weapons raised against you unless you show your blade first,' Catriona said stiffly.

'Do you think I believe him? Both he and his father would like to see me dead. You are no different,' came the callous retort.

'If my presence is so distasteful to you, why do you not allow me to return to my guests?'

'Because you are my safe conduct. With you beside me I know your brother will not chance a treacherous move.'

'Very well, if you are determined to be unpleasant, but I would be grateful if you would release my wrist. It feels as if it is about to break.'

She met his cold gaze challengingly and felt her fear of him suddenly slipping away. He emitted a soft expletive as his fingers fell away to reveal the painful red marks they had left on her soft skin. With a shrug she arranged the lace ruffles of her sleeve over them.

'It is no more than I expected from a MacDonald,' she said bitingly.

To her surprise a flush crept into those dark cheeks. Embarrassment? Surely not.

'I do not treat all women so thoughtlessly.'

'Only Campbell women.'

'Believe what you will.' He helped himself to another drink from a frull tray being carried past. 'It is of no consequence to me.'

All the time she remained at his side, Catriona expected to see Andrew reappear, drunken, blustering, spoiling for a fight. At last it dawned on her that James had somehow averted a disaster—no, two. One with the MacDonalds, the other with Andrew. When Murdoch was not standing outside the door through which she had last seen him disappear, two other clansmen lingered there, talking or watching the dancing. Always friends of her brothers, she noticed. Not once had the door opened again. Were they going to keep him out of the way all night? He would be like a raging bull when he was released, if he was sober. Knowing Murdoch's dislike of the man, he might have given him sufficient brandy to drink himself insensible—or forced it on him. Murdoch did many things these days he would never have dared do when he lived beneath his father's roof.

He was sarcastic and moody at times, given to long spells of solitude when no one dared go near him. He had changed drastically since the accident. Sometimes he refused even her company and that hurt her deeply for once she had been as close to him as she now was with James.

'Let's dance,' Rorie exclaimed. 'If I am to remain, I might as well enjoy myself too.'

'Have you taken leave of your senses?' she demanded aghast. People had been looking at her oddly since she came downstairs. The gossip tomorrow would be unbearable—that and her father's wrath. 'Dance with you! Before everyone!'

'Am I not man enough for the Laird's daughter? Perhaps my brother would suit you better. Or am I too much of a man?' The tawny eyes were amused as he stared down into her shocked features. 'I've noticed you have not been so pert with your answers this past hour. Are you losing your enthusiasm for this grand occasion? I have just discovered mine. Donald and I are being entertained by the Laird of Darna and not a hand raised against us. Faith, I could laugh aloud.'

'But you are not laughing, are you? You are not in the least amused by the situation, whatever you pretend to be.'

'Humour me then. Dance with me.'

She had no choice but to give him her hand again. This time his hold was gentle. Minutes later she realised what really lay behind his request when he said.

'I do not see your brother or Kirsty. They were by the french windows a moment ago.'

'Perhaps they have gone into the gardens, it is exceedingly warm in here,' she answered and wished she could have bitten off her tongue for such thoughtlessness as she was propelled firmly out onto the terrace.

The two missing people were clearly to be seen in the bright moonlight in a sheltered arbour in the gardens. Rorie blinked at the figure bending over his sister, dropped Catriona's hand with an angry roar and vaulted over the low stone balustrade towards them.

'James!' She cried a warning, but too late. As her brother whirled about he found himself face to face with the MacDonald's furious features. A clenched fist sent him reeling backwards to the ground.

'Kirsty's leg is painful again,' he shouted as Rorie bent to grab hold of him again. 'Look at her, man, can't you see for yourself? I've sent inside for Doctor McBain. He will tell you himself he thought she should rest in bed for at least two weeks. Both you and my father are to blame if she becomes ill again.'

'Was she running from you, Campbell?'

'Rorie, no. Listen to him.' Kirsty raised her head from the pillow James had fashioned out of his jacket. 'I twisted my foot on the path—the foot I hurt when my horse threw me in the mist. It hurts so again. He isn't lying, the doctor did order me to stay in bed, but what could I do? I was too afraid of what would happen . . . Don't be angry with James, it isn't his fault. I should not have tried to dance . . .'

Cautiously James came to his feet, rubbing a bruised jaw. He ignored Rorie, he only had eyes for Kirsty.

'Put your arms around my neck and I'll carry you back inside.'

'Kirsty comes home with me now . . .' Rorie began. Kirsty gave a soft cry and folded like a rag doll into the arms which held her.

'She is in no danger, you have seen that for yourself. Let her stay another few days,' Catriona begged. 'She is not a strong girl.'

'Do not presume to tell me about my own sister,' Rorie growled, but he wavered in his decision to snatch her away now. She had never been strong and this was the third time in as many months she had injured the same leg and suffered much pain.

'Are you blind to everything but your hatred of my family?' Catriona cried.

'One day that foolish tongue will be the death of you,' he replied grimly. 'Her safety is in your hands. If anything happens to her I will find you wherever you are and deal with you myself. Are you prepared to take that risk?' Mutely she nodded. 'Three more days and I shall come for her.'

He stood like a watchful sentinel as Kirsty was carried upstairs and put to bed. He paced the corridor outside her room impatiently while the doctor was with her and then dragged the man to one side to question him when he appeared. Apparently satisfied with what he heard he disappeared into the room, slamming the door behind him. When he emerged again, he looked pale and angry and once more voiced his intention of returning in three days. The onus was on James, Catriona realised, and wished with all her heart she could have borne full responsibility for what had taken place tonight. Her father would never forgive her, that did not matter, but if he alienated himself from the only person he had left in the world . . .

'This is the difficult part,' James murmured as the three of them descended the stairs again. He had intended it for her ears only, but Rorie's sharp ears had caught the words too and his hand was on his sword as he came face to face with Fergus Campbell, prepared to take his leave peaceably, or prepared to die if necessary for a treacherous turn of hand.

'The MacDonalds are leaving now, Father.' James intended his father to continue with the deception to the very end—for all their sakes.

The news of Kirsty's delayed departure brought to him by the doctor, who for several days had been trying unsuccessfully to convey to him how frail the girl beneath his roof really was, had not served to improve Fergus's temper and he did not even answer.

'My sister must remain until the end of the week, with your permission,' Rorie said, in a voice loud enough for everyone to hear. He wanted them to know if his sister was harmed, the blood of an innocent girl would be on the consciences of the inhabitants of Darna. His tone told them she would not go unavenged.

'She will be at the gate to meet you then. No Mac-Donald sets foot in this house again.'

Once again fingers began to steal towards swords and dirks, expecting the worst, but the man facing them was perfectly calm and seemingly untroubled by the fact that he was in the midst of the enemy. He said nothing, but inclined a slight bow in Fergus's direction and then, in defiance of all those wishing to plunge a dagger into his back, turned on his heel with deliberate slowness and followed his brother out of the Hall.

Catriona saw James swiftly issue orders to the men at his disposal, men who hurried after the departing figures. Her father turned away from her. Many other people followed suit. She was in disgrace. Then let them have something to talk about, she thought defiantly, and followed her brother after the MacDonalds.

'Catriona, you sly bitch.' A hand fastened in her hair and she was pulled abruptly to a standstill as she reached the door leading to the courtyard. Andrew's drunken voice prevented her from resisting. Somehow he had escaped the vigil meant to keep him out of the way until the evening ended. She cried out in pain as she was dragged backwards into the passageway. 'You are taken with him, aren't you? I've seen the way you looked at him.'

'Let me go, Andrew! I don't know what you mean.'

'The MacDonald, you treacherous little whore. Your brothers bundled me away before I could confront them. I saw the way you looked at him. I hear you enjoyed his favours upstairs too—it is no more than I expect from the likes of you. Nobility! Pah! You turn my stomach. Camp followers are more honest than you, but now you will pay . . .'

He pushed her back against the wall, cursing her as she fought to free herself from his excruciatingly painful grip. Her resistance maddened him and too much drink did the rest. His mouth crushed hers and the smell of liquor on his breath made her feel faint with repulsion. She felt his hands fumbling with her bodice and then the warmth of his fingers against her breasts.

Suddenly he groaned in her ear. For a moment she thought the amount of drink had overtaken him, then he staggered back and collapsed on the ground a few feet away. Desperately trying to rearrange her gown, she found herself looking into the mocking eyes of Rorie MacDonald.

'I take it you didn't want to be tumbled,' he murmured.

Catriona was glad of the darkness which hid the colour flooding into her cheeks at his crudeness.

'He—he is drunk . . .' she stammered.

'And my sister's future husband. You'll be damned lucky if he doesn't call you out over this, MacDonald. If he does I shall be privileged to be your second,' James declared, appearing from the shadows. His voice was light, but he came to Catriona and held her for a moment and she could sense the anger raging inside him. 'Are you all right?'

'Yes. He—he is drunk. It means nothing . . .' she tried to make light of it too, although she knew he would not believe her after the previous occasion.

'I did not hit him hard enough,' Rorie murmured. He stared at her with a fierce frown. 'If your amorous suitor has any score to settle with me when he comes round, tell him I'll be waiting. I have few virtues, but forcing myself on unwilling women isn't one of my vices. Once again I offer my thanks to both of you for your kindness to Kirsty.' His glance flickered down to where Andrew lay sprawled at his feet and his eyes gleamed with the devil's own mockery as he added, 'And my condolences.' He raised Catriona's hand to his lips and then, as an afterthought, turned it palm upwards and pressed his lips to her bruised wrist. Before she even thought of freeing herself, he had released her and was striding towards his horse.

Beside her, James gave a thoughtful frown as he watched the two heavy gates close behind the Mac-Donalds. He stood listening for some while afterwards, to the sound of orders being given, the clatter of horses' hooves . . . It was a long while before tension died inside him. Even then he could not believe it had really happened. MacDonalds had come to Darna, stayed before the piercing, unnerving gaze of all his kinsmen and relatives and still ridden away unharmed. Peace was possible!

'That man is dangerous,' he muttered, remembering how Rorie had forced his sister up the back staircase. Such hatred! And composure! For the first time in many years he began to think once again that he was not wrong. If he did not sleep at night because of the nightmares which plagued him, did the MacDonalds sleep any easier? Was it not possible they could now at least talk?

'I agree.'

He glanced at his sister, not sure of her interpretation of his statement. She was gazing at the closed gates as if they were an end to her own existence.

'What did you talk about when you and the Mac-Donalds were alone?' Her reticence to confide in him was puzzling. They had no secrets from each other.

'Nothing. Why do you ask?'

'He came to your defence against Andrew like a man who—who had an interest in what was happening.'

'Perhaps he is a gentleman.'

'Or a clever rogue. It would suit him to have a friend in the enemy camp.'

'Does he not already have one if I am to believe my own eyes? You—and Kirsty,' Catriona replied and James slipped an arm about her shoulders with a contrite apology.

'Don't take everything so seriously. I was only teasing. Andrew is no great catch and it is my hope that someone will soon dispatch him to the hereafter. He will not leave you a rich, mourning widow, but at least you will be free—free to return to Darna if you wish. I'd rather that than see your head turned by that devil MacDonald.'

'Tamsie suggested I find a diversion.' She tried to sound flippant and failed miserably.

'From what I have been hearing you took her seriously. No, no explanations now,' he said, as Catriona opened her mouth to protest. 'I think it best I am ignorant of what passed between you for the moment, or I might feel inclined to ride after him. You say he did not lay hands on you against your will and I believe that. I have been told by my steward it was with your consent. So be it, but you'd be better seeking a liaison with

D'hommil Dhu himself. MacDonald Ruadh is not for you!'

'What do you have against him—apart from his name?' she demanded. She was flabbergasted that James not only knew what had happened, but thought it was with her consent. Others would too. The servants— her father—Andrew had voiced his displeasure and earned himself a headache for his lurid accusations.

Rorie MacDonald had treated her roughly during the short time they were together but, she acknowledged, had it been Donald beside her she would not have fared so lightly and in those minutes when she had been struggling in Andrew's grasp, it had been the 'Red' MacDonald who had come swiftly to her aid. She would forget that no less easily than the sound of his voice coming out of the mist—the memory of his kiss that had both answered all her dreams and shattered them in one brief moment!

'Apart from that and the countless number of our people he has killed since he was old enough to hold a sword, the fact that his kinsmen from Glen Coe are still trying to destroy us for the folly of one of our own many years ago which also reduced Darna to ashes, he is the man who crippled Murdoch four years ago. You didn't know that, did you?'

Catriona shook her head in silent horror, and said when she at last found her voice,

'Murdoch always maintained he was set upon and could not defend himself. Is that not the truth?'

'We concocted that story hoping to satisfy Father, but once he realised Murdoch was crippled . . .' James paused, his mind dwelling on that encounter. 'Murdoch was waiting for me, that at least was true. The rest is fabrication, to save his hide as well as mine in the end, I suppose. He overheard Donald MacDonald boasting about an affair he was having with a girl from our village, and a married one at that. He challenged him, but the fight had barely started when the "Red" MacDonald appeared, knocked his brother away and . . . Oh, God, Catriona, a man of his experience against a mere boy! Murdoch, as good as he was, stood no chance. The MacDonald deliberately maimed him and then left him bleeding on the tavern floor.'

'Why—why did he not kill him?' Catriona forced the words through stiff lips, shutting her mind against the images forming there.

'Donald dragged him away. Another woman had taken his fancy—I don't know. Are you still anxious to be a friend of Rorie MacDonald, little one?'

'I know it won't happen, but I wish Rannoch Moor would open and swallow them both.' Catriona felt ashamed she had ever harboured decent feelings for such callous destroyers of human dignity and life. 'I pity poor Kirsty with two brothers like that! She is so gentle, James. You have seen that for yourself—and refined. An education in France among people who appreciate music and the arts must have made her feel that her brothers act like—like barbarians!'

'We spoke together only yesterday of the times we have spent abroad. It is something we have in common,' James said softly and Catriona looked at him in surprise. He had kept his visits to Kirsty well hidden from her. Had Nan been asleep or had he bribed her to be elsewhere when he arrived—even against her implicit orders? Somehow she could not find it in her heart to be angry with him.

'Catriona, don't look so alarmed, have I not made my feelings for her quite clear to you,' James said, with a smile. 'I shall behave like a gentleman at all times.'

'James,' she began apprehensively.

'Hush now. I think you should discreetly retire. If Father misses you I shall say Andrew waylaid you and I had to deal with him. He is so drunk, he will not know who hit him. Would you prefer to go back inside and face all those curious eyes? You do not deserve that.'

'I don't think I could.' Now the MacDonalds had gone, Catriona found she had no courage to return to the festivities.

'Then do as I say.' James bent and kissed her cheek. 'Trust me, I will not desert you now. And believe me, I really do find her most captivating.'

Catriona bade him goodnight and hurried upstairs to her appartments. Was James serious, or had he been schooled too long by their father? If he had fallen in love with Kirsty . . . She knelt at her prayers that night, her thoughts for him and no one else. Dear God, let him find happiness, she prayed. She asked nothing for herself. Why should she? What she had felt when she had been held in Rorie MacDonald's arms had been nothing! A passing whim! Why should she dwell more on that wonderful moment?

'Out, girl, and don't come back.'

Fergus Campbell strode into his daughter's bedroom as she was dressing to go on her usual morning ride and the young maid attending her fled from the room in tears as he bellowed at her furiously and flung her towards the door.

Catriona had spent a sleepless night preparing herself for the storm she knew must come—and could not be avoided. She sat in silence, staring at the carpet at her feet as she was upbraided for her wanton behaviour. Wanton! Her father flung the word at her time and time again. Not only had she brought his enemies into the house, but she had been seen in the arms of one of them, on the very night of her betrothal ball. He asked no name; that meant he knew, Catriona thought, growing more alarmed. A more intense questioning of the maid who had seen her would doubtless provide him with any information he lacked.

'If Andrew no longer wishes to marry me, then I will

quite understand.' She raised her head and stared un-flinchingly into the angry features confronting her. She had nothing to be ashamed of!

How was her future husband after the blow Rorie MacDonald had dealt him, she wondered? Sulking somewhere with a worse headache than usual after one of his drinking bouts.

'You would like that, wouldn't you? It isn't going to happen. I've already talked to Andrew and being a man of the world, he has accepted you were in no way to blame for the situation you found yourself in. He doesn't believe it any more than I do, but he's an ambitious man, among other things, and he needs this marriage almost as badly as I do. Did he make love to you, this "Red" MacDonald? Did he make free with you up here the way he would with a common serving wench?' her father thundered.

'No. He did not. How can you suspect such an awful thing?' Catriona's face flooded with colour. She had not forgotten the fierceness of Rorie's embrace, could still hear the unsteady pounding of her heart as he kissed her. It was racing now, just dwelling on that moment. She suspected she would never be able to erase it from her memory.

'There are bruises on your wrists. I noticed them last night,' Fergus continued accusingly.

'He forced me to bring him up to Kirsty's room and he was not gentle about it. His brother followed with his sword at James's back. I tried to fight him, but he was too strong.'

'Or he makes love in the fashion he does everything else—like an animal.'

'You cannot believe me capable of—of . . .' Catriona had thought she knew the extent of her father's loathing for her, now she realised differently.

'I believe you capable of anything after what you have done. You made it possible for the MacDonald girl to reach her brothers. You brought them into my presence, humiliated me before my guests, and I will never forgive you for that. You will remain in this room until she leaves Darna. You will not attempt to see or communicate with her, do you hear?'

'Yes, Father. Has Andrew left yet?'

'Yes, and in a foul mood too. It's little wonder after what he said your brothers did to him. He's arranging for his house in Perth to be made ready. When it is, in a month—two at the latest—the wedding will take place. They will be the longest weeks you will ever know, I promise you.' He paused in the doorway and looked back at her. A cruel smile touched his lips at the defiance already creeping back into her expression. She would pay and pay dearly for what she had done. When he had finished with her she would be glad to run to the Fraser. 'If you wish to communicate with me for any reason, do so through a servant. I will do likewise when I consider that odious task necessary. You are a traitor to your people and I intend to see you are treated accordingly. From this moment, I have ceased to have a daughter.'

Catriona had not moved from the bedside some ten minutes later when Nan appeared. She looked like a frozen statue, pale, unmoving, her eyes fixed on the door through which her father had departed, yet seeing no one, nothing, as she dwelled on that final, cruellest blow of all. He had disowned her. As easily as he would have dismissed an unsuitable servant, as callously as he had sent Murdoch away. Neither of them were of use to him any more. Only James, the right arm he needed so desperately as he grew old, remained. James, oh, my dear brother, Catriona thought, blinking back a rush of tears. I do not envy you.

'Mistress, what has happened? The Laird almost knocked me over going downstairs, sent me to the stables to have your horse unsaddled and now I've just heard him giving instructions you are to have all your meals served in your room.' Her face lined with concern, she caught Catriona's hands in hers. They were like ice. 'My lady, do you hear me? Sweet Jesus, what has that brute done to you.'

'Where is my brother?'

'Ach, so you've no' been struck dumb. He's with the Laird in the study and a fair old battle the two of them are having. I'm not surprised with the goings on in this place the last few days. I think the whole world has gone mad. Campbells and MacDonalds beneath the same roof and not an inch of blade shown and did you see that brother of his? Dancing as if he was an invited guest. I thought half the men watching would throw a fit.'

'When my brother is free ask him to come to me,' Catriona said. 'First help me to change.' How long was she to be deprived of her morning rides? Three days only, or longer? Her father, knowing how she enjoyed them, would use the knowledge to his advantage.

She would have to find something to keep her occupied every minute of the day, Catriona realised. She dared not attempt to see Kirsty, but Nan or James could carry messages for her. She suspected she would be watched, but could not believe that the servants, people she had known all her life, like Nan who had nursed her since she was a babe, the old retainer who attended to her father's every need, the groom whose help she had enlisted to free Kirsty and many others, could consider she had betrayed her own!

The thought appalled her. Were they willing to vent their anger on the head of a helpless girl just to satisfy the whim of an aging old man? It was more than possible she acknowledged, with a sinking heart. If her father dismissed any of them from Darna, he would also ensure they found no other worthwhile employment. Yes, they would obey him, whatever orders he gave. Slowly she forced herself to accept that in the whole world she had only two friends upon whom she could rely—James and Nan.

'Nan?' She looked questioningly into the matronly face before her. 'I am in disgrace. I deserve it, I know, for bringing death so close to my family, but I do not regret what I have done. In a few days, Kirsty will go home, safe and well. The MacDonalds know now we are capable of charity and compassion. Perhaps one day one of her kin will repay what I have done.'

'Heaven forbid!' Nan declared, ignoring the frosty look which instantly rose to her mistress' eyes. 'What good has it done you—this charity? Didn't I warn you how it would be?'

'You did and I no more listened to you than I did my own brother . . .'

'For which we have both paid the price,' James said as he pushed open the bedroom door. 'Leave us, woman, I wish to speak with my sister alone.'

He looked tired, Catriona thought, as she went to greet him. The arms which enfolded her gave only brief comfort.

'You made father so angry this morning, he told me of some wild scheme he was considering of sending you to Perth tomorrow and having you confined in the house alone until the wedding. I have managed to talk him out of it and convince him that three days alone up here will be punishment enough.'

'Thank God,' Catriona murmured weakly.

'He told me what passed between you. He will not accept you again, you realise that, don't you? Nor will he attend the wedding. I am to give you away.'

'Does he not wish to enjoy his final triumphant hour? After all his plans?'

'I suspect he will relent at the last moment—for the sake of appearances. We are a great disappointment to him so he tells me,' James said, with a wry smile.

'You! Oh, no, James. I am the only one to blame. I

will not have you condemned for my actions. You are all he has.'

'Is that supposed to bring me comfort? Do you think I want to be used as you have been? Before your wedding day I intend to let Andrew know how I expect my sister to be treated. One complaint from you after the wedding and I shall kill him. I can do nothing to prevent the marriage now, but I can offer you that small solace.'

'It is enough,' she said, laying her head against his shoulder. She would never tell him if it was not. She had risked his life once, she would not do so again.

'Are you and Kirsty in love with each other?' she asked softly.

'Yes, although neither of us has dared to put our feelings into words. She is all I have ever wanted in a woman, Catriona. Innocence, gentleness, shyness. Dammit, I love her!'

'Is there no way we could come to peace with the MacDonalds from Mamore? Kirsty could be our emissary. She knows full well you and I . . .'

'They would laugh in her face. I have said nothing to Father yet, but when I am sure she feels the same way I do, I will. He will have to accept it.'

Without James there would be desolation for Darna and only memories of the past for its Laird. Would Kirsty have the courage to live with the man she loved in such a hate-ridden atmosphere? It was a frightening future.

'I wish you both well.' Catriona laid her lips against her brother's cheek. How she envied him his happiness. 'Be careful. Guard yourself well and take care of those who have helped us. Alistair should leave before Father finds out his part in this affair.'

'I have spoken to him, but the boy is devoted to you, Catriona, and swore he was ready to do it all over again. I shall watch out for him, don't worry. Dear heaven, how thoughtless you must think me, talking of Kirsty and myself when you are a virtual prisoner here because of the help you gave her,' James exclaimed.

'You are happy,' Catriona whispered through a mist of bright tears. 'I am content, believe me. Do nothing to jeopardise your own future happiness, James, you can do nothing more for me. When Father learns how —you feel about Kirsty, you will lose what little sway you have over him. He will fight you all the way, but in the end he will give in to your wishes because he needs you and the children you will give him. Heirs for Darna—he lives only for that, I am sure.'

'What a pretty picture you paint of my future, but you are right, I know. This is my home and I wish for no other. I hope Kirsty loves me enough to live here despite Father.'

'Is there any way I can help?'

'She trusts you . . . she would listen to you . . . but not yet. Father has forbidden you to leave your rooms and you must obey him. I will watch over her and see her safely into the hands of her brother. I will give her your love when she awakes. I had the doctor give her a powerful sleeping draught. I want her to be really strong when she leaves here.'

He had so many questions to ask, but did not know where to begin. His sister at the side of the 'Red' MacDonald had been an odious sight. The knowledge that he had touched her, kissed her, made his blood boil, yet Catriona said nothing of the time they had been together, gave no indication of her own feelings. He found it puzzling, indeed worrying, that she had not confided in him. She should have been shocked—indignant—angry. But nothing!

'When Kirsty has gone will I be allowed to ride again, James? Or am I a prisoner until I go to Perth?'

'You shall ride any time you wish. He will not take that pleasure from you.' James kissed her and did not tell her how close she had come to losing even that. He wanted to give her more reassurance than he had, but could not find the words. As he turned away he thought how fragile and vulnerable she looked.

Before he had closed the door behind him, he heard the sound of her crying.

CHAPTER
FIVE

THREE short days felt more like three long weeks, but at last the final day of her confinement arrived. Tomorrow she would be able to ride again, perhaps go and see Murdoch and Tamsie, or take a picnic lunch on to the moors and linger there the whole day. She would tell James where she was going so that he did not concern himself over a prolonged absence. No one else mattered.

She had idled the hours away rearranging her suite of rooms until the constant alterations and critical comments had all but driven Nan mad. When she tired of that, unsatisfied with the results, she began the task of choosing the material for her wedding gown, but she had no real interest in that either and could not make up her mind. Eventually Nan persuaded her to take a trip to Glasgow to look at the latest cloths from France. She would need a complete wardrobe to entertain the ladies of Perth she was told, and then there would be parties and balls at the castle, attended by men of the garrison there.

The thought brightened yet another dull day. A few days away from Darna, new faces, the excitement of a shopping expedition. Yes, Catriona thought, that was exactly what she needed. It was time she began to show her father and Andrew that this marriage they had so carefully arranged between them to suit their own purposes was not going to break her spirit. She would make the best of it!

She would have Nan at her side. She would gather her own circle of friends about her . . . But she would not be able to ride free as a bird in the windswept countryside around Darna, and at night, there would always be Andrew!

'What is it, lass?' Nan watched the glow slowly fade from her eyes. For a moment she thought she had succeeded in rousing her from her despondent mood.

'Nothing. A passing thought, that's all. As I am not allowed to communicate with my father, you will have to do so for me. Tell him we wish to go to Glasgow for a few days and why. No, say a week, let us enjoy ourselves while we can. I can stay at Aunt Sarah's house, where I shall, of course, be suitably chaperoned.'

Catriona took up her sewing and retired to the window seat in her sitting-room. It was a bright, sunny day, but cold, and already she had ordered a fire to be lit, although it was not yet midday. She wore a grey woollen dress, the severity of the colour broken only by the dull fire of rubies at her throat and in her ears. Her hair had been brushed, her toilette completed every morning before ten o'clock, in case her father should suddenly appear, expecting to find her dejected and lonely, desperate for his forgiveness.

She no longer cared if he spoke to her or not. She had come to terms with the future and accepted it. Something she should have done months before, she realised, but somewhere at the back of her mind had always been the thought that her father would not be so cold-blooded. When it was possible she would return to Darna to see James and Kirsty. How wonderful that would be. A visit to her brother and his wife—and when her father had gone . . .

A frown furrowed her brow. He was an old man and they harboured no love for each other, but she did not wish him dead.

The sound of voices below the window drew her

attention from her work. Men were hurrying towards the main gate, arranging themselves on each side of it, and on the walkway which encircled the house.

She knew instinctively that Rorie MacDonald had come to collect his sister. She stood up, the breath catching in her throat. There were fifty, no, more— perhaps eighty riders approaching up the slope towards the house, converging on Darna at a slow, deliberate pace. Where were James and Kirsty? Had they been told or had her father cleverly sent James on some errand to keep him out of the way? She had not seen him all morning.

They emerged into the sunlight below her and she laid a hand against her wildly beating heart. Soon it would be over. Kirsty would be free and so would she, for a few more months at least.

The gates were opened wide, but only two riders approached. In the gateway Rorie MacDonald waved back his companion and dismounted, advancing alone into the courtyard.

He had an arrogant swagger to his walk, she thought, as if he cared not that he was in the midst of his enemies. Nor did he! His attitude on the night of the ball had proved that. He feared nothing, was forever prepared for a fight and trusted no man, woman or child. He had an irresponsible braggart for a brother and a headstrong young girl for a sister. He and James had much in common. So alike, yet they were enemies.

She watched Kirsty linger to speak with James, a gesture that brought a heavy frown of annoyance from the man approaching them. Then, painfully, she limped across to join her brother. James followed, extending his hand towards the MacDonald. It was ignored. His hand fell to his sword. Catriona knew for an instant it was in his mind to draw it and avenge the insult; instead he turned on his heel and returned to the house. He had promised her he would not lose his temper or act rashly, no matter how intense the provocation, and even thus alienating himself further from his father's affections—he had kept his word.

Rorie MacDonald began to lead his sister towards the waiting horses, but she paused and looked back, her eyes sweeping upwards for the face she had not seen since the night of the ball and her hand lifted in a farewell salute as she caught sight of Catriona watching. Her brother followed her gaze and his eyes lingered for a long moment on the slender figure framed in an upstairs window. With that single glance, before the gates closed behind them, everything that had passed between them came flooding back into Catriona's mind and she sank down onto the cushions, weak-kneed, trembling. It was some while before she realised the bedroom door was open. Her father stood there and the look on his face condemned her.

'I wanted to see your face when you looked on him again,' he said harshly. 'I have seen all I need to know. You ached just to see him—you whore!'

The room shook as the door slammed after his departing figure. Catriona laid her burning forehead against the window pane, forcing herself to consider the pain and sadness she had unwittingly brought down upon her own head. She could not defend her feelings, she did not even understand them. How could she think kindly of a man she knew to have killed her own kinsmen, perhaps women and children too, on raids into Campbell territory? It was beyond her comprehension.

Yet in the darkness of the staircase his nearness, his touch, had aroused in her feelings she had never known before. His kiss had been like a drug, one moment numbing her senses, the next firing them to an uncontrollable response. No one had ever made her feel this way! It was shameful, unforgivable and she would have to live with it for the rest of her life. Thank God she would never set eyes on Rorie MacDonald again.

James did not visit her as she expected. She saw him ride away from Darna some hours later and he had not returned by the time she retired. The next morning she learned he had gone to visit friends in the next glen and would be away for several days. Determined to keep her spirits high, she kept the promise she had made to herself and went riding, taking Nan and Alistair as escort, the latter only after her maid had refused to venture outside the house with at least one armed man riding with them.

Her imprisonment over, she once more resumed her duties in the house and again took all her meals downstairs, although at times, her little sitting-room would have been preferable to sitting to one side of the silent, grim-faced man who totally ignored her presence. He never knew the effort it cost her to maintain her composure beneath his contemptuous gaze.

For the next week, with no James to sit and talk with her, she spent more time on horseback than she did on her own two feet, and at night climbed into bed worn out in mind and body.

'Again?' Nan echoed in dismay as Catriona asked for her riding habit. 'My lady—no. Not me. My back is fair breaking from these tortuous rides. I'm not as young as I was and I swear that horse has taken a dislike to me.'

'Then you can stay here and begin packing for Glasgow,' Catriona told her with an amused smile. 'Last night my father informed me, through his steward of course, that I may leave at any time I choose and remain as long as I wish so long as I return with sufficient materials for the village women to start on my wedding gown and trousseau. I shall naturally have an escort there and my aunt will watch me like a hawk, but I don't care. I must wait until James returns though. I can't leave without seeing him. Perhaps I can persuade him to come with me.'

'Maybe he has a bonny lass hidden away somewhere who is keeping him occupied.' Nan threw open the closet doors and proceeded to take out dresses and shoes, not realising how close she had come to the truth.

Catriona smiled as she drew on her gloves. Not hidden, but momentarily inaccessible. Something that would be rectified, if she had her way, before she left Darna.

As she rode that morning her thoughts were full of how she might bring James and Kirsty together, but there seemed no solution. Kirsty's brothers would never allow him to present himself as a suitor. Their gratitude, if they felt any, would not extend that far. A Campbell as a prospective husband! She could imagine the incredulity and disbelief, the pressure if they so much as allowed him over the threshold, to cut his throat and send him back home as a warning to others with such high ideas.

'My lady, wait,' Alistair called urgently as she continued to ride, deep in thought and oblivious to the countryside about her. 'Do ye not realise how far we have come. We are almost to Rannoch Moor.'

Catriona had not realised and did not care. She had ridden further afield on her lonely excursions.

'We have nothing to fear from the MacDonalds, Alistair. I have ridden this way before.'

'Aye, without your brother's consent or knowledge. For pity's sake, my lady, I am your only protection so far from Darna. Turn back, I beg you. If anything happens to you I will never be able to face the Laird or Master James.'

'Very well, we will go no further. I would not have you on the receiving end of my father's anger because of me. Let us rest the horses for a while and have something to eat before we start back.'

Reluctantly Alistair dismounted and helped her down and then untied the small wicker basket which contained cold chicken and some of the cook's favourite sugared biscuits. He spread a blanket on the sparse heather and retired a few yards away, squatting on his haunches, his young face so serious that Catriona was moved to yet another impulsive gesture.

'Alistair, come and sit with me and eat something. If we are to be descended on by a horde of MacDonalds, you will do more good at my side.'

The boy flushed, hesitated and then moved closer, but still remained at a respectful distance. Catriona sighed, laid several pieces of chicken and some biscuits on a napkin for herself and then pushed the basket towards him.

'Finish this food. Cook will think me unappreciative of her labours if I take any home.'

As soon as James returned she would leave for Glasgow. Her eyes swept over the landscape about her, imprinting every tree, every bush, the flight of a bird, a hovering cloud above the pass of Glen Coe, upon her memory. She would remember days like this in the months ahead, in order to make her existence worth while, for it was doubtful if she would be as free as this for some considerable time—if ever. There would be other memories too; the fragrance of newly-grown heather as she lay on her back—in the most unladylike fashion, as James was always telling her—to watch the birds in the sky; their rides together, her visits to Murdoch and Tamsie. Pleasant memories no one could take from her. It was so peaceful here! She could find it, why was it not possible for others?

The sun was warm on her face. She removed her jacket, unbuttoned the neck of her blouse and relaxed back onto the blanket. If only her brother could have been with her today. Every moment she could spend with him was precious now.

'My lady,' Alistair's voice was a hoarse whisper. How long she had been lost in thought she did not know. Her eyelids felt heavy. She was drowsy, content, but the voice persisted. 'My lady.'

She sat up, pushing back loose strands of hair from her face—and froze in horror. The dirk at the boy's throat gleamed wicked and deadly in the sunlight. The terror on his face made her feel sick with apprehension. She should have turned back sooner.

Slowly, almost disbelievingly, she raised her eyes to the face of the man who held it. She had thought never to see him again.

'Release him, he is no danger to you. He is only a boy.' Her senses reeled. The very sight of him made her feel weak. She stood up and her blue eyes sparked like brilliant sapphires. 'Let him go, I say.' She must show no fear. Dear God, she had never known what fear was until she encountered this man.

'Now that is the fire I know.' Rorie MacDonald straightened, but the knife remained menacing the boy. 'Go and sit down by yonder bush and stay there with your hands where I can see them. Leave your sword and dirk with me.'

Catriona nodded assent and Alistair sullenly obeyed. Already she knew he was envisaging the disgrace for himself and his family when this incident became known. He had been caught off guard!

'Do as he says and you will not be harmed, Alistair— unless the MacDonald is less of a man than I think him to be,' Catriona said calmly. This was Nan's son and she would do nothing to endanger his life. She hoped, in return, he would make no rash moves in her defence.

Rorie's pale eyes locked with hers, registering mockery at her insulting words.

'So you have thought of me. Now I find that interesting.' As she stared disdainfully at his dirk, he sheathed it and lowered himself cautiously to the ground at her side. 'Sit down.'

'What do you want with me?'

'To talk. I thought it time I thanked you for caring for my sister.' The mockery grew and she realised he was enjoying her discomfort. He preferred to have her at a disadvantage!

'We have nothing to say to each other.' She sat down making sure there was a wide space between them. He was looking at her, but she knew he was aware of every movement around them.

'I have spent several days waiting for you. I thought you rode this way often.'

'I do, but not since . . .' *Waiting for her!* She swallowed hard. 'How is Kirsty?'

'I have just come back from Inverness. I have left her with my cousin for a few weeks. She needs to be well looked after so that her leg heals, and Mary is just the person to make sure she stays in bed and does as she is told. I have a good deal of thinking to do about that girl. More than ever now, I am convinced she should go to France. I said I waited for you,' he repeated at length.

'W-why?'

'To express my thanks. I was too angry and suspicious to do so when we met.' The lean mouth deepened into a smile. How different it made him look. 'I must have been everything you had been told a MacDonald would be—but my sister's safety came first and that's all that mattered to me at the time. I was rough with you . . .' The features were suddenly unsmiling. As if he cared, Catriona thought, growing more confused. That was not possible.

'As you say, it is no more than I expected.' She had to fight against the way this man made her feel. To listen to those contrite tones, looking into those green-flecked, bottomless pools of his eyes, made it impossible for her to gather her own thoughts and retaliate as she knew she should. She should be screaming for Alistair to defend her against this MacDonald who dared sit at her side and expect her to listen to him, but she could no more risk the life of the helpful young boy, than wish the death of this arrogant man. Her only defence, she realised, was attack.

'You crippled my brother Murdoch,' she said in a low, fierce tone.

'I did.' No pity in the deep voice, no show of remorse to ease the tension building inside her. 'He has grown into a man these past three years, although what happened between us will always be a wedge. I wish it were otherwise.'

'You speak so lightly of maiming a boy no older than Alistair,' Catriona returned with flashing eyes. 'If I were a man I would kill you for what you did to him. My father could not tolerate an incomplete son and so he disowned him. You didn't know that, did you? What would it matter to you anyway? Murdoch is an outcast from his own home because of what you did to him. If for nothing else, I hate you for that.'

'Do you?' Her wrists were seized in an iron grip. Alistair began to rise to his feet and she cried out to him to remain still. 'That was wise of you, I'd not want to hurt him any more than I did your hot-headed brother. On that occasion however, I had no choice.'

'An experienced swordsman against a boy of twenty.' She spat the words at him and saw his eyes narrow dangerously. She bit her lips in pain as his fingers curled more tightly around her soft skin. 'I know what happened. Your brother set upon him while he was in a tavern waiting for James. When he proved too good for him, you intervened, deliberately, cruelly crippling him, and then left him bleeding on the floor.'

'A most graphic description. Murdoch's, of course,' came the quiet reply. No anger—no denials. She tried to twist free of his grasp to no avail. He shook her quite violently. 'Now you listen to me, you little fool! I am still not sure if you are as innocent as you pretend. No one connected with the Fraser can be so pure, but in case you have not yet been contaminated by those about you, I will tell you the truth. Listen to me and listen well, for I doubt if you and I will ever meet again. I wanted to see you for one reason only and that was to thank you. Kirsty told me of your father's displeasure and what it had cost you. I knew nothing of it until the day after I had taken her home—and even now I find it hard to believe.'

Liar! He wanted to believe it as desperately as he had wanted to see her again!

'Then you too, are a fool.'

'I do not like to hear you call me that.'

'What should I call you then? My kinsmen call you the "Red" MacDonald with the black heart. You raid our land, steal our cattle, kill and plunder. You are well named.'

Rorie sat back on his heels. He wanted to hit her for the name which burnt deep into his heart and yet at the same time, grab her in his arms and kiss those soft lips into submission as he had done once before. She had fought him then out of fear, the knowledge that someone was watching, but what if he touched her now? Something must have registered on his face for Catriona drew back, straining against his hold even though he knew it hurt her.

'Don't touch me!' She was terrified of him. He felt suddenly disgusted and released her.

'No, I won't touch you. The Fraser is welcome to you!' He leapt to his feet, eyes burning, more anger inside him that he had known for years. Whether for her or for himself, he did not know.

'Murdoch Campbell was a loud-mouthed boy, too skilled with a sword for his age. Donald was no match for him. He was drunk. I was not. I stepped in to prevent my brother being killed. I could have killed him, but I didn't. I wanted to stop him becoming like Donald, especially when drunk—a braggart, a bully, incapable of taking care of himself. Murdoch is a man now, though he'll not thank me for the way it came about. Think on that, my girl, the next time you presume to judge my actions.'

There was a large gathering at the house of Angus MacDonald of Borradale. Together with many others, the chiefs of Clanranald MacDonald, of Keppoch and Glen Coe, Gordons and Camerons, stood drinking together in the comfortable sitting-room.

At first glance the young man seated in a high-backed chair at one end of the room looked incapable of rousing to passionate outbursts of fervour the wild Highlanders who were to flock to his standard over the following weeks. To follow—to die or spend years in hiding, half-starved in the mountains, or rotting in an English prison awaiting transportation to some distant place where they would never again hear the sound of the pipes. The luckier ones would wander as penniless exiles in whatever country would afford them sanctuary.

He wore a plain black coat and a plain shirt, a cambric stock fixed with a silver buckle, black stockings and brass buckles on his shoes. The simplicity of his appearance mattered not to any one of the gathering, many of whom had been waiting thirty years, since the defeat of his father James Stuart, to settle old scores with their hated English enemies. They had heard good reports of the twenty-four-old Charles Edward and had been touched by the first words he spoke to them. 'Gentlemen, I am come home!'

At fifteen he had been serving in the Spanish army, receiving a commendation from his uncle, the famous Marshall Berwick, for 'coolness under fire'. He was a keen sportsman, an excellent horseman and skilled in the use of both sword and pistol. He also spoke French, English and Italian fluently and had further delighted many an old campaigner with a greeting to them in halting Gaelic.

'A boy!' The leathery features of old MacIan from Glen Coe creased into a scowl. He was careful to keep his voice low enough not to carry beyond his companions. 'What does he bring with him? A fleet of French ships to blockade the English ports? Guns? Money? I've heard he has only £4000, less than two thousand muskets and not enough powder and shot to fill those. He's not only a boy, he's a fool and he expects us to put our necks in a rope for him.'

'Lochiel is no fool,' the man beside him returned in the same low tone, looking at the tall man standing beside the Prince's chair. He was a Clanranald MacDonald clansman. The Prince had landed on MacDonald territory and spent his first night ashore in the humble croft of one Angus MacDonald of Eriskay. They had been the first clan to give wholehearted support to his invasion plans for England and he had a personal guard of more than a hundred MacDonalds. The fiery young Ranald, son of the chief, had been the first man to declare his allegiance and had threatened to advance on London with his men alone if it suited the Prince.

The Camerons had fought for the Stuart cause since the days of Montrose. Lochiel, their present chief, had responded instantly to the summons he received and had already pledged some seven hundred men. MacDonald of Keppoch pledged three hundred, the Stewarts, two hundred men from Appin. More letters had been despatched further afield to all chiefs of 'loyal' clans.

MacIan sighed and swallowed his whisky.

'I haven't had a good fight in years,' he said dourly, thrusting his glass under the nose of a servant to be refilled.

That day in July 1745, it was decided to raise the Prince's standard at Glenfinnan, some twenty miles away, on the 19th August. Between that time, many men came and went from the house in Borradale, among them Donald MacDonald and his brother, Rorie.

'Nan, he's back!' Catriona threw aside her sewing with an excited cry. 'James is back! Didn't anyone know he was coming?'

'Be still and let me tidy your hair,' Nan chided, secretly pleased at her excitement. It was the first time in a week she had looked her old self.

'It doesn't matter. He won't mind what I look like.'

'Mistress, wait!' The maid's plea fell on deaf ears. Nan too, had looked out of the window and seen what Catriona had not stayed long enough to see. There were another two riders dismounting in the courtyard and the sight of them wiped the smile from her face. It was too late. Catriona had already gone.

She came running down the stairs, the golden cloud of loose hair streaming out about her shoulders, her eyes bright with happiness and flung herself into her brother's outstretched arms.

'James, oh, James, I've missed you! The house has been like a graveyard. Where have you been for almost two weeks?'

With a laugh James hugged and kissed her. It was good to be home again even though he was about to cause the biggest upheaval in Darna's history. Catriona raised her head, determined to have her curiosity satisfied and saw the shy-faced girl Murdoch was gently, but firmly ushering through the door.

'In you go, lass, no time to hesitate now. You are in the lion's den and it's your home.'

Catriona felt her mouth sag at his words. Silently she looked at James—at Kirsty—at Murdoch.

'They were married a week ago in Inverness,' the latter added with a crooked grin. 'Tamsie was a witness and I was best man, so it's all very legal. For heaven's sake, aren't you going to congratulate them? You started all this in the first place.'

'He's right,' Kirsty said, through trembling lips. Somehow James had made it sound so simple. They loved each other, so they would marry. They had spent one exhilarating week alone in Inverness, but now the dream was over and she was once more faced with reality. She had worked herself into such a state over the impending meeting with Fergus Campbell that she was near to tears. 'If you had not persuaded James to bring me here that first day I would never have known what love is, nor the true worth of the man I love. If you cannot bring yourself to look favourably on me again, surely you will wish your brother well.'

'Oh, Kirsty, I am so happy for you both.' There were tears in Catriona's eyes as she flung her arms around the girl's neck and kissed her. 'Married a week! James, it was too bad of you not to tell me your plans. Did you not think I would be eager to help?'

'I didn't have marriage in mind when I left here, only that I wanted to see Kirsty again, away from here where our every word could be overheard and our actions watched. I went to stay with Ian in Inverness and the very day after I arrived who do I see passing by in a carriage, but Kirsty. With a very matronly woman at her side, I might add. For a moment the sight of that sour face almost put me off.'

'Don't,' Kirsty said with a giggle. 'Mary is really very sweet. Poor thing, I don't envy her having to face Rorie and tell him the news. I left a note,' she added by way of explanation to Catriona. 'When James and I had made our plans—or rather he made them and I . . . I just wanted to be his wife.'

'In a few days Kirsty and I will ride to see her brothers,' James said. Then, with a frown, 'No, perhaps it would be wiser if I go alone.'

'And have them vent their wrath on you? We shall go together.'

'Married a week,' Catriona repeated softly. 'How that would have ruffled his feathers had I known.' James sent her an enquiring look but she chose to ignore it. 'Come into the salon, I want to hear every detail of how this came about.'

'Where is Father?' her brother asked, closing the door firmly behind them all. 'And the other servants? Alistair and Calum were the only ones about as we rode up.'

'Father is in the study. He's shut himself in there every morning for the past four days, ever since he heard Charles Stuart is in Scotland. Nan told me over an hour ago that most of the servants are downstairs listening to one of the Stewart men. He's talking of war with the English. Is that possible?'

'Of course it is.' Murdoch helped himself to a drink from a decanter close at hand and threw himself into a chair. 'God, I can't wait to get at the English for what they did to us after the '15.'

'Which is why men from Darna will never be raised for the Prince, Father will see to that,' James returned stonily and the smile died from his brother's face. 'We cannot go through all that again.'

'You are the eldest son. When we talked yesterday you were all for the Cause. You could bring them out.'

Catriona frowned at the sudden change in the atmosphere. Talk of war when there should have been congratulations, the making of plans? Angry expressions instead of smiles? She rang for a servant and ordered a bottle of champagne to be brought from the cellars. James had brought a case back with him on his last visit to France.

'We are all going to have a celebration drink before we descend on Father with the good news.' Deliberately she forced herself to sound unconcerned by the event. Even so, Kirsty paled and reached for the reassurance of her husband's hand. 'There is so much to do, why am I standing here? We must find Kirsty suitable rooms and a maid to look after her. We can introduce her to the servants after dinner tonight. Good, here's the champagne. Bring another two bottles, please, Morag.'

'Three bottles, to dull the minds of everyone in the house to what James has done?' Kirsty asked tremulously. 'Do they have to be bribed to accept me, or besotted with drink.'

'It is the custom in this house that the servants always drink the health of a new bride,' Catriona rebuked. 'Besides you both did me out of the pleasure of attending your wedding, so I shall make the most of it now. I am going to give you both a ball such as Darna has never seen before. We shall invite everyone . . .'

'If we live that long.' From his chair Murdoch was staring fixedly out of the window. 'We have visitors, James. I thought we were being followed . . .'

'In God's name, why didn't you say so. Your aunt lost no time in sending word to your brothers, Kirsty.' James strode to the window with his wife behind him. 'They must have followed us from the Stewarts'. Why didn't they stop us before we reached the house?'

'They were waiting for orders. There were only four before, there are six now,' Murdoch declared. He tested the sword at his side. 'Well, what do we do?'

'We receive them,' Catriona said as she backed towards the closed door. 'You will stay here and I will greet them. It is obvious why they are here, but there is nothing they can do. Kirsty and James are married and they will have to accept that fact.'

'They might choose to abduct you in place of their sister. You don't know Donald MacDonald or that black-hearted brother of his. I say we invite them in and see what happens. Taken by surprise we could deal with them between us,' Murdoch suggested.

'No,' Kirsty gasped. 'James, they are my brothers! You cannot allow it. You swore a most solemn oath to me never to take up a weapon against my kin. The bloodshed was over, you said.'

'It will never be over,' Murdoch snarled. He grabbed at the decanter with his crippled hand, could not hold it and swore violently as it crashed to the floor, the contents soaking into the carpet at his feet. His eyes wide with rage he wheeled on the white faced girl to whom he had shown the utmost civility until this moment. 'He did this—the "Red" MacDonald. One day he will pay.'

'No, Murdoch, you did that,' Catriona said, ashamed of the tumour which had been steadily growing inside her brother all these years. 'He said you were a man now. I don't think I agree. You harbour a grudge against him because of the stupid, misshapen pride you still retain. He could have killed you, but he didn't.'

Kicking aside broken glass, Murdoch stepped towards her, his eyes narrowing suspiciously.

'So suddenly my innocent little sister is an expert on the virtues of Rorie MacDonald. Perhaps not so innocent if I am to believe the tale I have heard. Caught in his arms, were you not—and enjoying his kisses.'

'That's enough,' James snapped. 'We will make matters worse if we quarrel among ourselves.' But Catriona saw the question in his eyes. It had been there many times since the night of the ball and she had chosen always to ignore it. She did not know how to answer . . .

'Yes, I was in his arms, with his dirk threatening me, and James was somewhere behind us with Donald Mac-Donald's sword at his throat. If you think I would have cried out under those circumstances, you are mistaken,' she cried fiercely. 'Father too believes he had a gay time making free with me. He is as blind as you.'

'Who told you about this?' The useless hand rose before her eyes. Until now she had always felt pity for Murdoch, anger and contempt for the man who had injured him. Now she found it possible to understand how it happened. He had grown older, harder over the years, but in a moment of crisis, no more in control of himself than he was then.

'He did. We—we met while I was out riding last week.

He had been waiting for me, to thank me for the help I gave Kirsty.'

'I'm surprised you found time to talk,' he sneered and a pink flush stole beneath her cheeks. 'What lies did he feed you? Were you in his arms this time too?'

She slapped him hard across his grinning features and said icily,

'I am going out to the MacDonalds. As everyone seems to think I am such a close friend of theirs, you need have no fears for my safety.'

She found she was trembling as she walked purposefully towards the open front door. Two servants, gawping at the riders outside, took one look at her face and disappeared from sight. With a deep sigh she emerged into the sunlight and stood with hands clasped loosely in front of her against the soft grey of her gown as she confronted the mounted assembly.

There were men all about them, but none dared make a move without an explicit order from James or the Laird himself. Twice before these same men had ridden into Darna and left unmolested. Catriona prayed the third time would be no different.

'Tell my sister I have come to take her home,' Rorie declared. The composure of the woman before him annoyed him. As on the last occasion they had met, he wanted to shatter it and discover what lay beneath. 'Be quick about it. I'm tired and in no mood to trifle.'

'She is home. I am sure you know full well she and James are married. Her place is here at the side of her husband.'

The shock of her words caused both brothers to grow rigid in their saddles. The agony of suspense Rorie had so carefully controlled for hours, the frustration of not knowing his sister's whereabouts, his fears for the worst, together with the thought that he had been too harsh with her after her return to the house, sending her to his cousin's when he should have kept her with him, watched over her himself, welled up inside him ready to be unleashed in temper at this woman.

Mary's message had been almost incoherent. Run away, was all he knew as he rode his horse unmercifully through the night to reach Inverness. Kirsty's note, left beside her bed had been more explicit. She had gone away with James Campbell. He had scoured the town for days, questioning friends, but she had vanished. He knew then she would come to Darna and so he had set men to watch the roads. Four long days of waiting, spending sleepless nights in a chair, snapping at brother and servants alike as his frustration grew.

They had planned it all before she left Darna, he suspected and no doubt enlisted the help of Tamsie Stewart and Murdoch Campbell. How that boy hated him. One day there would have to be a reckoning between them. He hoped the taste of revenge had been sweet for he would pay dearly for it. As for Catriona . . .

'You—you are behind this, I'll swear.' He leapt from his horse and came up the steps towards her two at a time. Alarmed, Catriona stepped back and found her brother's solid frame was behind her, giving comforting support.

'No.' James waved back the men who began to move menacingly towards the MacDonalds. Kirsty clutched at his arm as she saw the unsheathing of weapons. 'These men are here at my request. Go about your duties—all of you.' He looked into Rorie's murderous eyes and deliberately placed one arm about his sister's shoulders, the other about his wife. 'I will not fight you, Mac-Donald. It is a promise I made to your sister on our wedding day and I shall keep it. Catriona knew nothing until an hour ago. You owe her an apology and not only for your words this day.'

Rorie ignored him, although it was an effort.

'Could we not have talked first?' he asked his sister.

'What would you have done had I told you I loved the

son of Fergus Campbell? You would have locked me in my room and told me to come to my senses, or sent me away so that we never met again.'

'I want you to come home now,' Rorie said, his mouth tightening into a stubborn line.

'This is my home and this is my husband. Can you not understand that?' Kirsty answered bravely.

'We can come and fetch you,' Donald declared. 'When we've finished there'll be no home and no husband.'

'Does everyone here have their eyes closed?' Catriona cried. 'Can't you see they love each other?'

'Love?' Rorie echoed and laughed in her face. 'Is it a fairy story you want me to believe?'

'I doubt if you know anything about love, Rorie MacDonald. A pity, it might have turned you into a human being, capable of compassion.'

'Don't try my patience too far,' he flung back. 'If I did not think I still owed you for your help, you would be dead now for your part in this. Knew nothing! He has no secrets from you.' He wheeled about towards his horse. 'Let us be gone, Donald. Our sister prefers to stay with her new friends.'

'Rorie, no! Wait! Listen!' The cry was torn from Kirsty's lips. She would have run after him, but James held her fast. 'Donald, don't let him go.'

'Then come home with us.'

Mutely she shook her head, only the agony in her eyes betraying her painful decision.

'Your choice. Wife you may be in name, and that is all you will have. They will never accept you. Has Fergus Campbell welcomed you yet? Greeted the mother of his future grandchildren with a fond kiss?' Rorie demanded. 'My God, child, you don't know what you have done. One day you will wish you had come with us.'

'Take her! I want no MacDonald bitch in this house,' a harsh voice thundered out behind them.

Kirsty was pushed to one side so violently she lost her balance and fell heavily against the stone balustrade. Both James and Rorie moved simultaneously to help her, but it was to her husband she turned, locking her arms about his neck as he bent to help her to her feet. The look of rejection on Rorie's face, Catriona knew, would be forever imprinted on her memory. In that moment he acknowledged the fact that his sister was lost to him.

Slowly James looked around at the figure of his father in the doorway. He knew the eyes of every man in the courtyard, MacDonalds and Campbells alike, were riveted on him.

'If you lay a finger on my wife again, I'll kill you,' he swore. Now everyone knew where he stood.

'If she sets foot in here again, she'll not live to see morning.'

'Then I shall bury you both on the same day,' James returned. 'Believe me, Father, I will kill you. Kirsty is here to stay. Darna is now her home. If you cannot be civil to either of us, I suggest you remain in your rooms. I am capable of running the estate. I have been doing so for a good many years.'

'You—you dare to speak to me in such a fashion— before them!' Fergus was gripping tightly to the door frame. His face was bright red as if he had been drinking heavily and he reeked of brandy, but Catriona heard the falter in his speech, saw the difficulty he had in breathing, in focusing his eyes on those before him.

'He's ill, James. Don't aggravate him,' she begged. She knew he was near to collapse.

'Shut your mouth. This is all your doing.' Fergus spat the words at her. Even Rorie was appalled at the underlying viciousness he heard in the tone. 'A pity your MacDonald didn't slit your throat when he'd finished with you. Do you still fancy her, MacDonald Ruadh? Take her, she's yours. I have no daughter.'

'What an offer,' Donald chuckled. The sound made Catriona's blood run cold. 'If you don't accept, brother, I will.'

'My father is ill. Please go,' she pleaded. 'You have Kirsty's answer. There is nothing for you here.'

'Damn you, girl, will you never stop your interfering.' Fergus lunged at her, but never reached his objective. The hands raised to grip her by the throat never touched it. A glazed look crept into his eyes, a babble of totally incoherent words fell from his lips and then, clutching at the heart he had abused one time too many, he fell to his knees.

CHAPTER
SIX

'MY lady, wake up.' The voice in Catriona's ear was insistent and repetitive despite her groan of protest. 'Wake up or they will kill him with their quarrelling. Not that many will mourn his passing.'

She flung aside the bedclothes, her mind still fogged with sleep, but sufficiently awake to realise that Nan was referring to her father. How long had she been asleep? It was barely light outside the window. She had remained beside her father's bed until the doctor came and afterwards, when he had taken James outside, she had known from his expression when he returned that there was no hope.

'You will never refer to the Laird in that tone again or you will not come with me to Perth,' she warned.

'No, my lady. Forgive me.' Nan helped her into a robe, cursing her thoughtless tongue. She would have cut it out rather than cause her mistress further distress.

'What is this all about?' Catriona demanded as she hurried towards the sick-room.

'Your brothers—they are quarrelling with the master. Have been for the past hour. It's all this talk of war and on whose side our men will fight.'

Neither, if James had his way, and he had her full support, Catriona thought as she quickened her step. When she had left earlier, her father had not regained consciousness—or so she thought. Had he been deliberately ignoring her presence, condemning her to the last?

Kirsty rose from a chair in the passageway, her eyes red from weeping.

'Thank God you are here, perhaps you can stop them. They have all taken leave of their senses. Murdoch wants to join the Prince and he's trying to persuade James to go with him. Your father forbids it. They are both angry and he is like an enraged bull . . . He cannot be dying.'

'It's all right,' Catriona murmured as tears flooded into the girl's eyes at the realisation of what she had said. 'Nan, take her to her room and give her a warm drink. Put something strong into it and stay with her until my brother comes. Go to bed, Kirsty, there is nothing you can do here and James is going to need your strength. He loves his father and will not accept his death lightly. Help him—love him.'

For a moment she hesitated outside the bedroom door, listening to the raised voices from within. Even so close to death her father refused to relinquish his hold on Darna. It was all he cared for. No, that was not true. In his way he cared for James, and he had passionately loved her mother. To love someone so completely and then lose them must be the most shattering experience in the world. She realised she pitied, rather than hated him, but it was too late for them both. The clock could not be turned back. With a sigh she opened the door and slipped inside.

'What will you do, Father?' She heard James say. He stood beside the bed, his face white with anger.

Behind him Murdoch paced the floor like a caged animal, muttering under his breath. Brothers, yet so different in temperament—like the MacDonald brothers. As unobtrusively as she had entered, Catriona melted into the shadows at the back of the room, her eyes fixed on the figure propped up against a mound of pillows.

Breathing heavily under the exertion of raising his

voice, his pupils dilated from the heavy sedation he had received and which had had little or no effect, he shook his fist at his eldest son.

'Do? What do you suggest? Bend our knee before this upstart boy and bring ruin to our people again? Darna was built from the ashes after the old house had been razed to the ground in retaliation for Glen Coe. My father sided with King George in the '15 to ensure it was not destroyed again and I will do the same. Our walls will never be demolished by anyone again, do you hear me?'

'Side with the English?' James's lip curled in disgust as he spoke and Catriona saw her father wince as if he had been struck. At this moment he was more vulnerable than ever before in his life. And his eldest son, the only one upon whom he could rely, was opposing him!

'With the rightful king.' He coughed painfully and it took all her restraint not to run to him and beg him to be still. Seeing him so helpless she could bear no grudge. The past years of pain and humiliation might never have happened.

'James Stuart is the rightful king, and his son is here to represent him,' Murdoch retorted, wheeling on him.

'You! Go your own way. You always have.'

'You gave me no choice the last time. Aye, I'll go my own way and James will come with me and all the men hereabouts. For once the Campbells will not line their pockets with the gold of others. We will fight and die if necessary for the true cause, old man.'

The insult roused the last of Fergus's failing strength.

'You young pup. What use do you think you will be to him or anyone else? You'll not live to see your Prince on the throne of Scotland. James, you would not go against me?'

'Only if you make it necessary.' James had no heart for the merciless baiting which had been going on between them for the past hour, but it was beyond controlling. A decision had to be made and Murdoch was right.

This time it would be made with the heart, not provoked by money or the spoils of war on which the Campbells had grown so wealthy and powerful in the past.

'And what does that mean?'

'I can raise our people for the Prince and there's not a damned thing you can do about it. They look to me these days, Father, not you.'

'I'll have you killed before that happens. Do you think I have no loyal men left?'

'You have many of them. Father, the Prince has a fine army following him. Already Lochiel, Keppoch, the Stewarts and Glengarry and countless others have pledged their support. I hear rumours that there are many more willing to rise all the way to London—even in the city itself. I want to ride with him. I shall ride with him and I shall take any man who thinks as I do.'

'Why? In God's name, why have you turned on me like this?' Fergus gasped, his voice receding into a harsh whisper. 'Is it that MacDonald woman you have married? Is it because of her? When I am dead she will be mistress here, with my blessing if it pleases you.'

'I doubt if you could understand my reasons,' James began and then Catriona, who could stand no more, stepped out of the shadows declaring,

'Stop it, both of you. Do you want to kill him?'

A smile touched Fergus's slack mouth. He slid back onto the pillows and closed his eyes for a long moment. James moved closer to the bed. He could almost see his father's mind envisaging some new scheme to prevent him siding with Charles Stuart. The eyes which opened again were glazed with pain, but the voice was totally coherent, as he said,

'So, even my loving daughter could not stay away. All three of my children waiting like vultures for me to die so that they can go their own ways—only you cannot, can you, Catriona? I have seen to that.'

Such satisfaction, even now, at her discomfort, such a

show of malice even as he lay dying! Murdoch turned aside in disgust.

'Leave her alone, Father. Have you not harmed her enough?' James snapped. 'Is there no pity in you?'

'It doesn't matter,' Catriona said softly. She stepped forward and stared into her father's lined face. 'You have never loved me. I accepted that many years ago. You killed the love I had for you, but I don't hate you any more. You are my father. Can there not be peace between us now?'

Fergus gave a hollow chuckle.

'Aye, there's part of me in you whether I like it or not. One day it will show itself and I shall laugh in my grave. You will love as I did—too late! I want you to suffer as I have suffered all these years.'

Catriona recoiled disbelievingly from the fury in the harsh voice, the loathing in the eyes which stared up at her. No forgiveness—even in death! She could not control the tears which rushed to her eyes. Brushing aside Murdoch's restraining hands, she fled blindly from the room.

'You evil old man,' he snarled. 'You will surely go to hell for what you have just done. She is blameless.'

'Blameless? After being with MacDonald Ruadh?' Fergus was mustering all his strength to talk. He found he was actually enjoying these few minutes before he drew his last breath. He was not afraid of death. It would reunite him with the only woman he had ever loved, separate him from the disappointment of a crippled son, a wilful daughter whose resemblance to her mother had made him hate her since she was three years old. Only James—James the eldest—did he care for. He had a wife, now, was more susceptible than before. He would always defend Catriona, but what would he do for his wife? For them both? Two women he loved equally in different ways.

His heart was failing, the blood was slowing in his

veins, but his mind was still alert. Thank God! Fergus thought.

'I have seen the look in her eyes and so have you, though you may deny it, every time his name is spoken. She said nothing happened. Do you really believe that?'

'Catriona does not lie to me,' James returned stonily.

'Something happened. I know it.'

'Are you saying she has fallen in love with him?' Murdoch ejaculated. 'God's truth, Father, what other atrocities are you going to heap on the poor girl's head?'

'Perhaps she doesn't understand—or realise what she feels. She is young and Andrew Fraser is not exactly a perfect man for such an innocent.'

'One moment an innocent, the next a whore. You called her that.' James was tired of the innuendos and insinuations. 'What are you after, Father?'

'If—if I revoked the marriage contract . . . Signed papers to that effect here and now . . . She can have her freedom, marry anyone she chooses . . . A groom for all I care. Would you obey me? Raise our men against the Prince.'

'You would do that?' James was stunned. Be a traitor to what was in his heart—yet be instrumental in freeing his sister from hell.

'The choice is yours.' Fergus smiled—a terrible smile of triumph as his son hesitated. 'Call the servants, bring my scribe. I have things to write before I quit this world.'

Murdoch barred James's way to the door.

'No! Good Lord, man, you don't need his approval. When he is dead you will be the Laird of Darna, Kirsty will be mistress of this house and you can revoke Catriona's wedding match yourself.'

He could, James knew that, but his brother had overlooked one very important fact.

'I could, but I won't. I will do as he asks because I love him, Murdoch. That is the difference between us. I sacrifice little to gain much.'

'Your self-respect! You will not regain it in the arms of Kirsty MacDonald. Not after you have faced her brothers in battle.'

James did not answer. His face impassive, he tugged at the bell rope.

The servants filed silently into the room and stood, heads bowed, around the bedside. Angus, the scribe, drew up a document as dictated by the dying Laird and barely understood by those listening. James and Murdoch understood. When Fergus had signed it and it had been witnessed by his steward and two others, James knelt at his side and swore an oath upon his dirk. Murdoch spat on the floor and left the room.

'Is he dead?' He looked up at the gaunt-faced brother who came into the room later.

'Yes.'

'In heaven's name why did you agree?'

'You wouldn't understand.'

'Your talk of loving him? No, I don't. For Kirsty, then? No, she's mistress here now, she has nothing to fear any more.' Understanding slowly crept into his expression. 'For Catriona, wasn't it? Only for her.'

'I want her to find the happiness I have found. She deserves it. She is free now to follow the dictates of her own heart,' James returned tiredly. 'Give me a drink and let me go to my bed.'

Murdoch handed him a large glass of whisky with a scowl.

'I have to prove something to myself. Something that has dogged me day and night since I last faced Rorie MacDonald. I am going to kill him. Tell her that.'

'I cannot deny you that right. I won't tell her and if he is what she wants, I pray she takes the opportunity open to her now.'

'You will not change your mind?'

'No, I have given my word. Darna will not rise for the Prince. My heart goes with him, but not our men and that is an end to it. Are you staying for Father's funeral?'

'No. I am away to the Stewarts'. They ride to Glenfinnan for the raising of the Prince's standard. I shall be with them. I hope we do not meet over crossed swords, my brother. That would surely grieve me.'

'My blade will never be raised against you, Murdoch. You are of my blood,' James answered.

'Then you are a fool! On the battlefield I shall have no brother and I shall kill you.'

Darna had been a house in mourning for a week. Fergus Campbell had lain for two days in the study while friends and relatives paid their last respects, with four silent clansmen keeping a watchful vigil over the bier. Catriona wondered if they came out of respect for her father, or to inspect the MacDonald woman who was mistress now.

She thought Kirsty's courage magnificent in the face of the antagonism which could not be openly displayed at such a time, but which was still present. If she noticed the contemptuous stares, the air of suspicion and distrust which descended over a room whenever she entered, she did not show it. She was polite and courteous to all those about her, with a sufficient air of dignity to curtail any rash tongues. Only when Catriona found her in tears on the eve of the funeral did she realise the full extent of the girl's discomfort, the fear that James could be turned against her.

On a warm, brilliantly sunny day, with fresh heather and summer flowers blooming over the gentle slopes behind the house, over one hundred people gathered to watch Fergus Campbell laid to rest beside his wife, and none mourned his passing more than his eldest son.

Murdoch was not present and Catriona knew that fact and her own lack of tears attracted much attention and concern, for none but her immediate family, with the exception of Tamsie and Andrew, knew the relationship between father and daughter was not as it should have been. She was no hypocrite. She could not cry for a man she had never known. The sorrow she felt was for her brother and his wife. Never could they have envisaged such a tragic end to their honeymoon.

Catriona watched James throw a handful of earth on to the coffin and followed suit mechanically, as Darna's piper began to play a melancholy lament for his departed chief. It meant nothing to her except perhaps to show a solid front before the questioning eyes that were watching her every move.

How smug Andrew looked. There was a new air of importance about him and the rich brocade coat he wore, more befitting a banquet than a funeral, proclaimed he had had neither respect nor love for her father either. He had been a means to an end.

He and several of the men had got very drunk the previous evening after dinner and James had left their company in disgust. Before they had eaten Andrew had sought her out with changes to be made in the guest list for their wedding. Many names of her kinsmen and closest friends had been deleted and replaced by his own relatives. He would never have dared do such a thing had her father been alive, she thought, as she reluctantly agreed to every change he made. She was totally alone now. She would not go against his wishes now or later. She would say nothing, do nothing to arouse his childish, often vindictive temper and in that way perhaps he would soon leave her alone.

Poor James, who had loved and yet been at a different end of the scale from his father, stood like a statue beside the grave. Only Kirsty's insistent whispers eventually drew him away. She was glad he had found not only her, but also the courage to risk everything to keep her by his side.

She knew nothing of what had taken place after she fled from her father's room in tears. It had taken Nan over half an hour to calm her and the warm milk she had been persuaded to drink did not induce sleep. She tossed and turned restlessly the whole night and received the news of his death in the morning, heavy-eyed and with no compassion for the man who had so callously denied her her rights as a daughter. She wept in the arms of her unshaven brother, with misery in his eyes, not knowing the truth and misinterpreting his wretchedness.

She was not enlightened until several days after the funeral. All the guests, with the exception of Andrew, had departed and she spent the morning going through the house with Kirsty, acquainting her with everything she thought she should know in order to maintain control both of her new home and the servants. Secretly she had instructed Nan to tell each and every one of them she would tolerate no disrespect for the new mistress. If anyone wished to leave they were free to do so. If they stayed they must obey Kirsty's every wish, never question an order, and think of her as they would Catriona.

'You should not be wasting your time here with me,' Kirsty said, a tiny frown puckering her brows as they descended the main staircase. 'You should be making plans in your own house. Why aren't you? You've never once mentioned what it is like and you show such little enthusiasm for your wedding day.'

'It is a large, ugly old house in the middle of Perth. I shall be expected to entertain Andrew's fellow officers there, together with their wives or ladies. I shall listen attentively to their unimaginative prattling and the constant, boring boasting of the men. I shall smile and tell them how much I enjoy being a wife and look forward to being a mother. Dear heaven, within a month I shall be the most accomplished liar in the town.' The ghost of a smile touched her lips as she added in a lighter tone. 'How your brother would love to hear me say that. He told me the Campbells were already accomplished liars. I may very well prove him right.'

'There will be no need to go to that extreme,' James remarked quietly from the doorway of the study. 'Come down, both of you, I wish to talk to you. Yes, you too, Kirsty. I haven't seen you all morning and I am desperate for your company after what I have just been through.'

Mystified, the two descended the stairs and joined him. Puzzlement turned to bewilderment as a maid brought in a tray containing a bottle of champagne and three glasses. What were they to celebrate so soon after their father's funeral, Catriona wondered as she perched herself on the arm of a chair.

'Andrew has gone,' James said, waiting until they were alone before he spoke. 'He will never set foot in Darna again.'

Catriona stared into his hard, set features, watched them slowly soften as he waited for his words to penetrate her stunned mind.

'I—I don't understand, James. Why? We saw his luggage being loaded half an hour ago, but before he left we had to discuss the final wedding details. Despite all his alterations, last night he still was not satisfied and I had to revise the guest list again. I'm afraid some of our kinsmen were rather unkind to him the other night and made fun of him when he could not hold his drink. Neither they, nor their families are to be invited.'

'There will be no wedding,' James said. 'I have made Andrew aware of our father's dying wishes. You are not going to marry that odious lecher, Catriona. For the love of God, girl, do something, but don't stare at me as if I have taken leave of my senses. I assure you I have not. Scream—cry—throw a fit—laugh—anything!'

Catriona could say nothing. She could not take in what he had told her.

'Father's dying wish?' She forced the words out through trembling lips.

'At the last moment he realised his grief was self-

induced and always had been and you were not to blame.
He has released you from the marriage. It's true! Both
Murdoch and I were at the bedside, not to mention the
whole household of servants. He was quite coherent and
knew what he was saying.'

'How wonderful,' Kirsty breathed. 'Oh, Catriona, I
am so pleased for you. Your heart was never in the
match. You would have been so miserable. Now you can
stay here with us.'

'My father intended me to be miserable.' Slowly
Catriona rose and moved to her brother's side. With
tears in her eyes she took his face in her hands, forcing
him to look at her. 'Dearest James, no sister could have
such a brother as I have in you. We have always been
truthful with each other. Don't change now. What did
you promise him?'

James's hands covered hers, drew them to his lips and
kissed them. Watching, Kirsty saw again the unbreak-
able bonds, the depths of the ties which bound them, and
she blinked back helpless tears as she remembered the
brothers who had rejected her.

'Murdoch and I wanted to raise our men for the
Prince. We were determined on it.' James knew it was
useless to lie further. What he had to say would cause her
pain, but she was still free. One day when he was an
aging father and she, an old married woman with the
man of her choice, neither would regret the path he had
chosen. She said nothing, but clung more tightly to his
hands. 'Father gave me a choice. If the house of Darna
remained loyal to King George, he would revoke the
marriage contract.'

'James! Oh, James!' A sob rose in Catriona's throat.
Behind her Kirsty gasped at the implication of his words.
Campbells against MacDonalds—hurled into battle
against each other yet again. The brothers she loved
against the husband she would readily give up her life
for.

'Don't greet, either of you,' came the quiet, but firm command. 'The decision was mine. I could have refused and still revoked the marriage contract after he was dead, but that is not my way. You know why. A legal paper has been drawn up, Catriona, which he signed and it was duly witnessed. Andrew cannot hold you to the marriage.' He omitted to tell her that the language which had poured from the Fraser's lips at the news was more suited to a barrack-room than a house in mourning. No bride! No prestige at having the Laird of Darna as his father-in-law and worst of all no money to pay off his rapidly mounting debts which had trebled since the first plans had been made. He had spent recklessly, expectant of the day Catriona's ample dowry would fall into his hands.

'Father turned against both you and Murdoch. He gave you neither love nor recognition and there were times when I wished I was not his son for the harshness in him which made him deny you both. But I am his son Catriona, and in the end I could only remember how much I loved him. Murdoch has refused to join us. He rides with the Stewarts. We can only pray this madness does not last long before Charles Stuart gets what he wants.'

'And if he does not?' Kirsty whispered.

'I would have preferred to fight with your brothers, rather than against them, my love,' James returned, gathering her to him. She was trembling like an aspen leaf as her mind continued to dwell on what could possibly take place. 'But I have made my choice.'

'No! Catriona made it for you.' The words were torn from her lips before she realised what she was saying. She turned her face against his shoulder and wept uncontrollably. 'I shall lose one of you, I know it. Brother or husband . . . It is not fair. We have had no chance to live yet . . .'

'You did not question my decision when I whisked you

off to be married and put a wedding band on your finger. Do not question me now when I give my sister the chance to reach out and grasp a little of the happiness we have known,' James answered gravely. 'Would you have denied her the chance, in my place? Do you think your brother Rorie would have hesitated to act as I did if it had been you in Catriona's place? Would he expect recriminations from someone he loves?'

'James, you make me ashamed. Catriona, forgive my foolish tongue. I spoke in haste,' Kirsty begged.

'Dry your eyes. Both of you come and have some champagne,' James ordered, opening the bottle.

'Do you think we should—at such a time?' Catriona began. If this was a dream, dear God, please never let it end, she thought. No Andrew, no marriage. No dreary house in Perth, but Darna and the way of life she loved.

The face of the only man who had ever aroused her was suddenly in her thoughts. She lowered her gaze lest she betrayed herself before James and Kirsty. She was free, but he would never know it. He would ride off to war and might never come back. No! That must not happen. He had to come back, as James had to. Perhaps one day in the future they would meet again and then there would be truth between them. He had wanted her the last time they met. She had felt it in the arms which held her, the voice which so scornfully mocked her and she had deliberately sent him away so that he would not know she wanted him too! One day . . .

James handed them each a glass of champagne and then took up his own. For his wife he had a broad smile to dispel her misgivings. For his sister the truth was in his eyes, quickly veiled so that only she saw what was in his heart. He feared what was to come. The hardships and the suffering—and the aftermath, the penalties for the losing side.

'To all those who dwell within these walls. May we all find our heart's desires.'

He already had and he was leaving it all behind to fight a war not of his choosing, on the side of a king he neither liked nor acknowledged, Catriona thought as she sipped her drink. If anything happened to him she would never forgive herself.

Glenfinnan was a narrow mountainous valley to the east of Borradale. Just after noon on the 19th August, the sound of pipes heralded the approach of the first clansmen to the anxiously waiting Charles Stuart and his retinue. Camerons in their hundreds, MacDonalds from Skye, others led by Keppoch came striding proudly down the hillside to gather around the banner of red and white silk unfurled in their midst.

By the 21st August the army had grown as it marched to Invergarry. Men of Glengarry swelled the ranks, together with Stewarts from Appin and Ardshiel and many other clans who rose en masse to the call of their Prince.

The government in London ordered the commander of the King's forces in Scotland, General Sir John Cope, to disperse the rebels, but they were not yet destined to meet. As Cope and his two-thousand-strong force marched to Inverness, Charles Edward Stuart marched to Perth and promptly set about collecting money, horses and arms to replenish his already dwindling resources.

James began gathering men who had pledged to ride with him, but he delayed his departure as long as possible, unable to bear the look of misery on the face of his wife. Only when news reached them that the Highland army was advancing towards Edinburgh, did he realise that to delay further would dishonour the promise he had made to a dying man.

It was barely light on a chilly September morning when he took his leave of Kirsty and Catriona and rode away from Darna at the head of some ninety men, among them young Alistair the groom and two of Nan's grandsons from the village. Men from the household had also volunteered and there were only two aged retainers left. The rest were women.

Catriona felt her heart swell with pride as she watched, a white-faced silent Kirsty at her side. Long after he had disappeared from sight, she stood on the steps, hugging her arms about her for warmth and oblivious to Nan's entreaties to return to bed.

Dear God, keep him safe and bring him back home, she prayed over and over again.

'I am going to Edinburgh,' Kirsty declared, setting aside her tapestry work. 'Tamsie said a battle. James could be hurt—or dead!—Catriona, I don't know how you can sit there so calmly. I can't bear it. I must go!'

She had been on edge for days, ever since Tamsie Stewart, recently returned from Perth, had stopped at the house to give them the latest news. She had accompanied Murdoch and her father when they left to join the Prince and lingered in the town after the army left to march on Edinburgh, which it now occupied.

There had been a battle at a place called Gladsmuir, between the two villages of Prestonpans and Cockenzie, she told them, and her voice grew quite excited as she related the victory of the Highland army. In six minutes they had put to flight the English soldiers which numbered in the region of four thousand and primarily the MacDonalds and Camerons had been instrumental in doing so. Highland casualties had been light, perhaps no more than fifty killed and ninety injured, while the enemy suffered substantial losses. The prisoners taken totalled over sixteen thousand men, including many officers, and the death toll had been high. The Prince had been most magnanimous in his treatment of the wounded, however, she added, and the enemy wounded were being tended without distinction from his own men.

'My dear, I know how you must be feeling, but you cannot,' Catriona sat beside her concernedly. Kirsty had grown steadily paler and thinner since her husband's departure. He had been away four weeks now. Grey shadows beneath dull eyes accentuated her pallor and betrayed how little she slept each night.

Catriona had deliberately kept her occupied in the house and when that irritated her, had organised daily rides or invited friends of their own age to the house, in a determined effort to make her feel accepted—most of all to keep her mind off the war. Kirsty had shown little interest in anything. She wanted only to hear the latest progress of the Prince's army. Whenever she dared and when a sympathetic ear was available, she asked the whereabouts of the Campbell regiments loyal to the crown.

'Catriona, why are we not honest with each other? You wish to go as much as I do. Of course I want news of James, but I dearly want to see my brothers again too. I cannot bear this ill feeling between us, and what better way to gain news of my husband? They will tell me everything and then when I know, I will follow him— to London if necessary. Why should I not be with him?'

'You are not a camp-follower,' Catriona reproved, although secretly she agreed with everything that had been said. A battle, with the MacDonalds at the fore-front. Was he there?

'I will follow the man I love wherever it is necessary, for us to be together, Kirsty declared, eyes flashing defiantly. 'You are as feart for Rorie's life as I am for James's. Come with me, tell him how you feel. I am determined to go, with or without you. Without news of them I will go mad. What good are we doing here, pretending to ourselves we can go on day after day as if nothing is happening? We cannot! We have a small house in Edinburgh. Rorie and Donald will lodge there. Come with me.'

'You don't know what you are asking. If you had seen the way he looked at me the last time we met . . .'

'I saw the look in his eyes when I told him how you had cared for me, the risks you took. He is stubborn too. He would not accept it at first, but I knew he wanted to. He told me he would somehow seek you out and thank you. Donald made fun of him until they almost came to blows. I have never seen Rorie roused to anger over a woman before.'

He had kept his word and she, fool that she was, had scorned the thanks he offered and aroused fresh bitterness between them, afraid not only of him, but of herself and the love she continued to deny.

'I am persuaded,' she said with a heavy sigh. 'It will do no good, but I will come with you. On one condition. You will not think of going further. We will remain in Edinburgh until the army returns—whichever army that might be.'

'Yes—yes! Can we leave tomorrow?'

'The day after. I must try and find a trustworthy man to drive the carriage. Are you sure you feel up to the journey?'

'Of course. Let us go and start packing. I don't want to waste a moment,' Kirsty cried, and, for the first time in weeks, there was colour in her cheeks.

Right or wrong, Catriona had committed herself. She brushed aside Nan's incredulous doubts about the hundred mile long journey and the uncertainty of what lay ahead for them once they reached their destination. She ignored her recriminations that Catriona should allow the young mistress, who was clearly not herself, to attempt such a strenuous undertaking.

Catriona bit back the retort which rose to her lips at the last remark. This journey was for them both. She too, was seeking news of the man she loved and nothing now would deter her from doing so.

Edinburgh late at night, the cobbled streets full of kilted Highlanders, made Catriona uneasy. She was tired, her patience exhausted by Kirsty's determination to continue the journey throughout the day, even though they had started out at the crack of dawn. Whenever the horses were slowed to a walking pace or they stopped at a posting house for a change of team, she was irritable and impatient. The cook had provided a food basket for them, but she had hardly eaten anything. Catriona prayed they could obtain news of James. Only then might she be able to persuade Kirsty to return to Darna and wait for him in safety and comfort.

'My lady, is it far now?' Nan asked, trying to find a comfortable position to sit in. Every part of her body ached and sleep had been impossible.

'Do you know where we are Kirsty? Is the house near?'

'I'm not sure. Yes, this corner, driver. There—there at the end of this street . . . The red brick house with the shutters.'

Catriona heard the relief in her voice and said a silent prayer for their safe arrival. The sound of laughter reached them from within as she climbed out and helped Kirsty after her, frowning as the girl winced when she put her weight on the leg she had injured. Kirsty leaned heavily against her and she knew the last of her strength was gone. She herself ached in every limb and longed for the luxury of a hot bath to dispel the effects of a cold night wind that had chilled her, and Kirsty too, she suspected, to the bone.

'Nan, help me. Samuel, quickly, raise someone in the house,' she ordered.

His insistent banging brought someone to the door within seconds. She gave the startled manservant no chance for questions. Supporting Kirsty between them, she and Nan pushed past him and conveyed her to the nearest chair.

'Don't stand there like an idiot, man,' she snapped. 'Find your master at once. Tell him his sister is here and find some brandy for us all, we are near frozen.'

A door opened along the passageway and the sounds of laughter and voices grew louder. Behind Catriona the voice of Rorie MacDonald demanded,

'Who is it at this hour, John?'

'Rorie, you are alive.' Shakily Kirsty rose to her feet, stumbling towards him. 'We heard there was a battle. Where is Donald? Don't look so angry, I couldn't stay away . . .' Her eyes closed. As the last of her strength ebbed away she fell against him in a faint.

For a full minute Rorie stared at her, incredulity and disbelief registering on his face, then he was starting up the stairs with his unconscious burden. Half-way he stopped and looked back as if only then fully aware of the person who stood silently watching. Catriona saw no signs of injury and the relief which swept over her was so overwhelming, she leaned back against the tapestry-covered wall for support, near to fainting herself.

'Keep her here,' he said to the gaping servant. 'Let them warm themselves by the fire in the study, but watch them until I return.'

'Mistress, drink this,' Nan insisted, holding a glass to Catriona's lips. She drank a little of the port, grimaced and pushed it away.

She sat in a chair before a blazing fire, in a small room panelled in oak, on which were set old leather targets and basket-hilted claymores. Relics of the MacDonald past, she suspected. The fire had warmed her, easing a little of the tension from her weary limbs. Nan fixed a cushion behind her head and she allowed herself to relax for the first time since leaving Darna. It was the early hours of the morning! No wonder she was exhausted.

He had eyes for his sister only, had looked at Catriona as if she was a total stranger. She had come for nothing, harbouring foolish dreams not intended to be realised.

'Nan, what a fool I am. Let us leave here at once. Kirsty is safe and does not need us.'

'And where will we go at this time of the morning?' the woman declared indignantly. 'I'm fair dropping myself. My poor back.'

'I don't want to stay. Bring my cloak.'

Catriona swayed with fatigue as she stood up and then, suddenly realising they were no longer alone, turned towards the door. With a wave of his hand Rorie MacDonald dismissed the hovering servant.

'Where the devil do you think you are going?' he demanded harshly. 'You have some explaining to do.' There was not only anger, but fear too in his tone. Kirsty's collapse had greatly alarmed them both.

'I am too tired to fight with you, MacDonald. I have brought your sister to you because otherwise she would have made the journey alone and I care for her too much to have allowed that to happen. Just let me go. I cannot stay here.'

'You can and will. A room is being made ready for you now. Your servants will have to double up with mine, this is not a large house,' he answered stepping towards her. 'Tomorrow we will talk.'

'We have nothing to say.'

Catriona turned away from him, confused and vulnerable, determined not to give way to her weariness in his presence, but she could not control the tears which began to roll silently down over her cheeks.

Reaching out, Rorie took her by the shoulders, felt her immediately tense at his touch and tightened his grasp so that she was unable to free herself. She looked exhausted—dispirited. Her travelling clothes were streaked with dust and her hair, free from the confines of its ribbon, fell in a mass of disordered curls about her shoulders. The anger went out of him. She was so different from the proud young woman who had faced him at their last meeting, spat words of hatred and defiance at him, shattering the mood of gentleness that had been upon him when he sought her out.

He had wanted her from the first moment he set eyes on her, had ridiculed himself for the weakness in him which made him think of her constantly, which had caused him to raise his fist to his own brother for his mocking taunts—and he wanted her still, despite all the bitterness between them. Yet he knew he must deny the longing in him, or become the monster she already believed him to be.

Turning her, unresisting in his hold, his fingers brushed away all traces of tears in a caress as light as a breath of wind, before slowly lowering his mouth to hers.

'No,' Catriona moaned, but she did not resist, could not. She no longer had any defence against this man.

Behind her Nan brought down a string of curses upon the head of the 'Red' MacDonald for daring to lay hands on her precious mistress and she was just moving towards the poker in the hearth, when Rorie said quietly,

'She is in no danger from me, woman. Take her to the room at the top of the stairs and put her to bed.'

Flinging Catriona's cloak about her shoulders, Nan hustled her towards the staircase, muttering under her breath to a girl who was deaf to her words, oblivious to everything except the touch of Rorie's lips on hers. If she had betrayed herself, what did it matter? He had not been hurt in battle and she was with him. She had discovered the happiness James had spoken of. For the first time ever, her brother did not take precedence in her thoughts.

'Were my eyes deceiving me, brother, or was that Catriona Campbell?'

Rorie spun around to find Donald leaning against the

half-open door. In the room beyond were a dozen or more friends they had been entertaining when the thunderous knocking on the door had reluctantly dragged him away. They had all been drinking heavily, a relief from the boredom which followed their one and only real battle.

'It was.'

'Faith, has she decided to take her father's advice seriously then? Is that why you were hesitant to come with us this evening? Why, you sly old *sionnach,* you knew she was coming. You won't have to go looking for a woman to accommodate you now, will you? You have one right here.'

'Don't talk like a fool. Kirsty took it into her silly head to follow us and the Campbell girl didn't want her to travel alone. I find that quite acceptable. No other reason, Donald,' he added as a familiar smile touched his brother's mouth. 'She will be afforded the same courtesy as Kirsty was shown. Is that understood?'

'Perfectly. You are staying then, to show her true MacDonald hospitality?' Donald chuckled and, as several times before whenever Catriona's name was mentioned, he watched an angry gleam appear in Rorie's eyes.

'No, I am not. I am coming with you, but let one thing be understood between us, Donald—she is not to be touched.'

'So you are laying claim to her.'

'If you choose to put it that way—yes.'

'I'll vow she doesn't know it yet.'

'Remember what I say. So much as look sideways at her and brother or not—I'll break your neck.'

CHAPTER
SEVEN

WHEN Catriona awoke, she opened her eyes upon a strange room, smaller than her own at Darna, although it was pleasantly furnished and comfortable, with pink velvet drapes at the windows and around the huge bed in which she lay. She sat up, startled. And then memory returned to soothe her. The MacDonald house in Edinburgh! For a moment she had not known where she was.

The memory of the previous night flooded back to her and she grew quite hot as she remembered the intimate embrace in the downstairs room. Under the very eyes of Nan too! Would the time ever be right for her to tell him of her love, commit herself totally to what her heart demanded? She was so afraid of rejection, of being cast aside as she had been by her father. Her love denied—or abused—or rejected.

She longed to give herself freely as Kirsty and James were able to do, yet she held back. They were secure in their love, their marriage, the knowledge that nothing short of death could separate them and even afterwards, she somehow suspected if it was possible, they would be together. Such a love endured beyond the grave. Would it be the same for her?

She knew she must make a choice before she returned to Darna. Remain silent or declare what she felt. She would love only one man until she died, as her father had loved only one woman. He had been right. There was part of him in her. Would she lose Rorie MacDonald as he had lost her mother? He had cursed her with his last breath. Was her love doomed from the very beginning?

Pulling on a robe and slippers, she crossed to the window. Below, the street was even more crowded than it had been the night before. Open carts and wagons hauling supplies for the Prince's army rumbled over the cobblestones, the shops were bustling with people and everywhere the kilted Highlanders were to be seen. They dominated the scene with their differently coloured plaids.

Charles Stuart himself had taken up residence at Holyrood Palace and was exercising his full authority as Prince Regent, holding court, dining with his officers and entertaining the people of Edinburgh with lavish balls which in no way betrayed the lack of funds in the royal purse. The ladies adored him!

The noise was unbelievable after the peace and quiet of the countryside around Darna. Directly below her a woman was selling oranges and apples, a few yards away a knife-sharpener plied his trade from an old hand cart. In the gutter a one-armed beggar barely missed being trampled by a passing horse as he leaned forward asking for money.

She turned as the door opened and Nan came in with a breakfast tray. The smell of food made Catriona realise how ravenous she was. They had eaten very little on the journey the previous day.

The maid watched in approval as she ate every piece of the lightly buttered toast and the two coddled eggs.

'Is Kirsty awake yet?'

'You've slept late, my lady, it's almost noon. She and those two brothers of hers went out hours ago. The "Red" MacDonald said you are to treat the house as your own, but you cannot go out. Those were his very words.'

'Not go out?' Catriona echoed, her eyes widening. 'Am I a prisoner then?'

'I wouldn't know what's in his black mind, but he's left a man downstairs by the front door. You'll not get past that one. Built like an ox, he is.'

'We'll see about that. Bring me some clothes.'

Not only built like an ox, but with a face to match, Catriona thought as she came downstairs. His enormous frame moved to block the doorway as she approached.

'Stand aside, my mistress wishes to go out,' Nan said indignantly.

'Neither of you can leave until my master returns. Those are his orders.'

'What are you called?' Catriona demanded haughtily.

'My name is Colin, lady.'

'Well, Colin and how do you propose to stop me?'

'Any way I have to.'

The underlying threat in his voice told her neither wit nor guile would get her past him. She turned on her heel, found the sitting-room and sat herself down to await the return of Rorie MacDonald. It was over an hour before she heard voices in the hallway. Slowly she rose. Smoothing down the skirts of her pale blue gown, she adjusted a stray curl in front of the mirror over the fireplace and stepped determinedly towards the door. Opening it she was in time to see Kirsty hurrying upstairs, her cheeks wet with tears. Tight-lipped and unsmiling, Rorie stood staring after her for several minutes before he turned in Catriona's direction.

'Give me a moment before you fly at me with questions,' he snapped, brushing past her. She watched him pour himself a whisky and toss it back. Her first impulse was to slap his face for his high-handedness or at the very least, rebuke him for his lack of manners, but as he turned, she was struck by how drawn and tired he looked and the words died in her throat. 'Come in and close the door. We have things to say to each other.'

'It can wait.' She hesitated, then said boldly, 'I was only annoyed I was prevented from leaving the house.

Your reasoning is beyond me. However it is of no importance now. Kirsty looked upset, I think I should go to her.'

'Not yet. Sit down—please.' He indicated a chair and she seated herself full of curiosity. 'Will you take a dram with me?'

'Not whisky, but a little wine, please. I am finding it colder here than at home,' Catriona admitted.

'More cold and decidedly more unfriendly. Everyone smiles and speaks softly, but I wonder what is really in their minds? The Prince is determined to press on into England, despite much advice to the contrary. He thinks the reception he has received here is an example of what is to come.'

'You don't believe that is the case?'

Catriona sipped the full-bodied wine he had given her and found it helped instantly to warm her. Despite the sun outside, the woollen dress she wore and the fire not a few feet away from where she sat, she was feeling extremely chilly.

Rorie bent to throw another log onto the fire before sitting opposite her.

'The Prince has won people to his cause with his bravery in the field, his diplomacy in the face of constant opposition to his plans. Do you know what he said to someone who told him to go home not long after he had landed? "I am home". When Lochiel attempted the same thing he was told "Charles Stuart is come to claim the crown of his ancestors—to win it or to perish in the attempt!" Brave words, do you not agree?'

'By the sight of the empty crofts and the untended fields we passed on the way here he has roused every man in the Highlands.'

'Save a few,' Rorie returned dryly and she bit back an angry retort at the insinuation. He did not know the sacrifice James had made—or the reason.

'We saw only women and children or very old men,'

she continued, ignoring his pointed gaze. Was he seeking an explanation? 'It was most desolate and pitiful to
see. Perhaps some of those poor women are widows
now, or soon will be. It is too horrible to think of.
Women without their men, babies who will never know
their fathers. Families split apart because he came back.'

'It is his heritage and he has a right to claim it.'

There was no answer to that for it was the truth. She
put her glass aside, suddenly ill at ease with him. Rorie's
gaze narrowed as he watched the tension creep through
her body. Deliberately she avoided his gaze and stared
into the fire. Would they never be at ease together?
Damn it, what did her feelings matter? She was in his
house and he was master here. He could take her
whenever it suited him.

Abruptly he curtailed that train of thought. That was
Donald's way, not his.

'You know Kirsty is not a strong girl, was there
nothing you could do to keep her at Darna?'

'She has a mind of her own. She would have come with
or without me, and I will not deceive you, I came hoping
for news of James.' She saw his face harden, but he said
nothing. 'When she knew there had been a battle she
had to see for herself that neither you nor Donald had
been hurt, even though you had turned your back on
her. She wanted to heal the breach between you.'

'And for my foolishness I received a sound lashing
with that whip you have for a tongue,' he replied, but she
was surprised to see he was not angry at her words and
that gave her the confidence to continue.

'So many times I draw comparisons between us.
James and myself—you and Kirsty. We bear different
names, but we are alike.'

'You really are a most surprising—no, exasperating—
young woman, do you know that? You didn't believe me
when I told you how the fight with Murdoch really
happened, yet Kirsty tells me now he has been on the

receiving end of the truth for a change. That day I wanted to shake you until your stupid head fell from your shoulders, I was so furious.' He leaned towards her and she glimpsed flecks of green dancing in the tawny eyes, so provocatively mocking in their intensity.

'Murdoch is not the brother I once knew. When he came back from his travels, I thought he had accepted his injury. He had another good hand and he had learned to use it. He is capable with both sword and pistol again, but when I listened to him the other day I realised the hatred he has nurtured all these years has grown until it cannot be controlled. He means to kill you.'

'I'll remember the warning—with gratitude. You didn't have to tell me,' Rorie murmured with a smile. 'Are we friends, now that you have done so?'

'We can—never be friends,' she said, instantly on the defensive again.

'If only you were not so feart of me.'

'Afraid—me! What nonsense you talk.' The laughter in his voice stung her.

'Of yourself then. You are not in Darna now. There are no prying eyes watching us. When I kissed you . . .'

'It was against my will.'

'The first time, perhaps. Afterwards I think it was different, although it would take courage to admit it. Kirsty and your brother, although it is not to my liking, have found the necessary courage to stand against the rest of the world. Are you not made of the same fibre? I kissed you because I wanted to. Is there a better reason?'

'Because it amused you would surely be closer to the truth.'

'No. If you want the truth, then you shall have it. I want you. I have wanted you since that first night. Had you been more responsive when you arrived last night, you would have been in my bed. Isn't that what you want to hear? Doesn't that make it easier for you to stand on your dignity and decry this MacDonald savage and deny what I think is in your heart. For once in your life think of yourself! You are a free woman, aren't you?'

He was laughing at her. Kirsty had told him she was no longer to marry Andrew and now he considered her an easy conquest. In his bed! The words would not come, though a thousand retaliatory insults leapt to mind to hurl at him in reprisal for such an outrageous suggestion. But she wanted him, and he knew it. The humiliation which swept over her was almost unbearable. Hands clenched, she turned away from him. She had to leave now before he took advantage of her discomfort, of the vulnerability he had discovered and no doubt envisaged he could use to the full.

'You forget to whom you are speaking, sir.' She leapt to her feet, the colour receding from her cheeks. 'I am not one of your tavern wenches, eager to throw myself into the arms of one of the Prince's valiant followers. You will find plenty of them, I am sure—and cheap.'

'Even though you know you have wanted me from the first moment I held you?' The smile faded from Rorie's features.

'You have made it quite clear the only reason you are glad I came with Kirsty, is that I might be persuaded to warm your bed. You are mistaken.'

'Your brother was wounded at Prestonpans. At this moment he is in the Tolbooth.' The blow was delivered swiftly and without mercy.

The room spun around her. She lifted clenched fists to strike at the face before her, but it receded and there was only air. She heard an oath close by and then there was an arm tight about her waist, supporting her back to the chair. A glass was being held against her trembling lips.

She opened her eyes into Rorie's shocked features. She pushed away the drink he held so violently that most of it spilled down the front of his jacket, but he did not appear to notice.

'You—you are the most inhuman man I have ever met.' Her voice sounded unreal. Her vision was blurred and she closed her eyes again and was still.

'Catriona! For the love of God, look at me. The devil is in me today. In a moment of madness I wanted to hurt you. You've plagued my thoughts for so long and each time we meet—albeit the circumstances have never been in our favour before—we fight like cat and dog because it is expected of us. Can we not think of ourselves? Have I ever harmed you? Laid a disrespectful hand on you— apart from a few stolen kisses, which were very enjoyable. Can you hear me? I'm not given to apologising, but I am offering one now. Will you not accept it?'

Catriona's eyes flew open. Were her ears playing tricks on her? Was this Rorie MacDonald kneeling before her, touching her cold hands to his cheeks with a reverence and gentleness she had never considered possible in a man of his temperament? He sighed and drew back, but still held fast to her and she did not try to free herself.

James! He had spoken of James. The sudden rush of emotion which rose inside her, the urge to consolidate the unexpected honesty between them took second place as his words returned to her.

'My brother wounded and in prison! Is this Prince of yours an unfeeling monster?' she cried.

'Calm yourself. The Prince's own doctors are attending the wounded on both sides. I hope the English are as merciful with our men that fall into their hands. I've heard the Duke of Cumberland prefers hanging men to showing compassion. There's not one iota of feeling in that one.'

'James—tell me about James,' she pleaded. 'You talk of compassion, where is yours?'

'One day, you may find it in your heart to acknowledge you were totally wrong with all those black thoughts you had about me. I could vindicate myself now in your eyes, but I will not. I, too, have my pride.'

There will never be a right time for us,' Catriona whispered wretchedly. 'Can you not see that?' Was he mad to suggest such a thing, or were his motives, as she suspected, totally selfish?

'I refuse to accept what you are saying. Listen now and I will tell you of your brother. His wound is slight. He has received attention and been taken to the Tolbooth with other prisoners. I slept little last night wondering how to tell you both. He has attempted to escape twice. He is a brave and courageous soldier and I admire him for that despite all that has passed between us. Very early this morning I arranged passes for Kirsty and myself to visit him. Tomorrow afternoon I will take you. As his wife I thought she should see him first. I am not a fool. I know the real reason she made this journey, and Donald and I were only part of it. She is distressed now, but also pleased. For him the war is over. He is alive and will return to her. I swear I will do everything in my power to ensure that happens.'

'Are you so sure of the Prince's victory?' Catriona asked. How relieved Kirsty must be to learn James's life was no longer in danger.

'Either way it is possible Kirsty may lose someone she cares for.'

'You are not certain then?' His words jarred her moment of relief.

Outwardly her composure had returned, but she still felt a little light-headed. Most of this conversation was unreal to her. This man before her must be a figment of her imagination, exactly what she would have liked the man she loved to be. Yet he had spoken the truth. A few stolen kisses were nothing to what he could have extracted from her. That last day when he had found her alone, he could have killed Alistair, but he did not, abused her, but he did not. He spoke of fighting

Donald's battles. Donald, the braggart—the drunkard. So like Murdoch! Dare she believe him

'I—I am confused.' She raised trembling fingers to a head that had begun to throb abominably. 'I would like to go and lie down.'

It was no excuse to leave. She felt sick at the news he had given her, afraid for Kirsty, for her brother—for Rorie MacDonald.

'Of course. I will call your maid.'

'No. I can manage. You promise I can see James tomorrow? Please.' The plea broke from her lips and bright tears glistened in her eyes.

'Tonight we shall all dine together,' Rorie said as he raised her to her feet, 'and tomorrow you will see your brother and assure yourself of his well being. After that . . .' He shrugged broad shoulders. 'Charles Stuart is giving a ball in Holyrood Palace in four days. I would like you to persuade Kirsty to go—and come yourself. Afterwards I insist the pair of you return to Darna. I am satisfied my sister will be well cared for—whatever happens. Trust me.'

'I do. I wish I did not. You make everything sound so simple—uncomplicated,' Catriona answered. He did understand. He loved his sister still and did not hate James for taking her away from him. 'I, too, envy what James and Kirsty have found. My father tried to prevent it, but James was stronger than he realised.' She raised her pale face to his and a knife twisted in Rorie's heart. What he would have given to hold her and offer comfort. 'You know my father arranged a match for me with Andrew Fraser? Please, do not tell me what you thought of it. Your condolences were more than enough.' When Andrew had drunkenly tried to make love to her and the 'Red' MacDonald, the worst enemy of the Campbells of Darna had done no more that night than kiss her hand! 'James and Murdoch were—are—both for the Prince's cause, and they told Father so. His love for Darna, the desire to preserve it for future generations, decreed he should exact one final, binding oath from his son and heir before he died. Not Murdoch, whose disability sickened him—' Rorie's mouth tightened, but she knew she must not spare her words. He had to know how Murdoch had suffered, how James had endured a father who cared only for an heir, despite the love they shared. How she was of no importance, a package to be bargained off to a man of her father's choice. 'And whom he sent from the house as a useless form of life, lower than the beasts in the field. On his death bed . . .' She broke off, her lips quivering. Even now the memory of that last night was unbelievable. James had given her back her self-respect at the cost of his own!

'Father wanted our clansmen to remain loyal to the Crown. He never expected opposition. When James voiced his intention of fighting for the Prince, he used me. He never loved me. He hated me from the first day I began to look like my mother. She died giving me life and he never forgave me, although it was years before I realised the depths of his contempt—his loathing for me. Yet, to control James, he had to resort to using me. On his death-bed he revoked my marriage contract and gave me my freedom on the condition James did not ride with the Prince.'

'My God!' Rorie released her and slumped back into his chair, stunned. Such cold-blooded scheming!

'I think it is no more than you would have done for your sister, MacDonald. Did I not tell you how alike you are. Now because of me my brother is in a pest-ridden gaol in Edinburgh—and for that I will never forgive myself.'

She ran from the room before he could stop her. He started after her, then stopped, his brows drawn together in a fierce frown. Hours later, the whisky decanter empty, he was still seated by the fire when his steward cautiously opened the door.

'How many will there be for dinner, sir?'

'Lay four places, John,' he growled and the man withdrew with a respectful bow.

When he was in a solitary mood Rorie MacDonald did not like to be disturbed. As John said, when he returned to the kitchen, the last time he had seen the master in one of those moods was the day the old master had died, burdening his son with responsibilities far beyond his seventeen years.

'My lady,' Nan said in the frostiest tone she could muster, which was rather difficult in view of her mistress' happy expression. She had come upstairs like a walking statue, her face streaked with tears, and collapsed upon the bed. Yet when she awoke several hours later, she proclaimed her intention of joining the MacDonalds for dinner that evening. 'The journey has been too much for you. I will bring you a tray and you can have an early night. Why cause yourself further distress by staring at his ugly face across a table.'

Catriona was trying to decide which of the two gowns she had brought with her to wear for the occasion. A simple black taffeta, trimmed with sable fur or an emerald green velvet, trimmed with a darker braid. She raised her eyes to Nan's reproving features and said in a level tone.

'I shall be dining downstairs tonight and I will wear the green and my emeralds. I think I brought my necklace with me. Be good enough to prepare a bath, will you? I want to soak my cares—no, my suspicions, away. And don't dare to speak of him like that again.'

'Which one?' Nan stood her ground as she carefully laid the green velvet over a chair. 'Him! Or his brother?'

'You go too far.'

'Nay, not far enough. Dismiss me for my forwardness, curse me for what I am about to say, but hear me out.'

Catriona was silent. She threatened, but would never have parted company from the woman who had raised her from birth. Apart from the milk-mother who had nursed her in the beginning, Nan had been her mother. At night when she cried, she had been cradled against that matronly bosom, soothed and cossetted—and at times, spoilt. Until the age of seventeen, she had known no other confidante, save her brother James. When she had ached in the night from her father's ridicule and scorn, Nan had gently held her and lulled her to sleep.

'I love him,' she said simply. 'You can do nothing— say nothing to alter that. I love Rorie MacDonald.'

The woman stared long and hard at the young face, proud in its defiance.

'God bless you, mistress,' she exclaimed and Catriona was startled.

'Why do you say that? MacDonalds and Campbells, Nan! Two liaisons instead of one. What do you say to that? I will go with him wherever he goes if it pleases him. Be what he wants me to be.' Not long ago Kirsty had uttered almost identical words, she remembered. 'I have never felt like this before. It makes me act like— like an idiot when I am with him, but that changes nothing.'

'Nor did it for her—your mother.' Memories came crowding back as Nan stared at her. 'Your mother, God rest her poor soul, loved your father from the first day she saw him. He wanted her, but she was virtuous beyond his understanding of the word. The only way he could have her was if he married her.'

It took some while for Catriona to comprehend her words.

'He loved her! When she died he was lost!'

'Because too late he realised what he had lost. It was no love match, my dear child. She loved him, bore him two fine sons and he treated her like—like he treated you over the years. A useful commodity. When she was alive, he used her. He wanted another son even though he knew she was in ill health and the doctor advised against it. When you were born he disliked you on sight because you were a girl. Yet he could have accepted your birth if he had had the prospect of more sons in the future, but your mother breathed her last not ten minutes after you came into the world. When his disappointment over you had passed, he realised what he had really lost. How much he had loved the woman who was now forever lost to him.'

'Why did someone not tell me this before?' Catriona whispered. 'Nan, dearest Nan, I thought he hated me because my birth had killed the woman he loved most.'

'Aren't all men like that? Do you not understand what I am trying to tell you? You say you love this "Red" MacDonald. Perhaps you do, but have you ever known such an unscrupulous rogue before? He's had more women than . . . Oh, never mind! He's not for you. He'll use you.'

'I've had the same thought, but there's nothing I can do about it. Love is sometimes one-sided, isn't it—like my mother's.'

'Then think of his reputation.'

'I believe that came about protecting his brother. He said—no, he has never actually admitted it, only hinted, that he fights Donald's battles for him.'

'You are not yourself or you would not talk this way,' Nan said, crossing herself.

'Because of our long-standing friendship I will overlook your familiarity—and your presumptions,' Catriona retorted. 'You obviously have not heard my brother is a prisoner in the Tolbooth. He was captured at Prestonpans. Kirsty saw him this morning. Tomorrow, I shall be able to visit him and it is all due to the efforts of Rorie MacDonald. I will not have a word said against him, do you hear?'

'I hear.' Nan's tone was noncommittal and then,

without warning, she flung her arms about Catriona. 'You deserve happiness, my love. Grasp it now. Don't listen to this old biddy. I've never seen such a sparkle in your eyes as I see now.' She wiped her own eyes and looked rather abashed at such a display of emotion. 'The green, is it? And why not? It always suited you—although it was lost on the other one.'

She had worn it only once before, Catriona realised, the first time she had entertained Andrew at Darna.

'Be still now, your hair is in a mess. By the time I've finished with you, we'll have given the MacDonald something to think about.'

She was so careful with Catriona's toilette, the dressing of her long hair, smoothing sweet-smelling perfumes into her skin, that she could hardly believe that less than an hour ago, the MacDonalds had been Nan's most ardent enemies.

The dinner was over. It had been a pleasant meal which Catriona had enjoyed immensely, despite being conscious of Donald's sardonic gaze on her every time she raised her eyes. Afterwards they retired to the comfortable sitting-room, where they were served port and brandy.

'Rorie is taking you to see James tomorrow, isn't he?' Kirsty asked. She seemed quite recovered from the ordeal of that morning and had chatted quite excitedly about the forthcoming ball. 'I have some warm clothes for him, will you take them? And some decent food. The slop those poor men are being served is outrageous—fit only for pigs.'

'But good enough for traitors,' Donald retorted, glaring at her. 'Dammit! You'll be taking him in a clean white tablecloth to spread on the floor next and a crystal glass to drink from.'

'That's enough. Her concern is natural. He is her husband,' Rorie snapped, irritated by his brother's determination to ruin a pleasant evening. He, too, had noticed the way he watched Catriona, embarrassing her deliberately in the hope she would fly at him. Much to his relief, and admiration, she had not.

'My, we have changed in the space of a few short hours. Last night you were all for saying nothing about him and sending them both back to Darna immediately.'

'Is that true?' Kirsty whispered. 'Why?'

'Because of the pain I knew it would cause you,' Rorie answered with a frown. 'There is very little you can do for him and it upset you, did it not, to see him under such conditions?'

'I can give him a few comforts and tell him how much I love him, that I will wait for him no matter how long it is before he is released.'

'You are both returning home after the Prince's ball, even if I have to send an escort with you. I will not allow you to remain here when the army moves on,' Rorie warned. 'I will not be disobeyed. You will have to take my word that I will do all I can for him.'

'James would prefer you to be safely at Darna,' Catriona added, as Kirsty's expression became decidedly obstinate.

'How can you think of leaving him in that awful place? He needs me.'

'What he needs now is peace of mind, which he will not have if he knows you are here without protection,' Rorie said, with a nod of appreciation in Catriona's direction.

Donald gave a snort of disgust and rose to his feet.

'I'm going out.'

'Is it necessary to remind you we have a guest?' his brother asked.

Donald had been drinking heavily ever since the battle in an attempt to forget what it had been like. The noise of drums, the skirl of pipes, the cries of the Highlanders as they routed the English with devilish glee. Rorie had accepted long ago that his brother was a coward. Accepted it, lived with it and successfully managed to hide it from family and friends.

'I doubt if she will accommodate you as willingly or as satisfactorily as Jenny did last night,' Donald sneered, staring at Catriona with a meaningful smile. 'I'll give her your regards and tell her I've come in your place, shall I?'

'If you wish,' Rorie replied, tight-lipped, aware of a soft flush of colour stealing into Catriona's cheeks as she grasped the meaning of Donald's words.

He had spent the night with a woman he had never seen before, had no intention of seeing again. He had gained nothing from the association and left her before it was light. The city was full of accommodating women since the arrival of the Highland army. Soldiers' wives, prostitutes, camp-followers and the inevitable bored wives of business men and local merchants, who found excitement in brief affairs under the very noses of their husbands.

'I think I shall go to bed,' Kirsty said and Donald uttered a short laugh as he headed towards the door.

'Am I embarrassing you, little sister? And you an old married woman! The other probably doesn't know what a man needs yet, especially a fighting man, although with the Fraser as a teacher, she would soon have learned.'

'Take no notice of your brother, he's having delusions of grandeur because a few pretty girls smile at him these days.' Rorie took Kirsty by the shoulders and kissed her affectionately. 'Why don't you and Catriona go shopping in the morning? I owe you a trousseau, don't I, and you'll need something glamorous for the ball? Have all the bills sent here to me.'

'Oh, Rorie, you are sweet. I was right to come, wasn't I?' Kirsty exclaimed, hugging him.

'Yes, you were right, little one. Away to bed now. I'll see you in the morning before you go out. Do you have to go too?' he asked as Catriona rose to follow.

'I think I should, but before you accuse me of being afraid to stay with you, let me correct you,' she said softly. 'I am not, nor am I afraid of myself any longer . . . But everything has happened so quickly between us. Please, I need time to accept it. Tomorrow, if you wish to talk—we will.'

'Conversation is the last thing I have in mind,' Rorie mocked in equally soft tones as he touched her fingers to his lips.

She was caught in the light from the wall candelabra as he drew her to him. The rich fire of the emeralds glowed against her flawless skin, complementing the depth of colour in her gown. He could smell the fragrance of her hair which tonight she wore loose about her shoulders in a cascade of curls. He wanted to run his fingers through its silkiness, crush her against him and enjoy those soft lips. But he knew he must not touch her. Dared not!

Catriona was disappointed when he released her, yet at the same time glad he had not forced the issue too soon.

'I hate to break into this moment of tenderness,' Donald's sneering tones from the doorway shattered the idyllic moment. Rorie wheeled on him angrily.

'I thought you had gone out.'

'I was on my way, brother, but outside I met a search party.' His eyes turned derisively to Catriona. 'You'll not be seeing your brother tomorrow. He and several other prisoners have escaped tonight. We are asked to join in the hunt.'

'No,' she breathed. 'You cannot.'

'If your brother is captured, he'll have little chance of survival if Rorie isn't there. Four guards were killed in the escape, one of them a MacLeod lad of seventeen. His kinsmen are out for blood.'

Gently, but firmly Rorie removed the restraining hand Catriona had laid impulsively on his arm.

'I have to go.' The wretchedness in her eyes made him feel sick. 'Don't tell Kirsty yet.'

'No, I won't.' She moved to the fireside and did not look around as he left her. Despite the warmth of the fire, she found she was shivering.

CHAPTER
EIGHT

CATRIONA slept very little that night. She was haunted by visions of her brother being pursued through the city by bloodthirsty MacLeods, bent on revenge for the death of one of their own. When Nan brought her breakfast tray she had been up and dressed for nearly two hours.

'Is there news yet?' She had turned eagerly at the sound of the door opening, hoping to see Rorie.

'Nay, my lady, nothing. Neither of the MacDonalds has returned.'

'Perhaps it is a good sign. He would have come back to tell me if there was bad news, I know it.' Catriona looked at the breakfast tray and shook her head. 'I cannot eat now. Perhaps later.'

'So you trust him still,' Nan muttered as she turned away to tidy the room. Luckily she spoke too low for her mistress to hear.

'Hello, Catriona, are you awake early too?' Kirsty poked her head around the door. 'I have a long shopping list as Rorie is being so generous. It will probably take us all morning.'

'I am almost ready.' A look silenced Nan. 'Shall we come back for lunch, or not bother? I've always been so strictly chaperoned on my visits that I must have missed all those exciting little back streets Nan is determined I should not see.'

'Mistress!'

'Oh, poor Nan's face, Catriona. Just look! Tell her not to worry. I have a husband and as you have already made

your feelings plain about my brother, neither of us will
be looking for the attentions of any gentlemen. Besides,
Colin will be with us and he should frighten everyone
away.'

'Have I made my feelings so plain?'

'Not to Rorie, but I saw the look on your face when we
arrived. I don't remember very much else, mind you, but
the way you looked at each other after seven weeks of
separation . . .' Her mood changed abruptly and she
looked quite serious. 'Tell me I am right to go back to
Darna and leave James in prison. I know Rorie is right
and that James is in no danger any more, but I want so
much to stay close to him.'

Catriona uttered a silent prayer as she held the girl
close.

'He will be home before you know it. Now cheer up
and let us go out. We have materials to buy and presents
to take home. It is time Darna began to look like a house
again, with the touch of a woman about it.'

'Two women,' Kirsty said, with a grateful smile.
'What would I do without you?'

Ask me that when you learn James is a free man,
launching himself into the fighting again because of the
promise he made to his father, Catriona thought, and
the smile she bestowed on the other girl hid the
tremendous ache in her heart.

They were descending the stairs when Rorie came in
through the front door. He was unshaven and obviously
tired. Catriona saw this at once, saw too by the way
Kirsty looked at him as she stepped in front of him,
bright and beautiful in a dress of rich peacock blue, that
she had misinterpreted his absence from the house.

'Catriona and I are going out now.' Her tone was
quite disdainful. 'You did say all bills were to be sent to
you?'

'I did.' Rorie drew her against him and kissed her
cheek.

She grimaced and headed for the open door.

'I shall see you at dinner. I hope both you and Donald will be sober for the Prince's ball and not choose to seek your pleasure elsewhere that night. I shall be expecting an escort.'

Close behind her Catriona laid a gloved hand on Rorie's arm as his eyes glinted angrily at the insinuation.

'I have said nothing,' she assured him in a low tone. 'James—he is still free?'

'Yes, but I cannot control the blood-lust of the Mac-Leods. Their desire for revenge is totally justified, after all.'

'If my brother is killed—without mercy, will you be able to tell her you did nothing to prevent it?' Catriona whispered. 'I have told her we are visiting the prison this afternoon. She will be so busy with the dressmaker by then, she will not notice where I go. Please—please do whatever you can. I do not know what she would do if James was—killed.'

'You speak only of Kirsty. You ask nothing for yourself. He is your brother and I know how close you are.'

'Should I? Do you want me to beg for his life, Mac-Donald? I will do that gladly. If you demand me as payment for your help—and I think that is in your mind—then I agree, but not willingly. Such a bargain I assure you, would not be to your liking.'

Rorie stared at her, the proud stance, the eyes as tired as his, yet defiant.

'If you think I would have you under such circumstances, you are not the woman who danced with me at that farce of a betrothal ball, nor the woman I held in my arms a few short hours ago. I could take you that way, you might even enjoy it . . .'

'Is that why you set a man on the door, to keep me a prisoner here?' Catriona demanded.

'He was to ensure that before you set foot outside I had told those whom I thought should know that you were under my protection. You brought my sister to me with apparently no regard for your own welfare despite your brother's defection. I thought it a small thing in return.'

'It was not necessary. I am quite capable of taking care of myself.'

'When you are out with Kirsty, Colin will guard you both. Without him neither of you will set foot outside this house. Don't you think I have enough to worry about at the moment? Well?' The tawny eyes narrowed, threatened her. She drew back and found her wrists imprisoned. Slowly she was drawn against him.

She did not resist as before. His embrace hurt her, yet his lips on hers were gentle although nonetheless demanding. She allowed herself to relax against his hard body, abandoning herself to the sheer delight of being kissed by the man she loved.

'Catriona, have you forgotten something?' Kirsty's impatient tones made Rorie reluctantly release Catriona with a muttered oath.

He put her at arm's length, touched her fingers to his mouth and then laid them against her own. Without a word he turned and entered his own room. So much said—yet still unsaid! Catriona thought as she followed Kirsty into the street. That look! That touch! Was she being a blind fool? Was he using her as Nan so vehemently insisted?

Kirsty's desire to be the best-dressed woman at the ball was insatiable. Between them they visited every shop capable of providing them with suitable materials, but either the stocks had been drained by enormous demand or the supply was inadequate.

At the last moment Kirsty remembered a draper, vaguely related to her old nanny, who had always been able to find what she needed. It took an hour for them to find the place, but when they did, she found the white satin she required. She was so excited she did not notice that Catriona purchased very little. Certainly nothing good enough for the forthcoming ball.

'Please send it to the house of Rorie MacDonald. This is the address.' Kirsty thrust a piece of paper across the counter. 'Have you found what you want, Catriona?'

'I fear I have not, but there is time yet.'

'A few days!'

'I will find something,' Catriona laughed softly. Her brother was a hunted fugitive, how could she go to the ball? But it was better to say nothing until the last moment.

'My lady, the burgundy velvet you wanted . . .'

Catriona and Kirsty had left the shop some ten minutes' walk behind when a boy came panting up to them.

'My master has found it . . .'

'It is not important, but thank him,' Catriona said, moving on. She had asked for no velvet. He had mistaken her for someone else!

'My lady, will you not examine the softness of it? Look at the richness of colour,' the boy insisted. He was a lad of not more than ten.

Kirsty and Colin were ahead of her. The boy thrust the bolt of cloth before her, lifted the top layer of material and she froze as she recognised the crested gold ring staring up at her. A moment—and the cloth descended over it.

'Kirsty, it seems I have found the cloth I want after all,' she called. How could she be so calm? Look Kirsty in the eyes and lie so monstrously. The clansman who was their escort stared at her in silence. He did not like her, she suspected, but dared not displease her. 'You have finished your shopping and you look exhausted. Go home, this will only take a little while. If you think I shall be swamped by amorous advances from gentlemen of the Prince's army, by all means send Colin back for me, but I doubt it will be necessary.'

The shop was in a narrow side street where the houses seemed almost to touch each other as they leaned over the uneven cobbles. Catriona risked a look over her shoulder before she entered. Neither Kirsty nor Colin were in sight.

A man came from behind the counter, beamed at her and said in a voice loud enough for his other customers to hear.

'My lady, forgive me. I forgot to show you the new cloths which have just arrived from France. I am sure you will find something to your liking. Unfortunately I have not had time to put them on show yet and they are still in a back room.'

'That does not matter. I would like very much to examine them,' Catriona replied.

He led the way through the shop, opened a door at the far end and motioned her to enter. The door closed after her the moment she crossed the threshold. The panic which began to rise inside her was stilled by the soft, so very familiar voice which whispered from the darkness beyond.

'Catriona.'

'James, I can't see you.'

'Here. I'm here.' He materialised from behind bolts of cloth that reached to the low ceiling. She fell into his arms, trembling from head to toe. 'Don't you dare dissolve into tears,' he reproved as her cheek against his grew wet. 'We have only a few minutes and you must listen carefully to what I have to say.'

'Hold me a moment longer,' Catriona begged. 'James, do you realise the danger you are in? One of the men killed during your escape was a MacLeod—a young boy—and his kinsmen are out for blood.'

'You are remarkably well informed. MacDonald, I suppose. Does Kirsty know yet?'

'No.'

'Keep it from her if you can. If she thinks me still in

prison she will go back to Darna and not worry. Whose mad idea was it to come to Edinburgh—not yours? You are too level-headed for such an escapade. Or did the urge to see him again prove too strong?'

Catriona's cheeks flamed in the darkness.

'I love him. I don't deny it.'

She heard James's sharp intake of breath at the unexpected admission.

'Does he know?'

'Of course not.'

'Then tread warily, my little sister. He is not Andrew Fraser. This one is used to taking what he wants. If, as Kirsty tells me, he has accepted our marriage, then you may find he is eyeing you in a different light.'

'Don't worry about me, you know I can take care of myself.' She had said the same thing to Rorie a few hours ago—now she was not so sure. 'Are you safe here?'

'Not for much longer. It's only a matter of time before a house to house search is made. I need money and clothes to get out of the city.'

'The money can be arranged.' She had brought little with her, but she could sell a piece of jewellery. 'The clothes are the problem. No, wait, I have an idea. At the end of the week there is to be a ball at Holyrood Palace for the Prince. Everyone in the house will be out and the servants have been given the evening off.'

'You aren't going?'

'Would you expect me to under the circumstances? None of the others know yet. I shall say nothing until the night. There will be many people out in the streets, I could bring them to you then.'

'No, I will come to you. I will not have you out on these streets after dark.'

'To the house? James, that is madness.'

'One of the men who escaped with me was a spy awaiting execution. He had in his head a list of names, people working both for the Prince and the English, who would turn their coat for a handful of gold,' James told her in a low tone. 'He wanted to tell me all he knew, but died before he could do so. He had been shot and badly wounded as we scaled the prison walls. From what my friend the merchant tells me, I am believed to be in possession of that information. If the MacLeods don't cut my throat, the Chiefs will demand my immediate execution. They dare not risk that knowledge falling into the wrong hands.'

'But you know nothing,' his sister protested in horror. 'The man died.'

'Do you think anyone will believe he did not talk first?' James held her close again, and said reassuringly, 'I will come to the house at eleven. Is there a side entrance?'

'Yes, through the alleyway to the left of the front door. I will have it unlocked for you.'

'Good girl. Go now and try not to worry. You'd best buy some cloth to make it look good.'

Catriona purchased six yards of the velvet and was told it would be delivered with the rest of Kirsty's purchases that afternoon. She made her way back to the house in a daze. James had sounded confident enough, but had that been an act to keep her spirits high? If he was caught he would surely die and no one could save him. The room had been so dark she had hardly been able to make out his face. She had not even asked if his wound was healing. How thoughtless he must have thought her, but the shock of the sudden confrontation had dulled her senses.

She passed a pawn-broker's, hesitated and then re-traced her steps. When she came out of the dingy shop she was minus a ruby ring and bracelet. James had given them to her for her nineteenth birthday. She hated to part with them, but in her purse now was sufficient money for him to bribe his way out of the city.

*   *   *

By the time the night of the ball came, Catriona's nerves were strung as taut as a bow-string. She had endured Kirsty's non-stop chatter about the event and thwarted curious questions about what she was to wear by saying it was a surprise. She had comforted her after Rorie had cleverly averted a near disaster when Kirsty wished to visit James again in prison, by telling her there had been an attempted escape by several prisoners and until further notice all visits were cancelled, but that he would deliver any letter she cared to write to her husband. She had spent sleepless nights tossing in bed, praying James would not be recognised when he ventured from his hiding place or made his way towards the city gates. So much could go wrong.

'Catriona, what on earth are you doing down here and why aren't you ready?' Kirsty had come looking for her friend and found her curled up in a chair in the study, the book she had taken from the shelves lying unopened on her lap. She looked in a dream.

Catriona looked at the exquisitely gowned figure in the doorway.

'You look lovely. That white was a superb choice and it has made up so well.' Bright yellow ribbons adorned the ruffled sleeves, the curving neckline, others were sewn into the ruched skirt. Around her shoulders she wore a shawl woven in the MacDonald colours. The diamonds in her ears and around her throat had been James's wedding present to her. 'There will be many an eye on you tonight.'

'Go and change quickly. Rorie and Donald are coming downstairs.'

'I am not coming. The Campbells of Darna are fighting on the side of the English, Kirsty. I do not think it wise of me to flaunt that under everyone's nose, do you?'

'No one will say a word against you, not while Rorie is at your side. Did you hear her?' She turned appealingly to her brothers. 'She will not come. Make her.'

'She shows remarkably good sense,' Donald growled. 'Come on or we will be late.'

'The carriage is outside. Take Kirsty and wait for me. I'll follow in a moment. You will not change your mind?' Rorie stepped into the room the moment they were alone, masking the disappointment which gripped him at the news. For days he had thought of nothing else but the pleasure of dancing with her all evening. He had intended to monopolise her completely—selfishly—and now it was denied him.

How handsome he looked in his dress plaid, Catriona thought. The white frilled cravat at his throat accentuated the dark, arrogant features. It was not possible for her to go, but that had not stopped her from dreaming of how it might have been. To be held in his arms and dance the night away, indifferent to the stares and whispers because he was at her side. She felt a knot tighten in her throat. She loved him—yet she could not bring herself to trust him!

'No,' she said, with a shake of her head. 'I will not.'

'The servants have been given the evening off. You will be alone here.'

'And perfectly safe, I have Nan, remember. I shall have an early supper and go to bed,' Catriona assured him, fearful he might order Colin to remain behind. 'Is there no news of my brother?'

As once before, the casualness of her deception made her inwardly shudder, but it was necessary in order to remain the worried sister in his eyes.

'Not yet. Several of the other men have been captured and questioned. They said he separated from them immediately they were free, which means he had friends waiting to hide him. For their sakes and his, I hope they did not wait too long before getting him out of the city. T'would have been better had he remained where he

was. He's brought unnecessary grief to both you and
Kirsty,' Rorie said in a fierce tone. 'The man is a fool!'

'He is a man of honour. He is no coward to remain in a
safe haven, uncomfortable though it was, while his men
go off to fight without him.' Catriona rose immediately
to the defence of her brother. In a way she was glad he
had raised this issue between them before the pressure
of her nerves became so great she blurted out the truth.
'He raised the men of Darna to fight for a cause in which
he does not believe because of the promise he made to
Father. He has been hurt, imprisoned, and is now a
hunted fugitive because of his deep affection for me and
those who serve him. I am proud of the love we share,
but if he is killed his death will be on my conscience for
the rest of my life.' Catriona opened the book on her lap
and pretended to read with fierce concentration. 'The
others are waiting for you.'

She sat immobile long after the sound of the carriage
had died away in the distance, not daring to move for
almost half an hour. She was glad she was so cautious for
John, the steward, knocked on the door some while later
to enquire where she wished to eat supper.

'Your maid has prepared a tray, my lady. Would you
like it in here or in the dining-room?' His tone denoted
he did not like Nan or consider her his equal. Theirs was
a stormy relationship at the slightest encounter.

'In here, I think.' Catriona forced a smile to her lips. 'I
believe everyone is going to a party tonight.'

'A small celebration, my lady. Our own poor thanks
for the freedom the Prince has brought to the people.'

'Then go and enjoy yourselves. I shall be away to my
bed after supper. Goodnight, John.'

'Thank you, my lady. Goodnight.' The man withdrew, feeling almost sorry for the Campbell lass. She
looked so lost!

'Mistress, they've gone!' Nan poked her head around
the door and looked at the motionless figure staring into

the fire. 'Do you hear me? The house is ours. I've food upstairs for when the master arrives, lots of it, and if anyone notices it has gone, I shall say I had a late supper.'

'Bless you.' Catriona rose wearily to her feet. She had been almost on the point of falling asleep. 'Are you sure everyone is out?'

'I watched them when they left and twice I've been outside, carefully mind you, and there's not a soul about. Do come and eat something. I'll prepare a fresh tray and take it upstairs.' She looked at the food she had brought earlier—untouched at Catriona's side.

'When James comes. It may be the last time we eat together for some while. In it's way it is a very special occasion. The clothes, Nan, did you find some?'

'Aye. Not altogether his size, but in the dark they will do. Come away now.'

'Is the door unlocked as I instructed?'

'Yes, we can do no more than wait.'

Catriona reached the bottom of the stairs and then with a sigh, turned and sat down.

'A whole hour to wait. I shall go mad.'

'Nay, not a courageous lass like you.' Nan sank down beside her and drew her against her ample bosom. 'You are made of better stuff. He will come, never fear. Come upstairs. I'll let him in.'

Eleven o'clock came and passed. A quarter past eleven—half past. The hand was creeping towards midnight when Catriona heard hushed voices outside, flew to the door—and embraced her brother.

'You are late! Is anything wrong?'

'Everything. We have been betrayed. I suspect the man who helped me has been arrested by now. The soldiers passed within a few feet of the doorway where I was hiding,' James said.

He was dishevelled and breathing heavily. There were dark shadows of fatigue around his eyes and his chin was heavily bearded. It made him look so different.

'Will—will he talk?' Catriona gasped, a thousand imaginary horrors flashing through her mind. Arrest—questioning—the pressures that could be brought to loosen a stubborn tongue.

'Eventually. He is a brave man, but . . . Have you some wine? My throat is parched.'

'Here, sir.' Nan brought him a full glass which he drained immediately. Parched and half-starved, the woman thought worriedly.

Silently Catriona turned and looked at the small table beneath the curtained window. Supper for just the two of them, as it used to be. James took her hand and carried it to his lips affectionately. The wine, the cold ham and chicken were before his eyes and his stomach groaned for want of them. He had eaten very little in the last two days, but he dared not say so or he knew his sister would insist he stayed—and that would be suicide.

'I wish it could be so, but I dare not stay,' he whispered regretfully. 'Put something in a napkin and I will eat it the moment I am outside the city walls.'

'You have a plan to get through the gates?'

'Yes, but you shall be ignorant of it. I have involved you enough. The food, Catriona, quickly. I cannot linger.'

'Go with Nan,' she said with a smile that wiped some of the tension from his tired features. 'She has clothes for you and I have money.'

'Kirsty does not know,' he began apprehensively.

She laid a finger across his lips.

'No, nor will she. We are both returning to Darna before the army moves on. You will come back to us, do you hear? You will not do anything heroic. You have done enough to satisfy the whim of our father.'

'Dear Catriona, I have two of the best reasons in the world to live.'

As she sat waiting for him to return, Catriona realised their relationship was not as it had been before—not for him at least. He had a wife now! Her heart ached a little more for the happiness she felt was slipping away from her.

'Take this—and this.' She thrust a leather pouch full of coins into one hand, a bundle of food into the other. 'God go with you, James, and keep you safe. I will pray for you.' She pulled his cloak about him, stared at his appearance thoughtfully for a moment, then said. 'Wait here.'

When she returned she carried a tartan bonnet with a sprig of heather fastened to it by a silver pin. 'Wear this. Then no one will stop you if you are seen leaving the house.'

'By heaven, Catriona, are you mad? I'll be taken for a MacDonald! Besides it will be missed.'

'Let me worry about that. Now you look more like a young man on his way to the Palace. Go quickly before I make a fool of myself and weep all over you. I will see you at Darna.'

'At Darna,' James repeated softly as he kissed her. He held her close for a moment without either saying a word, then he was gone and she was left with the sound of footsteps on the stairs, the murmur of voices, the careful closing of a door. She ran to the window, fractionally drew aside the curtain, but could see nothing and was standing ashen-faced by the table when Nan returned.

'Mistress, you gave him all the food. I will go down to the kitchen . . '

'No, help me to undress, then take everything out of here. No one must see this table laid for two,' Catriona interrupted. 'I am not hungry. I want only to sleep. Pray for him tonight, Nan. Pray as you have never prayed before.'

Which was what she had been doing ever since she set

foot in the house, Nan thought, but was wise enough not
to mention it.

She was brushing Catriona's hair when they heard the
distinct sound of a door opening and closing. Catriona
sprang to her feet in alarm.

'James! No, it cannot be, he would have come to the
side entrance. Someone has come back. Nan—the
table!'

It was not yet cleared. The two places she herself had
so carefully laid, the decanter of wine and the silver
goblets—not touched. She froze as someone knocked at
the door. John—Rorie—Colin? Why had anyone returned so early? She cast a frantic look at Nan who stood
with her back against the table, but in no way shielded it
from view. She half turned, about to scoop the contents
into the tablecloth and bundle it under the bed, when the
door opened.

Rorie MacDonald stood there, a bottle of champagne
in one hand, two crystal glasses in the other. In silence
his gaze swept the speechless women—Catriona clad
only in her night attire, the tell-tale table. The corners of
his mouth deepened into a sardonic smile.

'Forgive me for intruding, you are obviously expecting someone else,' he drawled and watched Catriona's
face grow crimson with embarrassment. Or was it guilt?
You fool, he thought bitterly. You leave a place full of
your friends, with ample food and drink—and willing
women, because the woman you want is not there—and
what do you find? An assignation, no less—under your
own roof!

'How dare you think such a thing.' Catriona's eyes
flashed with the magnificent sapphire colour he loved to
see. It reminded him of their last meeting when she had
spat fire at him and sent him away. 'I was not expecting
you—or anyone, MacDonald.'

'A table laid with two places—wine . . .' he taunted.

'And a mistress so sick with worry she cannot eat or

sleep properly,' Nan broke in fiercely. 'I prepared the
table. I was going to keep her company, try to raise her
spirits—and make her eat something substantial. No one
else in the house bothers about her, do they? You take
yourself off to a fine ball without one thought for her
suffering. MacDonalds! You are all alike. Take—take—
you give nothing in return.'

'One more word, woman, and I will cut out your
tongue,' Rorie said, in a dangerously low tone. 'Get out,
I want to be alone with your mistress.'

'My lady, you can't . . ' Nan gasped and looked pro-
tectively towards Catriona.

She was staring at the tall figure who advanced purposefully into the room as if he was a ghost. He deposi-
ted the items he held on a table and, before the maid's
horrified gaze, he removed the sword at his side, unbuttoned and removed his jacket and tossed it over a nearby
chair, before turning to face them again.

'Leave us,' he thundered, advancing towards her and
she did not wait for Catriona's almost imperceptible nod
of approval. He slammed the door after her and turned
the key in the lock. 'That should ensure we are not
disturbed,' he added, ignoring the hammering on the
door which began the moment it was closed.

'You cannot stay here,' Catriona said in a hollow tone.
'Please leave at once.'

'In my own house I do as I wish. You have no say in the
matter,' Rorie returned, his eyes narrowing as she
stepped back from him, tightly clutching her robe about
her. Damn the girl! Did she think he had come to assail
her virtue? A nonexistent virtue if he was to believe his
brother's prolonged tales of the women Andrew Fraser
had known.

'Nor did I once before,' she reminded him.

'There is no dirk at your throat now.'

'And no one to come to my aid if I scream. What I
have been told of the MacDonalds is true then—you

have no regard for womanhood. I must admit you hid it well, I was almost beginning to believe . . .'

'If that was the case you would have been in my bed long ago,' he flung back as he moved towards her. She could retreat no further, for the wall was behind her. He was drunk, she thought, as his hands fastened over her shoulders, biting into her skin beneath the thin material of the robe—but then she looked into his eyes and knew he was not.

She raised her head and stared at him quite calmly. 'What do you want from me?'

'Honesty. Truth between us.' His mouth took hers by storm, forcing apart the stiff lips determined to resist him, bruised them with a ruthless force until with a soft cry, she surrendered to the dictates of her heart and melted willingly into his arms. She answered kiss for kiss, trembled, unashamedly awakened by the knowledgeable hands which caressed her body through the thin robe.

'Stop! Please, stop!' Catriona dragged her mouth free, her senses reeling. She was his and knew it! 'I cannot think.'

'I don't want you to think. Answer me, dammit, as you've wanted to from the first time I held you.'

Catriona sagged in his arms. She was in no way prepared for this onslaught on her already tired mind and body. With a low oath Rorie lifted her, carried her to the couch and set her down. His hand lingered on the soft cloud of loose hair as he drew back.

'Drink this.' He brought the bottle and glasses, filled the latter and gave her one as he sat down beside her.

'My brother tells me champagne loosens the tongue,' Catriona whispered as she drank a little. She was afraid—exhilarated and at the same time, tormented by guilt. 'What do you want to hear from me, Rorie Mac-Donald? Have my lips not betrayed me already?'

Rorie's eyes gleamed in the candlelight at her admission. She wanted to reach out and touch that fierce red hair, that proud mouth that had conquered hers, but she dared not. She was still trembling slightly as he refilled her glass. She had seen him drink before—nothing seemed to have any effect on him, but on an empty stomach she was already beginning to feel the effects of the champagne. 'No more, I beg you. I have not eaten.'

'Why not?'

'I could not.' The table beneath the window rose before her tortured gaze and she quickly looked away. 'Poor Nan, she went to so much trouble to try and please me.'

'Is it James?'

'James—and Kirsty—and . . .' Suddenly all pretence vanished as she looked at him, 'And you! A week, two—a month from now, we shall be women without our men as you all go off to fight the English. Kirsty wants a husband who will return to her. How can I tell her it might not happen?'

'What do you want, Catriona?' Rorie asked softly, putting aside his glass and leaning towards her.

She caught her breath. You, her heart cried. She could not say the word, but her eyes were bright with tears as she sought the courage to utter it. Tears which glistened like night stars in the lustre of her eyes spilled down over her cheeks until he could bear the sight of them no longer and gently wiped them away.

'I want you to hold me and tell me this is no dream. Don't lie—I don't want fancy words. If this is not meant to last, but is a momentary thing because you are lonely, then I will accept that and when I leave here we will never see each other again.'

'And if it is reality?' Rorie's lips traced the path of a tear on her cheek, before he allowed them to wander slowly down over her throat to the smooth line of her shoulder, the soft rise of her breast beneath the frilled robe.

'Then I will be waiting for you at Darna. Will you come for me?'

Her words stopped him. He lifted his head and stared at the limp figure cradled in his arms. He had returned with the bottle intending to make up for her spoilt evening, but Donald's taunts and jeers had lingered in his mind long after he left the Palace, overshadowing his original intentions and the sight of her in night attire had roused hostile suspicions in his mind. He had intended to force the issue between them into the open whether she liked it or not, but not to this extent! Or had it been at the back of his mind all along and he had refused to acknowledge the fact?

Two women without their men. Kirsty—and her! *Come for me at Darna!*

If he took her tonight she would have no regrets, Catriona thought as he gathered her to him, his lips against her hair, even though it went against everything she had ever been taught to believe was right and proper.

'I want to stay with you more than anything else in this world,' he muttered. He knew if he looked into those lovely eyes he would be lost! 'Do you hear me? Believe it! I have never spoken this way to any other woman. Soon I shall be going into battle, I would like to have taken the memory of what we might have shared this night with me—but I won't touch you, Catriona. Tomorrow—ask me why.'

He took her mouth once more, felt the instant response, the submissive softness of her body against his and it took all his will-power to rise from the couch and leave the room.

Nan found her mistress curled up on the couch, two empty glasses and an almost empty bottle on the table beside her. Her eyes were closed, her breathing even. She did not respond to questions or the insistent shaking

of her shoulder. She was sleeping like a babe! And all
due to him!

The maid tucked a thick coverlet around her, locked
the door and slept in a chair close at hand for the rest of
the night.

CHAPTER
NINE

THE house seemed unusually quiet when Catriona awoke. She stretched lazily, in no hurry to move from the bed, until Rorie's words returned to her. *Tomorrow, ask me why.* He had wanted her, but he had not touched her. Flinging aside the bedclothes she began to dress in a feverish haste. Where was Nan? she needed her to fix her hair. Eventually she tied it back with a ribbon to match her dress, pulling the curls over one shoulder in a profusion of gold.

She wanted to hear him say the words of love which would bind her to him for ever. What else could he have meant? No more pretence! As she made her way down-stairs, she was startled to see the time. Nearly eleven. Nan had overslept or was being kind in allowing her to enjoy the first good sleep she had had in a week to the very last moment.

The sitting-room door opened and Donald stepped out, catching her by the arm as she drew level. She gasped at his cruel grip and tried to pull free, only to have him shake her roughly.

'The charade is over, mistress. Listening at keyholes, were you? Come inside, you'll hear less to your liking in here.'

She was dragged through the door and pushed into the middle of the room. Kirsty sat in a chair, pale, tight-lipped. She stifled something which sounded suspi-ciously like a sob and turned her head away as Catriona looked at her questioningly. What was wrong with everyone this morning? An icy hand clutched at her heart. Had James been caught?

'You'll not receive any sympathy from my sister, so keep your distance from her.' Rorie rose from his desk and stood before her, arms folded across his chest. 'Nor from anyone in this house. No MacDonald has ever been known to deal lightly with a traitor who has abused the hospitality of his host after sharing his food and sleeping untroubled in his bed.' His eyes lingered momentarily on the red marks on her wrists left by Donald's fingers. He hardened his heart against the anger which rose inside him and would, under normal circumstances, have been directed against his brother for such unnecessary force. Nothing was the same any more. He was done with weakness.

'Traitor?' Catriona echoed. Was this stony-faced man the same one who had held her in his arms? It was not possible. He was a stranger who stared at her with contempt in his eyes, disgust in his expression. He knew! It seemed impossible, yet somehow he had discovered the help she had given her brother. Donald had closed the door behind her and was standing with his back against it. He stared at her with rude eyes, enjoying her discomfort. How he disliked her. She had come closer than any woman to stealing his brother's affections and he would never forgive her for that. He had been given a chance to destroy what had grown between them and he intended to make full use of it. One day Rorie would thank him.

Catriona fought and conquered the panic rising inside her. Bluff was out of the question. There was only the truth—up to a point. Now she could never ask him what his words had meant or confess her own feelings. That dream would never materialise. A coldness settled over her features and over her heart as she raised her eyes to look at Rorie.

'Why do you speak to me like this? Last night . . .'

'Did not happen.' The answer snapped back at her like a pistol shot.

'So you were only amusing yourself after all. My congratulations, you gave a convincing performance. So much so—' She forced the words out through stiff lips. She had to know, no matter what it cost her. 'I came down to ask you—why?'

Her voice shook and she could not control it. He could not have known anything then, but she had to attack. He had shattered her defences and she needed time to reinforce them, if that was possible, to find some protection against the scorn, the anger she was sure he was about to unleash upon her. She had protected her brother, but to him she had helped a traitor to the Prince's cause and so was one herself. She had given freedom to a man he believed had important information that could upset the carefully-laid plans of either side.

'And you shall know. I want everyone in this room to know,' Rorie said, his mouth tightening into a bleak, painful line. 'I did not take you last night because I was going to ask you to be my wife. I did not want to dishonour the love I thought we had for each other. That is the kind of blind fool you made me. Now I can see clearly again, thank God. Your sweet words and promises meant nothing.'

'What sweet words? What promises?' Catriona blanched, her hands clenching into tight fists at her sides. He loved her and she had destroyed his love! Kirsty raised her head and looked at her and there was not one flicker of warmth in her expression. 'I gave you no encouragement—ever!' she cried scornfully.

'Except that which a blind fool accepts when he is on the edge of a precipice. You did well, all wide eyes and innocence such as I have never seen before, and then passion, to make me feel unsure, indecisive.'

'Brother,' Donald said softly, 'I have saved you from a

terrible fate. She has bewitched you, but it will pass. Tonight I will find you a real woman, one who gives everything she has.'

'You!' Catriona wheeled on the grinning figure behind her. 'What have you done, you hateful devil?'

'I've had my faithful Colin dog your footsteps every hour of the day, my lying little Campbell bitch. We know all about your brother's sanctuary in the draper's shop, his visit here, the stolen food and clothes, not to mention Rorie's bonnet. By heaven, that was a cool piece of thinking. You planned it deliberately, cold-bloodedly, and lied to my brother blatantly day after day. While you were in his arms last night too by the sound of it.'

Colin must have returned after bringing Kirsty home, Catriona thought, watched her leave, followed her, saw her go into the pawnbroker. Of course he would have checked what she had sold and reported back to Donald. Despite all her precautions, she had been observed without her being aware of it.

'You betrayed my brother,' she accused and Donald laughed aloud at her indignation.

'You don't betray a traitor, you give him his just desserts. I hope they catch him soon so that I can watch him hang and you alongside him for your treasonous act.'

'No!' Kirsty had turned so white she looked as if she might faint, but with a tremendous effort she composed herself and looked up at Catriona. 'When I was told James was free and how you had helped him, that you had probably met him while we were shopping, I—I think for a while I hated you. He turned to you, not to me, his wife. He did not even think of me when he escaped. I was—am still—deeply hurt. I do not understand why.'

'Why he escaped?' Catriona's heart went out to her in her wretchedness. 'Because he is a man of honour. The easy way out would have been to remain in prison and let the men from Darna do his fighting for him. That would have been thinking of himself—of you. His men were without a leader and the promise he made to our father, who he loved deeply despite their differences, made it impossible for him to do that. He is duty bound to lead them if possible.'

'My, doesn't she turn a pretty phrase,' Donald jeered. 'I wonder how many men she has taken in before you, brother?'

'That's enough,' Rorie snapped, annoyed at the interruption. They were almost the same words she had spoken to him and he could not deny they had a ring of truth about them, but even if she was being honest now, nothing could condone the farce she had played out the night before. The grief-stricken sister unable to eat or sleep. The reticent innocent who begged him so convincingly to release her from his embrace, while not an hour before she had brought her traitorous brother into his house, given him clothes stolen from the servants' quarters, food ransacked from the kitchen. Donald was right—the theft of his bonnet was the work of a cool, devious mind.

What had she been thinking when he held her in his arms? How best to keep his mind from dwelling on that carefully laid table? Perhaps James Campbell had not left the house when he arrived, but had made good his escape after he retired—or, while she kept him occupied? The thought roused his temper to a dangerous level. As he watched the flecked eyes narrow, Donald's mouth deepened into a satisfied smile. The seeds of doubt he had sown were bearing fruit.

'He could have turned to me,' Kirsty insisted, although deep in her heart she knew that was not possible. On their wedding day James had sworn never to raise a hand in anger against her brothers or do anything which would alienate her from their affections.

'He told me of the promise he made and he has kept

it.' Catriona straightened her shoulders with a sigh and
forced herself to look once again into Rorie's accusing
eyes. 'If I am to be condemned as a traitor because I
helped my brother, then I am guilty. He is everything to
me. I love him above all things—all people.' She broke
off, her eyes widening as she realised what she had been
about to add, she had only just stopped herself saying—
And you!

'Even more than your life?' Donald asked, 'because
that is what you will lose when the authorities have tried
you and found you guilty. Two good men have been
killed because of James Campbell this week. If we don't
have him, then you will do in his place.'

'Two,' Kirsty echoed. 'Rorie, what else has been kept
from me. Am I a child that I am the last one to know
what is happening.'

'Colin was found in the garden early this morning. He
had been dragged behind some bushes and left for dead.
He had laid all night in freezing conditions. He lived long
enough to tell me of the Campbell's visit, how he had
followed him when he left, but had not been stealthy
enough. The rest I already knew.' Donald's face was
twisted with anger. 'I sent him back to watch you and he
met his death at the hands of your accursed brother. We
were close, Colin and I . . .'

'But you used him as a means to an end—to discredit
me,' Catriona cried. 'You did not care for him, you care
only for Rorie. Without him you would have been dead
long ago. Murdoch told me how the fight between you
really started, how you goaded him when you were
drunk and he proved too good for you. You had to feign
an injury so that someone else would fight your battle.' It
was a lie, but she saw by the reddening of his face that
her suspicions were correct. 'The same person who
always fights your battles, because you are a coward,
Donald MacDonald!'

'Liar!' Donald screamed the word at her and the blow

he dealt her sent her reeling backwards onto the settee. Kirsty cried out as he followed her, only to find Rorie blocking his path.

'Don't touch her again. I warned you once.'

'Haven't I convinced you yet what she is? You can't still care for her?'

'That is none of your business. The whole sordid affair ends here, Donald. She goes back to Darna unharmed,' Rorie said in a threatening tone and his brother stepped back, knowing he had provoked him too far.

'*We* go back,' Kirsty said. The lace handkerchief she had held to Catriona's mouth was stained with bright red blood. 'Make the arrangements for us to leave first thing in the morning, Rorie. I won't remain in this house a moment longer.'

The young sister who had blossomed into the wife he was only just beginning to acknowledge, was suddenly a woman older than her years, despising him and his hardness. She gave no thought to how it had been for him all these years, when he had rarely been able to be himself. She knew so little of those times and had never understood them, or his loyalty to a man who was a bully and a coward. Yet that man was their brother and Rorie would defend him to the death, right or wrong. The blood they shared surpassed all obstacles. They were brothers, and nought but death could separate them!

'That is your choice. We leave here in a few days anyway.' His eyes considered her for a long moment. He wanted to say more, but was still consumed with anger and complex emotions he had never known before. He could not ease his own suffering, let alone offer her comfort.

With Kirsty's help, Catriona rose to her feet. Her senses still swam from the blow and she staggered dazedly towards the door. Rorie did not move from her path. He stared impassively at her bruised mouth, the imprint of Donald's fingers on her skin.

'Consider yourself lucky to get off so lightly. Come to
Darna for you, isn't that what you asked of me? I'll come
and we'll have our reckoning there. Let her go,' he
ordered curtly, turning aside and Donald moved from
the door with a none-too-polite oath under his breath.

At the end of October the Highland army began to leave
Edinburgh, to make a new camp at Dalkeith. By the
third of November, almost all the men were on the road
to England, but even the prospect of another fight after
six weeks of kicking their heels with nothing to do, did
not prevent many from deserting, longing for their crofts
and the old ways, as was the Highland temperament.
The roads to Stirlinghsire and Lanarkshire were full of
clansmen returning home.

The ranks of the Prince's army had swelled during
those past weeks of inactivity. Lord Ogilvie, son of Lord
Airlie, had brought in six hundred men. Lord Pitsligo
arrived with a contingent of 'mounted gentlemen', raising the number of cavalry to around five hundred. Lords
Kilmarnock, Balmerino and Elcho joined the cause, and
Gordon of Glenbucket came with four hundred Aber-
deenshire men. Another three hundred recruits were
enlisted in Edinburgh itself.

The advancing army was well clothed and supplied.
Taxes had been exacted from Glasgow amounting to five
thousand guineas. Edinburgh had parted with six
thousand pairs of shoes and various other items for the
troops, along with one thousand tents. They marched to
the continuous skirl of pipes, on full stomachs, well
rested and eager for battle. In the midst of the Mac-
Donalds marched Rorie MacDonald who had been put
in charge of a body of men from among his mother's
people, the MacIans of Glen Coe, after the exemplary
courage he had shown at Prestonpans.

The town and then the castle of Carlisle surrendered
to the Prince. As he pushed on towards Derby, the

fighting spirit of the clansmen rose to fever pitch. England lay open before them. It seemed the English had no heart for fighting after their humiliating defeat.

King George's government had not been idle, however. It recalled troops from Flanders, and the Duke of Cumberland, the King's son, had returned from the Continent bringing with him infantry and dragoons. In the north of England fourteen thousand men had been assembled, together with ten thousand disciplined troops in Staffordshire. Another army was being mobilised at the camp on Finchley Common for the protection of London.

In Derby the two opposing camps were separated by only a few miles and as battle seemed imminent, all the necessary preparations were under way. Highland expectations rose! Broadswords were sharpened while the pipers played of their last victorious campaigns.

But there was to be no battle—only a retreat. It was the beginning of the end for the Highlanders' dream—demoralisation of their fighting spirit and comradeship as Charles Stuart bowed to the advice about him. It was argued that five thousand men, however stalwart and courageous, however willing to give up their lives for a cause, would be slaughtered if launched against an army of thirty thousand men, which now confronted it. Skilled, disciplined soldiers who were accustomed to rigorous forced marches, gruelling drilling, bad food, officers who had not one iota of feeling for the men they commanded, men who often saw their comrades flogged or hung for a wrong word—and all for sixpence a day!

Discipline for the English army was a matter of progress, a slow, necessary train of events that brought together the dregs of every town, old soldiers, officers of long standing, raw recruits—into one indomitable force. They were well trained. They would stand and fight against impossible odds because they were ordered to and to disobey the order meant the 'cat'. To desert and be caught, and most of them usually were, meant hanging, so that the remainder might learn loyalty and obedience to the Crown that paid its pathetic pittance.

So the Highland army left Derby, many still believing there was to be an encounter with the enemy. Not until they realised they were on the road back into Scotland did they fully comprehend what was happening, and it was then that the malaise set in.

Had Charles Stuart only known the alarm his determined march had caused in London, he would probably have ignored all advice and continued southwards. There had been a run against the Bank of England which aroused a natural widespread panic. Shops closed and people fled to the country. Even the King had a fleet of ships organised to sail at a moment's notice, and his most treasured possessions on board. But the Prince did not know how close he had come to the throne of England, and the immediate pursuit by the Duke of Cumberland with all his cavalry and one thousand mounted infantry, another four thousand following in his wake, left no time to dwell on what might have been.

Twelve days later, the rear of the Highland army was attacked by the English.

'Your mind was elsewhere,' Donald said sourly as he bound his brother's arm. Rorie had refused the attention of a doctor, insisting the sabre slice was merely a scratch, but he had lost a considerable amount of blood and he felt weak—both from that and from the amount of brandy he had consumed since he arrived back at the encampment.

The MacDonalds had fought a fine rearguard action against Cumberland's mounted cavalry, and stood their ground until broken wagons under the command of Lord George Murray were repaired and on the road again. Only then did the MacDonalds give ground to join them. They fought all the way to Penrith until Lord

George sent back reinforcements, and he and his Macphersons repulsed the pursuers.

Rorie looked at his brother, who, because of the suddenness of the attack, had for the first time as far as he could remember been forced to stand and fight. There had been nowhere to run to, no cover in those first bloody moments, but as the wagons moved ahead, he had seen Donald using one of them for cover, had yelled at him in disgust and anger and then an English Cavalryman bore down on him and the tip of his sword sliced Rorie's cheek. Incensed with pain and rage, shame at his brother's weakness, he turned to engage the enemy.

Some time later, perhaps half a dozen faceless, nameless men were dead from his claymore. One arm hanging uselessly by his side, it was one of the MacIans who helped him along the road to Carlisle—not his brother, the coward who always ran away, whom he had protected for countless years; but a smooth-cheeked lad of eighteen who had fought alongside him most of the day.

'You'll have all the ladies after you now, sir,' he said cheerfully, looking at his companion's bloodstained cheek. 'Battle scars always fascinate them.'

A tight smile twisted Rorie's lips as he recalled the words. One good arm, for the moment anyway, and a scarred cheek. He was no prospect for any woman; besides he wanted only one and she was miles away. A true Campbell with her lies and deceit but her day would come. She would pay for the pain she had inflicted. The wounds were deep and infinitely more painful than any he had received in battle.

'I said your mind was elsewhere,' Donald took the bottle from him and completed the task of emptying it. 'Thinking of her, were you?'

'Where did you get to this time?' Rorie ignored the comment. The brandy had warmed him and eased the nagging throbbing in his face and arm. Drawing his plaid around him he tilted his head against the back of the wagon and stared at his brother. Donald's face was grey and drawn. His hands were still shaking. 'For God's sake, go and get drunk before someone sees the state you are in.'

'I've found lodgings for us in the town. You'll freeze if you stay out here tonight,' Donald insisted. It was beginning to snow again, quite heavily, but Rorie appeared not to notice. 'Come on, man, get to your feet.'

'Damn you, I needed your help back there, not here,' he snapped, brushing aside the hand outstretched to help him to his feet. He got up alone and stood swaying perilously. 'We are not children any more, Donald. And the English aren't hot-headed boys like Murdoch Campbell. They are good—very good. You'll have to make a stand sometime—or turn tail and run before everyone. I don't think even you could live with that. Soon, I know, we are going to have to fight and it's going to be the bloodiest battle any of us have ever known. I would like my brother to be by my side.'

'I can't run from them—and the ties between us are too strong to be broken. Though you know I can't beat this devil that rides upon my back. God knows I've tried.' A strange look passed over Donald's face. 'The next time I shall have to make sure I'm an easy target, won't I? That should solve the problem. Now, give me your arm and let's away to a warm place and get drunk together.'

The news filtering back to the Highlands was slow. It was the middle of January before news of Falkirk and the continued retreat across the swollen river Esk reached Darna. It was brought by two deserting MacLeods on their way home. Catriona gave them shelter for the night and a hot meal and more food for their journey the following day and wished, with all her heart, she had never seen them.

Kirsty plied them with questions for hours, until one of the exhausted men who had lost a hand in the battle—the last victorious battle for the Prince's army—begged to be allowed to sleep.

The Highland army was retreating! It seemed impossible after such a grand march and victories all the way. It could have entered London without difficulty! Had James been at Falkirk? Was he now pursuing the Highlanders back into the mountains from where they had come, Catriona wondered, and looking at Kirsty, knew the same fears haunted her too. Was he safe? Where were Donald and Rorie? Dead? Captured. Lying injured in some roadside ditch?

For several days after their return home, the atmosphere between them had been strained. Kirsty could not hide the fact that she resented James's turning to his sister and not his wife, but as the days slipped by into snowy, frozen winter weeks, when they huddled before the fire in the salon and remembered Edinburgh, and she saw Catriona grow noticeably thinner and pale, sympathy rose inside her, and in the wake of that came understanding. For her, and for love of James, Catriona had sacrificed the only love she had ever known, had borne ridicule and scorn from the one man who had ever meant anything to her, had been struck in anger by Donald who saw her as a challenge to the deep relationship he shared with his brother. And she herself, in her selfishness, had done nothing to ease the torment she must have endured.

For Catriona their reconciliation brought brief comfort. She knew, if he lived, that Rorie would find her again at Darna. She would not try to hide from him, although there were a dozen families who would have given her refuge in the glen and none would have surrendered her to a MacDonald—whatever the threats. She loved him still, nothing could ever change that. She had done everything she did out of love for her brother.

Rorie did not believe she loved him, so he would never understand the fierce loyalty in her which demanded she gave everything for those she loved. James and Rorie—two men in her life, each in his own way tearing her heart apart. She prayed nightly for the safe return of them both, whatever the consequences for herself.

'My lady, he's back!' Nan burst into the bedroom where Catriona and Kirsty were discussing the changes they were planning for the sitting-room. Most of the women in the house were busy sewing curtains for the windows, making bright cushions for the chairs. Whether they were doing it out of a sense of duty or to please the laird's new wife, Catriona did not care. Kirsty was happy. For the first time in many weeks she had forgotten her troubles and found something to occupy her time.

Her mind elsewhere, Catriona raised her head, a frown puckering her brow. He's back! Her heart stood still. Which one?

'The master,' Nan gasped. 'In the courtyard—and not a scratch on him. What are you both waiting for? Go and greet him.'

Kirsty flew to the window.

'Oh, look at the man, waiting for us to go down to him!' Tears spilled down over her cheeks. Catriona wiped them away with her handkerchief and said in a quiet voice,

'Go and greet your husband.'

'And you?'

'I will come in a moment. He cannot hug two women at the same time and I know it is you he is hoping to see first. Go to your husband, Kirsty.'

'That was kind of you, mistress,' Nan murmured, when they were alone. 'The child has fretted for him so.'

'You did not tell me Andrew Fraser is with him,' Catriona said, turning away from the window. 'What does he want here?'

She had not seen him since the day James had told him the marriage contract had been revoked. She knew little of the details, although she assumed some kind of reimbursement had been made for his loss of face. Her brother had told her nothing, never made her feel the cancellation of the wedding extracted any more from him than he was willing to give. She surmised it had cost him dear! Not only would Andrew have extracted a maximum amount to cover his hurt pride and the disillusionment of his schemes, but he would also have made it known far and wide that he was a rejected suitor, not good enough for the daughter of Fergus Campbell. He was a fop when it pleased him, a fool when it suited him, but above all he was an ambitious man who would never forgive the man who had betrayed him on his death-bed, nor the son who condoned the action and released his sister from an unwanted alliance—or Catriona herself.

Nan watched her carefully inspect her reflection in the mirror. As much for the brother she loved as to give a bold front to the man she loathed, she realised and was suddenly afraid. For all his faults the MacDonald had made her happy—the Fraser never could! Sweet Mary, bring our men home safe, she prayed, whoever they are! One look into Catriona's face told her she went to greet her brother with love in her eyes and questions in her heart about the only man who had ever owned it.

That night the dining-room in Darna was alight with a hundred wall torches. The food was impeccable, served by familiar faced servants that made James relax a little more in his chair as the evening wore on. He had changed, Catriona decided, in a way she could not define. Older somehow—harder. Was it only in her eyes? He looked no different, yet as she studied him she became aware of new lines beneath his eyes, around his mouth. Once he acknowledged her long, studious gaze and they were one again, but after that all his smiles and compliments were for Kirsty.

Strangely enough Catriona did not mind as much as she thought she would to have her brother ignore her and pay attention to another woman. That one look had told her so much. He was worried. He could hide it from his wife, but not from the sister who knew him so well.

He sat at one end of the long table, in the chair once occupied by Fergus Campbell, Kirsty at the other end. Catriona and Andrew faced each other. Upon his arrival he had been quite charming and mentioned only briefly their broken engagement. It had been a shock to learn he was in command of the soldiers now relaxing in the courtyard, instead of her brother, but James bore his humiliating status well and was magnanimous in his civility. As Andrew began to consume first wine and then aperitifs before dinner, more wine and then brandies, the change in him began. The casual talk of war turned into detailed descriptions, of Cumberland and the attack on the rear of the Highland column outside Falkirk. He enjoyed every minute of Kirsty's discomfort, and was roused to further descriptive recollections by the black look on James's face.

'No,' Catriona said as Calum hovered with the brandy decanter. 'It has been a long day for everyone, I think we should retire early. Especially as you intend to start for Inverness at first light, James. Forgive us, Andrew, but these two young people have scarcely had any time together since they were married. You may, of course, make yourself comfortable down here if you wish. Calum will serve you anything you want.'

She looked into the red face opposite her, at the eyes which had been insulting her with their boldness for most of the evening and thought of the time in Edinburgh when Rorie had held her in his arms in her room and his kisses had brought her to a point of surrender— and then he had left her! How she longed to be in his arms now—longed for his strength. The love she had denied!

Shyly Kirsty looked at her husband. James rose and took her hand and led her from the room. Catriona followed them, but not until the door of her room had been bolted behind her did she feel safe.

James and the soldiers were ready to leave. Upstairs Catriona could still hear Andrew bellowing at his servant.

'Don't fret, lass, Inverness isn't so far away.' He held his wife close. 'I shall be back soon to see you and my bonny sister.'

'James,' she hesitated to ask, but she could contain the questions no longer. All night they had been in her mind. 'Is it true the Prince's army is encamped outside the town?'

'So I believe.'

'Then there is to be another battle?' Kirsty whispered. 'Dear God, no!'

'It may not come to that,' he reproved, but his eyes told Catriona differently. That was the reason he and his men were going there. To fight. With a stifled sob, Kirsty tore herself from her husband's grasp and ran inside. 'Take care of her, little sister.' His mouth twisted in pain as he gazed after her. 'And yourself. If we lose this time, you'll not be safe here. Her brothers will come for her. He will come for you.'

He will anyway, Catriona could have said, but she did not want to add to the burden which already weighed upon his mind.

'If I think we are in any danger, we will go to Aunt Sarah, but I doubt if that will be necessary. If the Prince's army is retreating, that means they are beaten . . .' Her voice trailed off into a miserable silence. If that happened the consequences for the clans who had so valiantly followed him were too awful to contemplate—the fines and destruction of land and homes, the appropriation of livestock and crops.

'I swore I would never lift a blade against her brothers,' James groaned. 'How can I not do so if we come face to face. Try to make her understand—prepare her, as you must prepare yourself. I tried last night, but she was so happy as she lay in my arms, I could not hurt her. Lord knows, I don't want to hurt either of you, but if I meet Rorie MacDonald or his brother on the battlefield, we shall try to kill each other.'

The two opposing armies were drawn up on Drummossie Moor—only five hundred yards separating them. It was a bleak, cold morning. Although barely light, the Duke of Cumberland's men already made a formidable picture as they began to fall into formation. Six regiments in the first line, another six in the second. Most of them had been marching throughout the night to reach the moor, accompanied every step of the way by the continuous, monotonous, tap-tap-tap of the drums.

The Highland army was also drawn up into two lines, and had been watching for five hours the approach of the English columns in their red and white, banners streaming in the wind. In the first line to the left, forfeiting the hereditary right bestowed on them by Robert Bruce at Bannockburn always to fight on the right in battle, were the MacDonalds of Clanranald, Keppoch and Glengarry. Alexander MacIan from Glen Coe had merged his small fighting force with the men of Keppoch, among them Rorie and his regiment. The centre was composed of Clan Chattan, the Clan 'of Cats', the Frasers and smaller clans like the MacLeods, the Grants and men from Glen Moriston and Urquhart, and to their right, the men of Atholl, the Camerons and the Stewarts of Appin. In their midst, Murdoch prayed once more to meet the 'Red' MacDonald.

Stretched out in a thin line behind them were the Irish

Piquets, the Duke of Perth's mixed assortment of men, among them many English deserters still wearing their red coats, and Charles Stuart astride his grey horse, surrounded by what remained of his bodyguard. Fitz-James Horse.

As it grew lighter, the brilliant scarlet coats of the English were challenged by the plaids of the Highlanders facing them. Blues, greens, reds and yellows, each a different sett. In every bonnet was worn the badge of their clan; many too sported the silk knot of five bows which was the Stuart emblem—the 'white cockade', and they carried assorted weapons, basket-hilted broadswords, targets, dirks and ancient pistols bestowed on them by their forefathers. Looking at them, some of the English soldiers remembered Prestonpans when they had turned and run before such men, remembered too, those who had hung from the gallows afterwards as an example—and they stood their ground.

When the bombardment from the English cannon began, the air was thick and black with smoke in a matter of minutes, blinding the Highlanders. The first salvo landed among the men of Glen Chatton, into the ranks of the Frasers and Stewarts from Appin. In five short minutes Tamsie Stewart unknowingly lost three brothers and a father. Within half an hour, some of the clans had lost up to one third of their men. They could not see the enemy through the smoke, were unable to use the broadsword until close range, and so charged heroically forward. Grapeshot cut them down in their hundreds. They dropped to the heather and more took their place. Athollmen and Camerons. MacDonalds and Frasers. Leaping over their fallen and dead comrades. The air was filled with the screams of the wounded and dying, the roar of cannon, the blood-curdling war cries as each clan launched itself forward, the skirl of the pipes competing against the English drums.

The three regiments of MacDonalds came sliding over

the wet heather towards the right of Cumberland's first line, but were driven back continuously by the onslaught of grapeshot which landed in their midst. Rorie lost sight of his brother in the first hectic minutes, searched vainly for him as he ran, but could not see him and cursed him for the coward he was. The battalions before them, drawn up in three ranks, poured continuous fire onto the advancing Highlanders, who were unable to come within a hundred yards of them. Three times they charged and were repulsed, and stood angrily waving their broadswords at the enemy in despair until Kingston's Horse bore down on them from their flank—and the clans broke and began to run.

Rorie became aware of someone yelling obscenities at the fleeing men, somewhere off to his right. He stumbled over a dead MacIan and saw, with a feeling of intense pity, that it was the young lad who had helped him after the column had been attacked—and then he saw his brother. Donald was standing alone, with grapeshot and musket fire falling all about him, waving his sword above his head and screaming at the English to come and get him and in the next breath, cursing his fleeing companions.

'Cowards! Women! Charge, I say. Charge!' He saw Rorie and ran to him, his eyes burning with rage. 'They're running, damn them. Running! I try to get myself killed and here I stand without a scratch, and what happens? They run like women! God, what a sight we must be for the English.'

'Do you blame them? We've no chance of breaking through here. Fall back and find another place. Fall back, we can do no good here,' Rorie cried.

'No, dammit! At least one MacDonald will die honourably today.'

A bullet whined past his ear as he spun away from his brother, another caught him in the side and he pitched forward onto the purple heather with a groan.

'Get up, man.' Rorie pulled him upright, his face hardening as he saw the blood seeping through his brother's plaid. 'Put your arm around me, the cavalry is coming.'

'Leave me,' Donald begged and there was no fear on his face. He had come seeking death and it had found him. The coward was to find peace at last. 'Do you want them to kill you too? You fool, go!'

'I'll not die yet, I have things to do—a certain reckoning if you remember. Put your arm around me, I say. That's it. Your dying will have to wait for another day.'

The men who began to trickle back into the Highlands, to their homes and families, were a pathetic remnant of the proud, stalwart Highlanders who had bravely followed their Prince to war. They were half-starved, their clothes in rags, many had lost limbs in the bloody encounter at Culloden, had watched their friends, brothers, kin, being butchered by the English soldiers who marched onto the moor in the days that followed the battle and killed the wounded without quarter. One detachment so ordered to do was under the command of James Campbell. The order itself had come from Andrew Fraser. He had not accompanied the men on their mission; the satisfaction of seeing the horror in James's eyes at the order was the beginning of the revenge he intended to inflict on the man who had robbed him of wealth and power.

James never carried out his orders. Among the first group of dead he came across he found his brother Murdoch. He rode from the moor in silence and half his men followed him. The following day he deserted and they followed him homewards, each and every one of them knowing that the end of a rope awaited them should they be caught. James had only one idea in his mind, to reach Darna and prepare for a siege. It could

withstand the onslaught of an attack for many months
and whatever happened in the end, he would have spent
the time with his wife and sister.

For the past week Catriona had not dared venture
outside the main gates, for fear on her morning rides she
would be accosted by one of the bands of roving clansmen who scoured the countryside in search of food and
clothes and plunder. After Falkirk, she and Kirsty had
freely given shelter to any man who came to Darna, but
after Culloden it was different. Sullen faces, hatred in
the eyes and some, learning it was the home of a
Campbell, spat in her face and turned away, even
though they were so weak they could scarcely stand.

Tamsie Stewart came to tell them of Murdoch's death.
She had been told by one of her father's clansmen who
had brought the dreadful news that all her family were
also dead. She had aged ten years since they had last
seen each other, Catriona thought as she watched the
woman ride away. She was returning home to gather
what able-bodied men she could and defend her home
against the English troops she had heard were advancing
towards them, destroying homes and property, killing
without distinction anyone who opposed them. She had
lost everything, she said quietly to Catriona. Her own
life was unimportant now.

Kirsty was still sitting beside the fire where they had
left her when Catriona went back inside. Her arms
folded against her chest, she rocked herself to and fro,
staring with sightless eyes into the flames.

'Are you all right?' Catriona knelt beside her concernedly. She had said nothing when she heard the news.
Not a word. 'Why don't you go and lie down until
dinner?'

'All her family—and Murdoch too. Did you see that
look in her eyes? She said the MacDonalds were slaughtered as they charged. They're dead, I know it—both my
brothers—and James too. I know it!' Her voice began to

rise shrilly. 'I will never see any of them again.'

'Hush now, you know these things are nearly always exaggerated. It's almost impossible in all that confusion for a soldier to say how many fell about him, whether they were dead, or merely wounded. Nan's nephew, the one that is married to the MacIan girl? He's home, and he was with the MacDonalds. Go and rest, my dear, and try not to think of what Tamsie told us.'

'Why don't you cry, Catriona?' Kirsty demanded frostily, pushing her away. She stood up. 'You have lost a brother—you may have lost two for all you know, as well as the man you profess to love. Have you no tears for them?'

'Would it help you to see me cry?' Catriona asked patiently. 'Go and lie down, you will feel better in a little while.'

She could give way to tears, Catriona thought, as she watched the girl walk slowly from the room, but she would not. She would not believe either James or Rorie had been killed at Culloden—to do so would have meant the end of her world.

The sound of a cry brought her running out of the room. Kirsty lay at the bottom of the staircase, her leg twisted beneath her.

'What happened? Oh, my poor dear, don't try to move,' Catriona begged cradling her against a shoulder as she attempted to rise.

'My leg, I can't move it,' Kirsty whispered in agony. 'Catriona—have I broken it?' Her face was taut with fear.

'No, of course not,' Catriona hastened to reassure her. 'Nan! Come quickly and help me. Kirsty has had a fall.'

She would send for the doctor in any case, Catriona thought, as between them the two women managed to support the girl to her room. For over a week Kirsty had vehemently denied her leg was troubling her; now it had led to an accident. She could not afford to take further risks.

It was well past midnight when Catriona left Kirsty's room. The doctor had not been at home when Calum arrived: being a staunch Jacobite, he had gone to help some wounded men hiding in the mountains, so his wife had been brought instead. She had a way about her which instantly soothed Kirsty's fears. She accepted in silence the advice given, that she should rest in bed for several days and not walk far for at least a week. She drank the warm milk Nan gave her, heavily laced with something stronger, and fell into an exhausted sleep. Catriona remained at her side until her eyelids began to droop, and Nan ushered her firmly out through the door.

'I'll stay with the lass,' she whispered.

'Bless you. Watch over her carefully.'

She was in her room about to undress, when she heard a movement outside the door. She had barely been away from Kirsty's side ten minutes—what was wrong? Even as she moved towards the door, it swung open and she recoiled in silent terror from the three figures which confronted her. She did not know the middle-aged man who closed and locked the door behind him, but she knew the scarred face of the bearded, raggedly dressed man who held another, barely conscious, in his arms.

'Come for you at Darna, you said. I have come for our reckoning,' Rorie MacDonald said harshly.

CHAPTER
TEN

CATRIONA stood immobile, struck speechless, as Rorie shouldered his way past her and laid Donald on the bed.

'Find something to make bandages,' he ordered brusquely, 'he's bleeding again. Hurry, woman—and not a sound. Ian there will have his dirk in you if you so much as look towards the door.'

In a feverish haste, Catriona pulled open drawers and closets, took out a spare petticoat and some linen cloths and began tearing them into strips. The man on the bed was hardly breathing. His face and clothes were streaked with mud and blood. His eyes opened as she began to remove the plaid wrapped around him and he swore at her for the pain she was causing him.

'Stand aside, he'll die from loss of blood before you've finished,' Rorie said, pushing her away. 'Gently, man, we're safe for a while. Can you raise yourself a little? That's good. Lie still now and let me do something with this mess.'

'Ach, what's the use?' Donald growled. 'I'm finished. I'm too weak to go on.' His eyes flickered to Catriona and a bitter smile touched his lips. 'Tell her how it was, brother. Tell her Donald MacDonald is no coward.'

'She's of no importance just now. For God's sake, lie still.'

'It needs cleaning first or it will become infected,' Catriona said, pouring water from a pitcher beside the bed into a hand bowl and holding it out to him. Donald's shirt was stuck to him with matted blood and he cried out as Rorie eased the torn material away. 'For goodness sake, is that what you call being gentle? Let me,' Catriona exclaimed.

Rorie wheeled on her so violently she thought he was about to strike her. But the hand upraised before her face slowly dropped back to his side.

'Gag her, Ian, and keep her out of the way.'

'Is your hatred of me more important than your brother's life?' she flung back contemptuously as the clansman began to move towards her. Rorie motioned him back.

'Why should you help him? Have you not forgotten he struck you?'

'He is Kirsty's brother. That is my sole reason for what I do.'

Without a word he turned aside and flung himself into a chair, and remained there while she cleansed and bandaged the ugly wound in Donald's side. By the time she had finished she felt sick. She had never seen anything so terrible before.'

'Grapeshot,' Rorie muttered as she emptied away the soiled water and poured fresh into the bowl to clean her hands. 'They mowed us down like sheep. Then the cavalry came after us, pursued us through the heather all that day. At night as we lay hidden in a bothy we could hear the wounded crying out for water. The English denied them even that, and in the morning they marched out—to bring them in, we thought—but no!' The tawny eyes were murderous as they turned on her. 'They shot them where they lay, or bayoneted them and then stripped them of personal belongings, sometimes even their clothes—left them lying naked on the moor. A few women managed to find their men before they were bundled into graves like the carcasses of diseased cattle. Have you something to drink up here?'

'No, but there is brandy in the study downstairs.'

Catriona sank down onto the edge of the bed. As yet she had given no thought to her own safety. Rorie was alive and well. Gaunt and exhausted, but alive.

'Ian—find it. Bring two bottles. If anyone sees you, kill them.'

'No,' she cried, 'let me go. There are only two men in the whole house and they are too old to harm you. Apart from them, there are only women.'

'Are you expecting me to believe your brother left only two men here to protect his wife and sister?' Rorie's narrowed gaze held no friendliness. He had done with weakness the day he left Edinburgh and marched towards England—though the sight of her had roused him as he had never thought possible and his first impulse had been to pull her into his arms and kiss the soft mouth that had once answered his so willingly—so treacherously!

'It's true! There were more, but several were killed last week returning from the village with supplies. Those who killed them took everything. I was going to send Calum out tomorrow because we are so short of food in the house and with Kirsty in bed . . .'

'What's wrong with her?' Rorie was on his feet immediately. 'Is she ill?'

'She had a slight fall, but the injury is not serious—at least we hope not, but the doctor was away and I can't be sure . . .' Her voice trailed off as he ejaculated,

'A fall? Her bad leg again?'

'Yes. It was painful when she was in Edinburgh. Did she not tell you?'

'She would not—under the circumstances, would she?' he retorted dryly.

'Did your brother know?'

'I thought it best neither of us mentioned it to him. He had worries enough.'

'Until you gave him his freedom. Fetch us something to eat and drink. Go with her, Ian.' He fixed Catriona with a warning look. 'If you have lied to me yet again . . .'

Catriona ignored the sour-faced clansman who dogged her footsteps as she descended to the kitchen, warmed some soup left over from dinner and hastily prepared a tray with a bottle of her father's best French brandy and a large plate filled with bread and cheese and cold chicken. It left very little in the larders for anyone else, but she suspected none of the fugitives had eaten well since the battle. She had expected Rorie to come, yet now he had she realised the foolhardiness of his action. Why had he not gone home, especially as his brother was wounded? From the Forest of Mamore it was not a long ride to the coast. He could have taken a ship to one of the islands, even France! But he had come to Darna. Her heart sank as she went back upstairs. He had come for revenge!

He was not in the room. She set the tray down on a table and went to inspect Donald. He appeared to be sleeping.

'Leave him, he's had no rest for days. He can eat later,' Rorie ordered, appearing in the doorway behind her. He quietly closed the door behind him and relocked it. 'Ian, help yourself, man, you're as starving as I am. That soup looks good and it's hot. Sit down where I can see you, Catriona. If you are wondering where I was, I went to see Kirsty. She's sleeping. When can she be moved?'

'Are you mad? Move her after a fall—in her condition? The doctor's wife said bed-rest for several days and she must stay off that leg as much as possible when she does get up.'

'So her foolishness finally caught up with her.'

'That's a terrible thing to say.'

'Don't preach at me, you don't have the right. She isn't staying here for the English to find. God knows what they would do to her,' he answered, pushing away his empty soup bowl. He could feel it warming his frozen limbs. If only he wasn't so tired. He could hardly think!

'Nothing will happen to her,' Catriona said, frowning. 'She is James's wife. They would not dare touch either of us.' She remembered the help they had both given to wounded Highlanders, but refrained from mentioning it. If he knew that he would surely take Kirsty with him. It could kill her!

'We're in need of clothes and food for when we leave. Donald will be stronger in a few days and then we move on.'

'Are you going home?' He made no mention of what he intended for her and she dared not ask.

'We have no home. A few days ago the Fraser and your brother burned my house, killed my servants and put to the torch every croft for twenty miles around.'

'I don't believe you,' Catriona said, her voice a whisper. 'He swore never to raise a hand against you—he would not, even if he was ordered to.'

'He was there. Ian saw him, watching as the soldiers burned and raped and looted. Not a man left alive, women and children slaughtered or turned out to die of exposure in the mountains. Campbell promises! You make a pretty pair!'

'You are mistaken. I know it. When he comes, he will tell me how it was—the truth!'

'Only if you are alive.' Rorie rose to his feet and moved in front of her. 'Why should I not leave you for him to find as Ian found his wife and daughters?'

'If that is already in your mind, then nothing I can say will change it.' The lack of fear on her lovely face took him aback. She had expected him to come! Yet she had not run.

'He can no more harm you than he could leave me back on the moor.' Donald's eyes were open, a strange look in them as he watched the two of them together.

'You are weak in the head. Give him some soup, Ian,' his brother said, and Donald gave a mirthless laugh.

'Am I? We could have reached a safe haven by now, but you had to come here—to see her! A reckoning you said. Well, let's have it then. Put your hands around her lying throat, or use your dirk, it matters not to me, but settle with her.'

'Stop talking like a fool and lie still or you'll start to bleed again,' Rorie snapped, glaring at him.

To kill her! Was that why he had come back to Darna? His reasons were no longer clear. He knew he had wanted to hurt her, force the truth out of her. Had wanted to hear from her own lips how she had lied to him from the very beginning, never loved him and deliberately deceived him as she lay in his arms in Edinburgh. Somehow it no longer seemed important. She had not killed his love that day. It would remain with him for the rest of his life, wherever he went. She would remain with him! He would never care for another woman as he did her!

'Now who is the coward?' Donald jeered hoarsely. 'You can't touch her! Let Ian do it then, he has reason enough after what the Campbells did to his kin.'

'That's enough.' Rorie wheeled on the mocking figure on the bed, his expression furious. 'Have some food and then start on the brandy, it might put some sense into your head or at least send you to sleep so that the rest of us can have a little peace. If she is dead, who will care for our sister?'

'She comes with us.'

'She's nearly lame . . . In this freezing weather? She would never make it to the coast. She can't run from the dragoons hunting us, can she?'

'We can take horses from here.'

'Even so Kirsty's life would be at risk. I don't know what is best—I can't decide now, I'm too damned tired.' His eyes came to rest on Catriona and the look in them made her inwardly shudder. 'I haven't decided anything yet.'

She sat silently in a chair as Ian fed Donald some soup. He took only a few mouthfuls and then pushed it away, reaching instead for the bottle of brandy. She watched him swallow great gulps and he chuckled as he saw the apprehension which crept into her expression.

Rorie threw several large pieces of wood onto the fire and stood warming himself for some while before he unwound the remnants of the plaid around his shoulders and removed his jacket. He was still wearing the same shirt in which he had been injured when the rearguard was attacked by Cumberland's men. Catriona caught her breath sharply at the sight of the torn sleeve which exposed a vivid red scar, searing the brown skin practically from elbow to shoulder.

'You were hurt.' The words were spoken before she could stop herself.

He turned and looked at her, puzzled, suspicious.

'Are you disappointed the sabre did not find my throat?'

'How can you say such a thing? I have never wished you harm.'

'You once told me that had you been a man you would have killed me for what I did to your brother Murdoch,' he reminded her in a callous tone.

'I was angry. You made me say things I did not mean,' she whispered, through trembling lips. In an almost inaudible tone, she added, 'Murdoch is dead. Tamsie brought the news. She lost everyone . . .'

'I know.'

'How?' she gasped. 'Oh, no, not you? You did not . . .'

'Kill Murdoch? No, the Campbells did that. They were hiding behind a stone wall which ran across the moor just before the river. Donald and I went that way to avoid being run down and cut to pieces by the cavalry.

We found Murdoch and the others, men from Appin mostly—some Ogilvies—watched the Campbells strip them after finishing them off, poor devils. For all I know your brother was there too.'

'And he would do nothing because of me,' Donald interrupted. Already the brandy was beginning to affect him and his speech was unsteady. 'Next time it will be different.'

'Why don't you finish the bottle and go to sleep, then perhaps we can all get some rest. Where does that lead to?' Rorie pointed to a side door.

'My sitting-room. There's a couch in there if you want to rest—or rooms upstairs.

'I'll sleep anywhere tonight. In there will do. Stay with my brother. The bandages may need changing before morning. Ian will remain too, to ensure you do nothing foolish.'

He reeled, rather than walked, into the darkened room and Catriona heard him throw himself down on the couch without bothering to light the lamp. Under the watchful gaze of the other clansman, she moved her chair closer to the fire. Three o'clock. Four hours at least until it began to grow light—and what then? As Donald fell into a drunken sleep and began to snore loudly, she closed her eyes and tried not to think of tomorrow, but it was impossible.

Would the English come to Darna next? Would James be with them? No! He could not have participated in that terrible act committed upon the MacDonalds, could not have been at the scene of Murdoch's death. Or could he? Soldiers obeyed orders, and in war men did things—sometimes unspeakable things—that would have been dishonourable to them in times of peace.

A tear seeped through her tightly closed lids. Try as she might she was unable to snatch even a few minutes' rest and when Rorie awoke at seven o'clock and inspected his brother, she was still sitting by the fire she had kept alight—tired, pale, and, unknown to him, terribly afraid.

'My sister's room is three doors along from here. Go and bring me the woman there, but do not disturb my sister,' he ordered the clansman, helping himself to a leg of chicken which still remained on the plate. He had been too exhausted to eat much before and was now realising how ravenous he was.

'Don't hurt her,' Catriona begged.

'Say her mistress is with MacDonald Ruadh, that should bring her quick enough,' Rorie said, and Ian slipped cautiously out of the room.

Reaching for the bottle Donald had been drinking from earlier, he grimaced to find it empty. At least it had kept his brother quiet for a few hours, he thought, staring across at the sleeping figure. There were fresh bandages around his chest, he saw. Words of thanks rose unbidden to his lips, but remained unuttered. One show of weakness and he was lost! He had admitted defeat to himself, but never would to her.

'You cannot stay up here,' Catriona said, rising to stretch her cramped limbs. 'You will be seen.'

'You will ensure we are not. This should be an easy situation for you to lie your way out of.'

'That's unfair. I have only ever lied to you once and that was to help James. Never before, not now. I have no reason. Once I asked you what you wanted of me and you said honesty. I will be honest with you now. I have not changed since the night of the Prince's ball when you held me in your arms and my dreams became reality.'

'Liar! Your only thought that night was to keep my mind off that table laid for two. Was he still in the house while I was holding you? Listening to us perhaps? You deserve a medal for the performance you gave,' Rorie said scathingly, his mouth tightening into a bleak line.

'You are wrong.' Catriona shook her head. 'I gave you the truth you wanted.'

'Pretty words, perhaps, but not truth. Not once did you mention the word love,' he flung back.

'No more did you,' she reminded him.

'You forget the following morning I told you I loved you, wanted you for my wife . . .'

'After you had learned James had been to the house, that I had given him clothes and food. Who gave a good performance that day, may I ask?'

He stepped towards her, roused to anger by the scornful words, but just then Ian ushered Nan through the doorway and he turned aside. She would never know what he had been about to say, Catriona thought sadly. If he had held her—she knew she would have been able to convince him of her love, but the few feet separating them now was like a mile—she saw that by his face.

'My lady—are you all right? These scum haven't hurt you.'

'Hold your tongue, woman, and listen to me,' Rorie ordered. 'Do everything I say and no harm will come to you or to any of the women in this house.' Was she included in that statement, Catriona wondered? 'Tell the manservant called Calum he is to go to the village for supplies today. Bring him up to the sitting-room. Is that clear?'

'Do as he says,' Catriona added as Nan looked at her for confirmation. 'We are short of fresh vegetables and meat. We can hardly feed ourselves, let alone three more mouths.'

'You are allowing them to stay?'

'She has no choice,' Rorie snapped. 'Get you gone. Speak only to Calum.'

Donald began to move restlessly on the bed and Rorie bent over him axiously. His brother's face was suddenly grey, his skin wet with perspiration.

'These bandages—are they too tight?'

'No, I left them deliberately loose, with extra wadding beneath,' Catriona said, joining him. Her hand brushed his as she leaned over the unconscious man and Rorie abruptly drew back. He could smell the French perfume she had worn the first night they met—like sweet-smelling apple blossoms. She laid a hand across Donald's forehead. 'He is feverish. He will have to stay here now. I'll fetch some more clean water and towels.'

'Nan will fetch them when she comes back. You remain in my sight.'

'Where are you afraid I will go?' Catriona asked sarcastically. 'I haven't been outside the gates of Darna for almost a month. What makes you think I will risk my life just to run from you?'

'Perhaps I should give you a reason,' he growled, his fingers fastening over her wrist in a painful grip. He dragged her close until her lips were only inches from his, before thrusting her roughly away. 'You have nothing to interest me; perhaps the English will find you more attractive.'

Catriona blanched visibly at his words. From what she had heard of the soldiers rampaging through the coun-tryside since the Battle of Culloden, they cared little which side the men they killed or the women they abused, claimed to be on. She and Kirsty would be alone in the house with only two aged manservants to protect them, until James returned with the men from Darna.

When Calum came, Rorie remained in the bedroom, the communicating door not quite closed. She knew his pistol was aimed at Nan as she gave her list of require-ments and sent him on his way. It would be dusk before he returned—if he returned.

'Ian is waiting for him out by the stables,' Rorie said, as she stared concernedly out of the window to watch him leave. 'He'll not be stopped by our men now. They'll have to take their chances if they are seen by the English.'

As you will once you leave here, she thought, looking into the bearded face.

'We need clean water, Nan, and towels, plenty of them—and fresh sheets for the bed. Bring my brother's shaving things too.'

'Aye, it would be nice to feel like a human being again,' Rorie said, touching the growth on his chin. 'You think of everything, don't you? That's why I don't trust you.'

Catriona ignored the taunt. With Nan's help she stripped the bed and put on clean linen and for most of the morning sat by the bedside, sponging Donald's burning skin with cold water. It did nothing to ease his fever and she grew quite anxious as the day wore on and he seemed no better.

Rorie sat in a chair by the window, staring out at the countryside, ever alert for the first tell-tale hint of a red coat that would herald the approach of English soldiers.

Towards late afternoon Catriona slept, curled up on the settee where he had spent the night. When she awoke it was dark and Nan was alone in the bedroom with Donald.

'He's gone to see his sister. Says he's taking her with him when they leave,' she snorted. 'The fool! With her delicate health, he'll kill her.'

'He fears for her safety if she remains here when the soldiers arrive,' Catriona returned. 'I am beginning to think he could be right. I wish James was here—then everything would be all right.'

'Only if the MacDonalds have gone, otherwise they will cut each other to pieces.'

'How is he?'

'Weak. He'll be going nowhere for a while.'

Catriona looked at the clock on the mantel with a frown.'

'Six o'clock! Hasn't Calum come back yet?'

'Not a sign of him, and cook is getting suspicious about your absence. You intended going through the store cupboards with her this morning. I told her you had been

up all night with Mistress Kirsty and were sleeping late
and that I'd bring both your meals upstairs tonight. She's
been fed, I've seen to that, though she'd take no more
than a wee drop of broth. Sit down, lass, he'll not come
back quicker for you staring out of the window. My lady,
did you hear me?'

'Dear heaven, no!' Catriona stepped back, her hands
against her mouth in a gesture of horror. 'Soldiers. I can
just make them out . . . coming this way. They are
coming to Darna, Nan!'

Picking up her skirts she ran from the room and burst
into Kirsty's bedroom like a whirlwind. Rorie sprang
from the bed, his hand reaching instinctively for his
sword.

'Soldiers, about a dozen of them, I think. On their way
here. Look for yourself if you don't believe me.' She
wanted to scream in frustration as he stood still with
shock and just stared at her. They were trapped! They
could not leave without being seen and even if that were
possible, Donald in his present condition would have to
be carried and so slow down their progress. Had he
survived Culloden to be killed in this place, Rorie
wondered?

'Less than a dozen I'd say.' He stood at the window for
a full minute and she waited in an agony of suspense for
him to turn. 'That makes it about even odds.'

'You—you can't mean to fight,' she gasped. 'That's
madness. If you are found here they will give no quarter
—to any of us.'

'Run,' Kirsty begged. 'Take your chances. We will be
all right. I am the wife of James Campbell. They won't
touch me, or Catriona.'

'It's too late to run, you must hide. Downstairs—one
of the store-rooms,' Catriona urged. 'Are you going to
trust me, Rorie MacDonald, or are you intending to
answer the door to them yourself when they knock,' she
cried as he did not move.

'Show me!' A fleeting kiss on his sister's ashen cheek and then he was close on Catriona's heels as she ran back to her own room. He didn't trust her, yet his life was in her hands. It was not the first time, he remembered as she flung back the bed clothes and ordered him to pick up his brother. Thank God, Donald was not conscious, he thought.

'Nan, go downstairs and delay them as best you can. They must not come up here. When I come, go and warn the women to stay out of sight.'

'You'll not reach the store-rooms, mistress. There are soldiers at the door already,' Nan wailed, peering out of the window again. 'I'll do what I can, but for the love of heaven, don't try to get downstairs with them!'

Catriona hurriedly rearranged the rumpled bed-clothes and pulled the coverlet into place, snatched up plaid and jacket and the bottle from the table. A supper tray looked innocent enough except when there was an empty brandy bottle beside it!

The sound of voices drifted up from the direction of the doorway as they eased themselves out into the corridor. A finger against her lips, she slipped silently back the way they had come into Kirsty's room and closed the door after them.

'You will have to stay in here. I'll tell them Kirsty is ill and cannot be disturbed, if they wish to search—though why they should wish to do so is beyond me—in here.' She opened the door leading to a small dressing-room. Rorie laid his unconscious burden down on the bed against one wall and followed her back. His clay-more was in one hand, a dirk in the other. Catriona looked at the trembling girl in the bed and said quietly. 'Try to look ill. Pull the covers about you and be still.'

She turned and looked into the suspicious features behind her and managed a brave smile.

'This may help if they do come up here.' She held out

to him the pistol she had secreted into the pockets of her skirts.

'Have you had this all the time?' His voice belied the incredulity her words aroused in him.

'It was in the cupboard beside my bed. James left it for my protection.' Her smile grew as he realised she could have used it against him at any time, had she wished to do so.

'Keep it. You may need it more than me.'

'Are you trusting me at last? Oh, MacDonald of little faith, what can I do to convince you of my love?'

Leaning up on tip-toe, she put her arms around his neck, her lips against his and kissed him as she had done that night in Edinburgh when he had brought her to the point of surrender. Before he could speak, she had stepped quickly through the door and closed it behind her.

'I think they are coming up here,' Kirsty said, huddling beneath the bedclothes, her face white with fear. 'Catriona, they must not!'

Pausing only for a moment to smooth down her skirts and pat her dishevelled hair into place, Catriona went outside, ready to remonstrate with whoever was in charge in the haughtiest manner she could muster for intruding into the privacy of her home without permission. The words died on her lips. There were three men on the stairs. Two troopers and an officer—Andrew Fraser! The sight of him shocked her into silence and she remained rooted to the spot as he came face to face with her.

'Catriona, my dear, how nice to see you again. A pity it is under such unfortunate circumstances.' He did not sound in the least sorry, she thought, on the contrary . . .

'What are you doing here? How dare you come into my house like some scavenging rebel in search of food, with no regard for property or privacy,' she said scathingly. If Fraser was here, then James would not be far away.

'Hardly the comparison I would have drawn. We are not after food, only rebels,' came the cool reply. 'I believe you have some here. MacDonalds if I am not mistaken.'

'Here! Are you mad? They would not dare come here.' She hoped he would think the unsteadiness in her voice was due to anger—not fear.

'My men stopped a cart on the way here. It contained one of Darna's servants and a MacDonald. An odd alliance, don't you agree? Unfortunately the fellow attempted to escape while we were questioning him and he was shot. A pity, as I'm sure he could have given me all the information I required.' He spoke of killing a man as lightly as if he was discussing the weather.

'Calum! Where is he?'

'The old fool tried to drive off when he saw us approaching. He, too, was shot.'

'He was an old man. He had gone to the village for supplies.' The news sickened her. Calum had been at Darna since the age of ten. He and James had taught her to ride.

'To feed your extra mouths, no doubt. How many are there and where are they hiding, or would you prefer my men to search the house? They are inclined to be on the rough side, Catriona, an uncouth lot actually—hard to control. Light-fingered too and many of them haven't seen their wives in months. You still have women in the house, don't you?'

The implication was only too clear. She had the choice of betraying the man she loved or seeing her beautiful home ransacked, the maids and kitchen women brutally assaulted. It could happen anyway, she suspected and her expression became stubborn.

'They may search, but you will instruct them to do so in a seemly manner—and quietly.' She motioned to the room behind her. 'My sister-in-law has had a bad fall and is confined to bed. I do not want her disturbed by your—rabble. Is that too much to ask? I shall not forget or forgive this unwarranted intrusion and James will hear of it the moment he returns.'

'Why not tell him now,' Andrew chuckled. 'He is below.'

Catriona's eyes widened in disbelief. She flew to the stair rail and looked down into the Great Hall. He was there! But something was wrong. There was an armed soldier standing at his side—and his hands were bound behind his back. Nan was cowering on the floor behind him, another soldier standing over her. Tears were streaming down over her cheeks and there was a vivid bruise on one of them where she had been struck when she attempted to warn Catriona that the soldiers were making their way upstairs.

In a daze she descended the stairs, brushing aside the trooper who tried to stop her, and flung herself against James's chest. He looked exhausted—bearded, his clothes dirty and torn, a bloody gash just visible beneath his hairline.

'What does this mean?'

'He's a deserter! A traitor to his King and country and tomorrow, after I have finished here, I am taking him to Fort William to stand trial. He'll swing on the gallows along with the others who ran from the field of battle,' Andrew sneered from above them.

'It isn't true. I didn't run. Yes, I confess I deserted rather than have you turn me into a butcher.' James laid a dusty cheek against hers. Instinct told him the Mac-Donalds had come to Darna. He had recognised Ian immediately as being one of Rorie's men. Was she hiding them? If only his hands were free—if only he had a pistol. He was helpless to protect his wife and sister from a man he knew intended to exact a terrible revenge upon him and his family for the humiliation suffered

over the retracted marriage contract. He had hinted at it
many times as they rode towards Inverness. The order to
go out and callously murder the wounded lying on
Drummossie he knew had been intended to provoke him
into taking a road of no return. And it had succeeded. 'I
was ordered to take my men—men from Darna, Catriona—and go and shoot or cut the throats of the poor
devils wounded after Culloden. Slaughter them in cold
blood. We rode out, but at the first bothy we came to, I
found some Stewarts—and Murdoch. I didn't go any
further. I turned my horse homewards and many followed me. It was as if I had killed him myself.'

'Tamsie told me he was dead and her father and
brothers too. Oh, James, what you must have suffered.
We heard of some terrible things—homes burnt, people
killed without quarter . . . James, you were not part of
it, were you?'

'How could I have been? I was on my way here. I've
been hiding for a week, not daring to come too close
because of the soldiers patrolling this area. Most of the
men drifted back to their families—God help them. For
many there was nothing left. He had seen to that.' James
glared, red-eyed at the smiling figure watching them.'

'James!' The cry came from the bedroom doorway
and Catriona gave a gasp as Kirsty limped painfully into
view. James started forward, cursing his bound hands,
only to be struck roughly on the back by a musket butt
and felled to the floor.

'My, what a scene of domesticity,' Andrew jeered.
'Sergeant, let the lady see her husband. Perhaps she will
tell us where the MacDonalds are. Kin, no doubt. You
have three minutes, you MacDonald bitch. Tell me, or
I'll have a bullet put through his head and then yours.
That should bring them out of hiding.'

Catriona started towards the staircase with a cry of
anger as Kirsty was seized by one of the soldiers and
thrust against the banister so violently she thought he

was going to throw her over. He held her doubled over it, his fingers twisted in her loose hair—she was sobbing with pain and fear.

'Three minutes.' Andrew took a gold enamelled snuff-box from inside his coat, oblivious to Kirsty's moans of pain. Catriona thought he looked as if he was enjoying the sight. 'I think one of you will tell me. No?'

The bullet came from behind him and struck the man holding Kirsty in the head. As his companion started forward, Rorie's dirk entered his chest and he, too, died instantly.

'Turn around, Fraser. Unlike you, I don't have the habit of attacking men from the rear.'

'It will give me great pleasure to kill you, MacDonald Ruadh. I knew it had to be you here. I shall console Catriona tonight for her loss,' Andrew sneered. As he came about, he flung the contents of the snuff-box at the Highlander with vindictive force.

Half expecting such a move, Rorie had side-stepped, but still some of the powder found its way into his eyes, momentarily blinding him.

'Kill him,' Andrew bellowed to the man below and drew his sword, but he made no move to use it. Why should he when he had others to do his killing for him? Instead he wheeled away, grabbing hold of Kirsty and dragging her in front of him as a shield. As Rorie watched helplessly, desperately trying to clear his streaming eyes, he backed against the wall to watch the annihilation of his enemy.

One of the remaining soldiers took aim with his musket and fired. It was a wild shot and glanced off the woodwork above Rorie's head as he ducked back into the bedroom. Before he could reload, James flung himself forward and butted him full in the stomach, winding him. His musket fell to the floor and was kicked out of reach. The other man had already started up the stairs to get a better shot at the kilted Highlander while Andrew railed at their bad marksmanship, threatening to hang them both on the spot. James fell to his knees, grabbed the knife from the fallen soldier's belt and buried it deep in his back.

'Cut me free.' He thrust the bloodstained blade out towards Catriona. 'Hurry! There's more outside.'

Catriona's gaze swept upwards as she snatched it from him and applied it to the ropes. The other trooper was cautiously approaching the bedroom. She saw him smile as he stepped through the open doorway, his musket coming up to fire and she choked back a cry as there came a single report.

'Take this.' She pressed the pistol he had left her into his hand. She saw the skin on his wrists was chafed and bloody where he had made repeated attempts to free himself. There came shouts from outside. The sound of running feet.

Rousing herself from her stupor, she threw herself against the door and secured the heavy bolts across it. Only just in time. It shuddered under a great weight and then glass shattered somewhere off to her right and a volley of shots echoed through the Great Hall.

'Quickly, before they reload. Nan, get to the kitchens and warn the others. Make them hide.'

James grabbed Catriona's hand and dragged her upstairs. At the top he thrust her to one side, the pistol he held rising to menace Andrew Fraser, but he dared not risk a shot for fear of hitting his wife, who sagged barely conscious in her captor's grasp.

Catriona reeled blindly towards the bedroom, steeling herself for what she would find, and stood in the doorway, not believing what she saw. Eyes still streaming, Rorie was leaning against one of the bedposts, supporting Donald whose meagre strength had been taxed to the limit as he dragged himself from hiding and plunged his sword into the soldier about to kill his brother.

'Andrew—has Kirsty,' she faltered. 'And there are

more soldiers trying to break in. Hurry . . .'

He came to her, held her in silence and the kiss which passed between them wiped out all suspicion, all hatred and distrust. She trembled in his arms, awakened by the passion the kiss contained, brief, but more eloquent than a thousand words.

'I leave my woman in your care, brother,' he said and stepped out to join James in the passageway.

Looking at Donald, Catriona saw a fierce glow of pride burning in his eyes. Whatever had happened in the past, he had redeemed himself in his brother's eyes and had at last come to terms with the devil that had dragged him down into the pit of hell for the last time.

'Let her go, and fight like a man,' Rorie said coldly.

Andrew Fraser looked from James at the head of the stairs to the man who stood on his right with murder in his eyes.

'Take her then,' he snarled and thrust Kirsty towards her husband with such force, he was knocked off balance. By the time he had recovered, the other man was past him and starting down the stairs to freedom. With a cry of rage, Rorie followed and was only a step behind when they reached the Great Hall. His claymore sliced through the tail of Andrew's coat bringing him to a halt. Rorie leapt in front of him, barring his way to the door.

'Fight,' he yelled and attacked fiercely.

The clash of steel upon steel brought Catriona and Donald to the door. But above that she could hear the sound of screaming.

'They have come through a side door,' she gasped.

The words were barely out of her mouth when two more troopers appeared from the direction of the kitchen, they took one look at the men battling in front of them, saw it was impossible to get a clear shot at the wild-eyed Highlander and so turned their weapons on the figures above them.

Without hesitation James killed the man nearest to him before he could fire and heard a bullet fired by the man's companion whine close to his head. He heard a soft cry behind him and knew with horror in his heart where it had found a home, even before he turned and saw the motionless figure of Kirsty behind him.

'My God, no.' His anguished cry brought Catriona down on her knees beside him. 'They've killed her, damn their black hearts!'

'No—no! Help me lift her.'

'She's dead! Leave her. Leave her, I say.' Leaping to his feet he spun around on Donald, hand outstretched. 'Give me your sword. Let me avenge her.'

It was tossed to him without argument. In this moment of shock and grief, they were no longer enemies, but two men who shared the suffering of the loss of a loved one. James ran to meet the oncoming trooper. The man had been one of those who had been at Prestonpans for the first encounter with the Highland army. He had run alongside his companions and afterwards seen his best friend hung for desertion as an example. This time he had no chance to run, or to reload the musket in his hands as the enemy bore down on him.

'Quarter,' he begged. 'It was an accident. I did not mean to hit the woman.'

Catriona closed her eyes as the claymore descended. When she re-opened them the man lay huddled against the wall and her brother was running towards the stairs which led below, shouting at the top of his voice for whoever was there to come and meet him. Had he been confronted by an army of soldiers, he would have fought them all.

'A bonny fighter—for a Campbell,' Donald murmured weakly as he lurched towards the banister to watch his brother deliver the blow which ended Andrew Fraser's life. He was breathing heavily and the exertion of killing the trooper had reopened his wound. He could feel the life-blood ebbing out of him, knew he would never leave Darna.

Rorie saw it too as he came upstairs two at a time. He paused for a moment to briefly grip his brother's hand, before kneeling at his sister's side. Taking one of her limp, lifeless hands in his, he touched it to his scarred cheek. The rage died out of his expression and the grief which replaced it made Catriona's heart ache. She laid her hand over his, but doubted if he was even aware of her touch. She said nothing. There were no words capable of giving him the comfort she knew he needed.

James found the three of them in the bedroom. Rorie had carried Kirsty back to the bed and lain her on it, smoothing the hair from her face and covering the ugly stain on her nightgown with the coverlet. She looked so peaceful it was hard to believe she was not sleeping, Catriona thought. She watched Rorie grow tense as her brother appeared to stand a few feet from them.

'There has been enough killing,' she whispered. 'There must be no more.'

He stared past her and his fingers were tight about the hilt of his sword.

'There are no more soldiers for the moment. I've told the servants I can no longer protect them and they must fend for themselves.' James's voice was without emotion. 'You must leave immediately. The rest of the troop will be here by morning. By then they will have carried out Fraser's orders to the full.'

'What orders?' Rorie demanded harshly.

'Tamsie Stewart and twenty or thirty Appin men barricaded themselves in the house. They refused to surrender. His orders were to get them out by any means and hang them. Failing that, to burn the house and every last one of them in it. As it was with your home, MacDonald.'

'And where were you on that occasion?' Donald

growled, sliding down into a chair as his legs threatened to fold beneath him.

'Astride my horse, bound and helpless, forced to watch for the Fraser's amusement. I was captured the day before trying to get food for one of my injured men. When he had finished with your house and people he dragged me with him to witness the end of the Stewarts, then he was taking me to be hung for desertion. If you don't believe me, then let us settle our differences now and be done with it. Then take my sister from here and save yourselves while there is still time.'

'Tamsie, Murdoch, Kirsty! Isn't that enough for you?' Catriona cried, stepping away from them. 'Rorie—he has no reason to lie to you. Did you not hear what Andrew said? He was bound. Look at his wrists. Andrew said he would stand trial and hang in Fort William. All because he would not murder the wounded on Drummossie Moor after the battle. He saw Murdoch too. But for me he might have been there with him.'

'That's the first time you have ever called me by my given name.' Rorie turned slowly and looked at her. He seemed only to have heard the first part of what she had said. His hand reached for hers and she gave it hesitantly. 'Am I no longer the "Red" MacDonald to you?'

'By whatever name you are called you are the man I love, but if you harm my brother, I will not go with you.'

'You will, even if I have to tie you on a horse myself. The English must not get her, MacDonald. Promise me that,' James interrupted.

'They will not, nor any of us if I have my way. If we can reach the coast . . .'

'Not me.' James looked down at Kirsty's serene features and a wave of pain washed over him, so terrible he found it almost unbearable. He wanted to cry, but that would not help her. He would kill the English who had been instrumental in causing her death and then he too, would die—and join her. 'I have things to do here. I shall stay and wait for the others.'

'James, no!' Catriona tried to go to him, but Rorie held her fast. She was near to breaking point herself, he realised.

'It is his choice,' he said quietly. 'Accept it.'

'Go and put on some warm clothes, quickly,' James ordered. 'Take your jewels and whatever money you can find. I'll pick out three of our best horses.'

Catriona wept as Rorie propelled her firmly into her bedroom, she refused to change into the clothes Nan produced for the journey, insisting she would not leave Darna without her brother. Only when Rorie threatened to dress her himself, did she acquire some small proportion of composure and obey him. It was Nan who gathered together money and jewels, thrusting them into a leather pouch and handing them into the safe keeping of the man who watched her mistress with worried eyes.

'It will pass,' she whispered. 'So long as you are with her. Leave her and my curse will haunt you for the rest of your days.'

It was dark as they gathered in the courtyard where James had three horses, the best from Darna's stables, saddled and waiting. Nan cried unashamedly as she held Catriona in her arms. The rest of the household had fled to friends or relatives for sanctuary. She would go to her brother in Inverness, Nan said.

For Catriona there were no more tears—no words of parting. She wanted to say so much to her brother—and could not. By tomorrow he would be dead—and she was abandoning him!

James took her face in his hands, pressed his lips to her cheeks, her forehead, finally her mouth, then spun her around into Rorie's waiting arms.

'Care for her well, MacDonald. You will never find

the like of her again.' His voice broke and he was unable to continue.

'Well I know it. I will protect her with my life, you have my word.' She stood facing him in a stubborn silence, refusing his order to mount. He had to lift her into the saddle. 'Will you give me your hand, James Campbell? Let us part as friends—Kirsty would want that.'

'Please,' Catriona whispered as her brother stared at the outstretched hand. Once before he had offered his own in friendship and it had been refused.

He clasped the brown fingers in a fierce grip and then with something which sounded very much like a sob, he turned and strode back into the house.

'Mount up, man. By the looks of it there will be a full moon to guide us to the coast. We should make good time,' Rorie urged his brother.

Donald coughed. The hand which came away from his mouth was stained with blood and he gave a crooked grin.

'I'll not make it a mile and you know it. You—woman! Take my horse.'

Nan needed no second bidding and hauled herself awkwardly into the saddle, fresh tears streaming down over her face at the realisation she was not to be parted from her beloved mistress.

'Get you gone, brother.' Unsteadily Donald moved to Rorie's side.

'We've fought many a good fight together,' Rorie said, his voice harsh with emotion he could no longer conceal.

'No, brother. You fought them and usually on my behalf. The next fight is mine—although I must share it with him inside. I'll not deny him that right. I am about to make history by fighting of my own free will alongside a Campbell.' He coughed again, a painful sound that made Rorie wince. 'Take your woman and go.'

Catriona sat like a statue, staring back at the house. It

was Rorie who took the reins from her unresisting grasp and urged both horses out through the gates with Nan following close behind. He did not look back.

The French frigate which had been moored for a night and a day in the small cove that joined the shore of Moidart with that of Arisaig, the same spot where Charles Stuart had first set foot on the mainland nearly a year ago, slipped silently out to sea under the cover of a blanket of mist. It passed the English man o'war patrolling the coast, and headed homewards. It had come to rescue a Prince. It was returning instead with over sixty Highland men, many with what was left of their families. Those of rank huddled alongside common men on the decks, desperately, vainly trying to get a last look at the homeland they were leaving behind.

Rorie, an exhausted Catriona, barely able to stand, and Nan had been among the last to board. They would have to remain on the cold deck for the days spent at sea. The limited accommodation below was already overcrowded.

'Will we ever return?' Catriona asked tremulously. The mist was soaking her hair, but she was oblivious to it. Gently Rorie drew the hood of her cloak over her head and face to afford her some protection and drew her close against him. His concern for her had grown during the harrowing escape to the coast. Not one tear shed, not a word of the brother left behind—or his dead sister!

'Yes,' he said. We are better off than some of these poor devils about us. At least we have a little money and your jewels. They will give us a fresh start. But I swear to you, here and now, my love, we will come back. Perhaps not for a long time, but one day we will bring our children home.'

She turned her back towards the shore and laid her cheek against his plaid. And then she began to cry . . .

How to join in a whole new world of romance

It's very easy to subscribe to the Mills & Boon Reader Service. As a regular reader, you can enjoy a whole range of special benefits. Bargain offers. Big cash savings. Your own free Reader Service newsletter, packed with knitting patterns, recipes, competitions, and exclusive book offers.

We send you the very latest titles each month, postage and packing free – no hidden extra charges. There's absolutely no commitment – you receive books for only as long as you want.

We'll send you details. Simply send the coupon – or drop us a line for details about the Mills & Boon Reader Service Subscription Scheme. Post to: Mills & Boon Reader Service, P.O. Box 236, Thornton Road, Croydon, Surrey CR9 3RU, England. *Please note: READERS IN SOUTH AFRICA please write to: Mills & Boon Ltd., P.O. Box 1872, Johannesburg 2000, S. Africa.

Please send me details of the Mills & Boon Subscription Scheme.

NAME (Mrs/Miss) _____ EP3

ADDRESS _____

_____

COUNTY/COUNTRY _____ POST/ZIP CODE _____
BLOCK LETTERS, PLEASE

Mills & Boon
the rose of romance